**The Movie Palace Mystery Series
by Margaret Dumas**

MURDER AT THE PALACE (#1)

MURDER AT The PALACE

A *Movie* PALACE MYSTERY

MARGARET DUMAS

HENERY PRESS

Copyright

MURDER AT THE PALACE
A Movie Palace Mystery
Part of the Henery Press Mystery Collection

First Edition | February 2019

Henery Press, LLC
www.henerypress.com

Trade Paperback ISBN-13: 978-1-63511-463-8
Digital epub ISBN-13: 978-1-63511-464-5
Kindle ISBN-13: 978-1-63511-465-2
Hardcover ISBN-13: 978-1-63511-466-9

Printed in the United States of America

For Dolores. Of course.

ACKNOWLEDGMENTS

I come from a family of movie people. That doesn't mean actors or directors or screenwriters. It means people who love the movies. My mother was incapable of hearing the title *Now, Voyager* without emitting a sigh that sprang from the depths of her soul. She brought me up on musicals and "women's pictures." I knew Elizabeth Taylor and Bette Davis as well as I knew my own aunts. And Katharine Hepburn? Don't even get me started.

My dad loved musicals as well, but his heart belonged to the swashbucklers and sleuths of his childhood. Errol Flynn was a god in my house. I cannot count the number of times I saw *The Adventures of Robin Hood*. And Burt Lancaster? Humphrey Bogart? Please. They were obvious. Talk to me about Wallace Beery or Alan Hale. Then I'll think you have an idea of the kind of people I come from.

I didn't realize until later in life how precious that legacy is. What a gift it was to be surrounded by people who conversed in movie quotes, who — in the case of my mother and her sister — would bust out a few bars of 'People Will Say We're In Love' or 'The Hills Are Alive' at the slightest provocation. I thought everyone's mother got them up in the morning doing Judy Garland's greatest hits.

So when the fabulous team at Henery Press asked me for an idea for a series, the world of classic movies was obvious. It was like going home. I owe huge thanks to Rachel Jackson, Maria Edwards, Art Molinares, Christina Rogers, Kendel Lynn, and a bunch of people I haven't met yet who are all amazing and supportive and wonderful.

Massive thanks as always to Denise Lee, Erick Vera, and Anne Dickson for your early and insightful comments, and to Claire M. Johnson and Michael J. Cooper for your sort-of-every-other-Thursday critiques and support.

My mother thanks you, my father thanks you, my brothers thank you, and I thank you. (And if you know what movie I stole that line from, you must be a movie person too.)

Author's Note: Spoilers Ahead!

I love the movies, and I hope you do too. This book is filled with references to movies, quotes from movies, and thoughts about movies. With all that going on, it's inevitable that there also lurk some genuine spoilers about movies.

Now, since most of the spoilers involve films that date from the 1930s and 1940s, I'm not going to apologize. If you haven't seen *Random Harvest* yet it isn't my fault. You should. Right after you read this book. Hopefully this book will make you want to see it, and a lot more. But if you're the type who absolutely can't stand a spoiler, here's your fair warning. Proceed with caution if you don't want twists revealed about *Jezebel, The Awful Truth, Random Harvest, Double Indemnity, Gaslight, Sorry Wrong Number, Dial M for Murder, How to Steal a Million, Family Plot,* or *San Francisco.*

Proceed with caution, but proceed. And enjoy.

When we are young
We read and believe
The most Fantastic Things.

When we grow older and wiser
We learn, with perhaps a little regret,
That these things can never be.

We are quite, quite wrong.

Noel Coward
Blithe Spirit

CHAPTER 1

It all started because of the séance scene in *Blithe Spirit* (1945, Rex Harrison and Constance Cummings). But before that it was because I got bonked on the head by that stupid light. But before that it was because I took the job at the Palace movie theater when Robbie offered it. But before that it was because Ted left me. So everything, ultimately, was Ted's fault. For better or worse. Ha.

But I should start at the beginning. Or at least one of the beginnings. So I'll start with my first day at the Palace.

I was walking at a brisk pace in the brisk October air, talking briskly on the phone with Robbie. Or at least I was listening as Robbie attempted to convince me, once again, that everything was going to be fine.

"You'll love San Francisco," she enthused from her office, safely back in Hollywood. "You'll make all kinds of friends, and people will get to know you as Nora, just Nora, not Ted's-Wife-Nora, or—"

"Or that pathetic wretch that Ted Bishop left for Priya Sharma," I interrupted. "The woman twice voted most beautiful actress on the planet."

I heard Robbie take a patient breath. "Okay. One—that vote was by a stupid frat boy Internet site and has no standing in the Hollywood community, and two—" she continued quickly to hold off my reply. "The only person who refers to you as pathetic is you, and I thought we placed a permanent ban on that."

"We did." I stopped to wait for the light at a crosswalk and took a deep breath. "Thank you. Again."

She knew I was thanking her not only for talking me down—again—but for whisking me away from the press and the paparazzi who had stalked me ever since the news of my husband's madcap love affair with his gorgeous co-star had gone public. It had been a month of live-streamed humiliation and I didn't know what I would have done without Robbie and the very few friends like her who had stuck by me despite Ted's considerable fame and power.

It was Robbie who had presented me with a getaway plan. I wanted to get out of town, but I needed more than that. Not just somewhere to go, but something to do. Something to keep me from going crazy.

Robbie had figured it out. She'd offered me somewhere to go: San Francisco. More specifically, the cozy guest house behind her Presidio Heights vacation home. And she'd given me something to do: run the classic movie theater that she co-owned just a few blocks away.

"*Running* it is really an overstatement," Robbie had explained to me back in my Beverly Hills kitchen the week before. "It practically runs itself. I mean the staff is amazing. And it's turning a nice little profit. So it's really just something fun for you to do—no pressure—until you figure out your next step."

"It will keep your mind off things." Robbie's daughter Tia had said soothingly, handing me a cup of herbal tea. "And you're the only person on the planet who knows as much about old movies as my mom." She rolled her eyes in Robbie's general direction. I'd known Tia since she was three years old. The eye rolling was new, but the underlying affection had always been there. In my current state I found it excruciating.

"*Classic films*, please," Robbie corrected her tolerantly. "You'll be helping me out," she told me. "Kate ran the place for years. Everyone thought she'd be there forever, and when she died in that accident it devastated us, obviously, but it also left us without a manager, so you would really be doing me a favor."

We both knew who was doing the favor. Robbie and I had been

through a lot since we'd met in the writers' room of a doomed sitcom a decade ago, when she had just ended her marriage and I'd just started mine. I'd given up writing as Ted's career had taken off, but Roberta Prowse was now one of the most successful showrunners in TV, and she was offering me refuge and distraction 300 miles away from the public spectacle that had become my life.

"You guys, I just..." My eyes welled up and before I knew it I was on an airplane.

Now, about to make Robbie's plan a reality, I summed up the situation. "Okay, so I'm crashing in my best friend's guest house, about to start a job I know nothing about in a city I've never even visited, with people who are still grieving the beloved boss I'm about to replace. Is this my life now?"

"I think you meant to say, 'strong black queen of a best friend,'" Robbie said. "But aside from that, yes. At least for a while. Until you're ready for whatever comes next."

What would come next would be a divorce, and I was, despite my misgivings, very glad not to be facing that under the unblinking eye of the Hollywood press and public.

I hung up the phone, squashed an instant flare of panic, and kept walking.

My first thought, rounding the corner at Sacramento street and getting a good look at the Palace, was that it was considerably less than palatial. It stood mid-block, between a boutique and a yogurt shop, and whatever remnants of its former glory it still possessed were largely obscured by the grimy wear of decades.

The marquee, angled out over the sidewalk like the prow of a ship, advertised a double feature of *Frankenstein* (1931, Boris Karloff) and *Young Frankenstein* (1974, Gene Wilder and Madeline Kahn). Appropriate for mid-October, I thought, and probably a good indication of the schedule leading to Halloween. But also a little whimsical, pairing the James Whale directed classic with Mel Brooks' loving and hilarious parody of it.

If this was an indication of how the former manager's mind had worked, I probably would have liked her a lot.

On a closer look, there was much to like about the Palace. The marquee seemed to be original, surrounded by a border of large clear incandescent light bulbs. They weren't lit this early in the afternoon, hours before the first show, but I imagined they'd look warm and welcoming on a foggy San Francisco evening. And the ticket booth was an actual freestanding booth, with dark blue velvet curtains behind the glass.

A walkway with an arched roof and tiled walls funneled moviegoers past the booth to glass lobby doors. Posters of classic Universal horror movies were displayed on the angled walls. From a distance they looked original, but they couldn't be. An original *Frankenstein* poster would cost more than the theater made in a year.

I stood outside the lobby doors and fished around in my backpack for the keys that had been left for me at the cottage, then hesitated, not ready to use them yet. As long as I was still outside maybe I could still run away.

Oh, right. I didn't know where else to go.

Someone quietly cleared their throat behind me and I nearly jumped out of my skin.

"Oh, dear." An elderly man regarded me from behind thick round glasses. "I didn't mean to startle you."

He was bone thin, dressed in a gray suit and navy blue tie under a heavy wool coat, all of it somewhat rumpled and worn, and his expression was of benevolent curiosity. "I only meant to welcome you," he said, stepping closer. "That is, if I'm correct in assuming you are the new manager?"

He held out a hand, and although it was covered in age spots and gnarled at the knuckles, it was firm and somehow reassuring when I shook it.

"Nora...Paige," I told him. Not Nora Bishop. Not anymore. "And yes, I'm the... um...at least for a while...until we figure out a more, a permanent..."

He saved me from what threatened to become a full-on babble. "I am Albert Lockhart. I work here." He stood a little taller. "And have for the past twenty-one years."

"Oh!" Robbie hadn't mentioned that the staff was as old as the movies. "It's so nice to meet you."

He rubbed his hands together and nodded. "I had a feeling you might be early on your first day, and I was presumptuous enough to think you might like someone to show you around."

"Thank you." I had thought to check things out by myself before anyone else showed up for work, but now that he offered…"I'd really appreciate a tour."

"Excellent." He produced a set of keys from his coat pocket, but I held up the heavy and ornate key ring already in my hand.

"I have these," I said. "Although I'm not sure which one—" I stopped when I saw the stricken look on his face.

"Ah," he said, sounding a little strangled. "You have Kate's keys." He blinked several times, suddenly looking much, much older.

"I'm so sorry," I said. "I didn't know Kate, but I've heard she was amazing." I knew my words were feeble. But any words would have been, under the circumstance. "I can't imagine how difficult this must be for you."

Albert nodded. "For all of us," he said, pocketing his keys. "We are something of a family here." He peered at me. "With all the blind loyalties and simmering jealousies that implies."

That was a little daunting. Robbie had talked me into this with the promises of seclusion and distraction. She hadn't described the place as a hotbed of suppressed emotions. I had plenty of emotions of my own to suppress.

"It's the large silver one," Albert said, eyeing the keys.

"Got it." I found the right key and turned to the doors. This was happening. This was my life now. At least for a while. For better or worse. Ha

CHAPTER 2

The doors opened to release the scent of magic. Or at least the scent of ninety-odd years' worth of popcorn, spilled sodas, dust, sweat, and dreams. It was the scent of the movies and I took a deep breath.

I loved old movies. I have since I was a kid, watching them with my mom. That love was one of the first things Ted and I shared together, way back before he got famous. I loved the black and white and silver of the images. I loved the strong, struggling characters from the golden age of Women's Pictures—the Joan Crawford and Bette Davis and Barbara Stanwyck characters who didn't let anything from murderous offspring to brain tumors get in their way. I needed to channel those women now as I started my life over. I needed to be as strong as they were. And, standing in the dim glory of the Palace lobby, I wanted to believe I felt their strength.

"It's quite a place, isn't it?" Albert had slipped behind me to open a small metal panel on the wall next to the door. "Just wait." He punched a code into a keypad and flipped a few switches to bring the Palace to life.

Lights came on inside the long wood and glass counter of the concession stand, illuminating the display of everything from gumdrops to chocolate truffles. Then, the star-shaped pendants above the counter winked on, lighting the vintage popcorn maker and the wall of shelves behind the counter. Next, wall sconces lit the way up the sweeping staircase to the balcony, and finally a chandelier sprang to sparkling life in the center of the ceiling, turning the lobby into something much grander and more beautiful than Robbie had ever led me to expect.

I turned around, looking up at the elaborately carved ceiling, down at the carpet—deep blue with a pattern of tiny gold stars—taking it all in. Then I caught Albert's eye.

"I think I'm in love," I told him quite seriously.

"That can happen," he nodded gravely. "I give you fair warning. You may never want to leave."

An hour later, having toured the main auditorium with its 800 seats, the vast backstage area behind the screen—the theater having been built when vaudeville acts still sometimes shared the bill with movies—and the not-at-all glamorous basement, a warren of rooms containing everything from old advertising paraphernalia to heating and electrical equipment, I collapsed with Albert in the front row of the balcony.

"It's amazing," I said. "How has it lasted all these years?"

"By hook or by crook," he said. "Since 1927. The same year I was born."

"I can't imagine what it must have been like back then." I leaned back in my seat and regarded the filigreed ceiling, trying to see it as it had been when the gold leaf had gleamed and the proscenium arch had been draped with plush velvet curtains.

The velvet currently covering the seats was decidedly not plush. It was, in fact, quite threadbare in places. I ran my hand over the seat next to me. "How do you manage the upkeep on a place like this?" I wondered aloud.

Albert cleared his throat delicately. "I think that will be up to you from now on."

Oh. Right. The word "manager" suddenly took on new and terrifying dimensions, and with perfect timing, a light above the aisle began to dim and sputter alarmingly.

Albert and I glanced up in unison as the light gave one last flicker and died.

"Is there a maintenance crew?" I asked with faint hope.

"A handyman," Albert answered. "One day a month. Kate kept a punch list of things for him to do." He shot me a glance, his sparse white hair a fluffy nimbus around his head. "I used to help with what I could, but I fear I'm not up to anything very strenuous anymore."

"Oh, of course..." The last thing I meant to suggest was that the ninety-some-year-old Albert should start scampering up ladders.

"I've been coming here all my life," he said with some pride. "Some of the most meaningful events of my life have taken place within these walls. My grandfather brought me to see *Captain Blood* here on my eighth birthday. Later I brought my children and grandchildren here, and when I retired twenty-one years ago I knew I wanted to spend as much time as I have left here, surrounded by my memories."

I was touched by Albert's words, which raised a dozen questions, but before I had a chance to pursue any of them I jumped at an insanely loud rat-a-tat-tat of drums followed by the triumphant fanfare of horns announcing the beginning of a 20th Century Fox movie.

"What was that?" I put a hand on my racing heart. It was still at least an hour before the first show, so a movie shouldn't have been starting. And anyway, there was no light coming from the projection booth, and nothing followed the blast of music.

"That was Marty," Albert said. "Our projectionist. He's an incredibly valuable asset to the Palace, but he can also be—if you will pardon my language—a complete ass."

"No worries," I told him, recovering. "After a decade in Hollywood, if there's one thing I know, it's how to handle an ass."

That came out wrong, but it didn't matter. Albert was already on his way downstairs.

Three people were gathered in the lobby. A young woman looking at her phone, an even younger man gazing at her worshipfully, and a fortyish guy wearing faded jeans, a once-red t-shirt, and an unzipped gray hoodie.

"Nora," Albert said. "May I present Marty Abrams, our projectionist and the perpetrator of the daily assault on our ears."

The hoodie guy glared at me. He had dark shaggy hair and a salt-and-pepper stubble and looked like he hadn't had a decent night's sleep in years. "I like an overture," he said. "Do you have a problem with that? Do you have a problem with me continuing to start my day the way I've been starting it for the past seven years at this theater? Do you? Because Kate didn't." He crossed his arms, still glaring.

Right. I'd seen people lead with aggression before. It was more or less the default setting for many of the agents and producers I'd worked with on Ted's behalf. I'd learned it was usually best to treat them like toddlers throwing tantrums. Respond to the words, not the tone.

"I liked it," I told him. "It seems like a fun way to start the day."

He blinked, momentarily thrown, I thought, before he responded. "Fun? It isn't *fun*. It's a call to greatness—it's a call to arms!"

The young woman sighed theatrically. This was probably directed at Marty, although she hadn't looked up from her phone so it was a little hard to be sure.

Marty pointed a finger at her. "Do *not* start with me." Then he turned back to me. "And do not waltz in here thinking you know anything about anything just because you saw *Some Like It Hot* once on Turner Classic Movies." He held up a hand. "Do not *start* with me on Turner Classic Movies, and do *not* get me started on Ben Mankowitz!"

He seemed to expect an answer to this. I didn't give him one. Although part of me was dying to know what the charming movie host Ben Mankowitz had ever done to deserve this level of hostility.

"He knows what he did," Marty said meaningfully.

I raised my eyebrows and he sniffed in satisfaction. "I'll be in the projection booth," he announced. And with one last fierce look he stormed up the staircase.

"He's not as bad as he seems." This was claimed by the teenager, who blushed bright pink to the roots of his ginger hair as soon as I turned to him.

"Brandon Dunbar," Albert introduced him. "Our latest addition to the Palace family. Brandon will be manning the concession stand today."

"Marty's just been angrier than usual since Kate died," the teenager explained. "We've all...I mean..." He flushed ever more deeply as he trailed off.

"I get it," I told him. "Robbie told me how close you all were to Kate. How much she really *was* the Palace. Believe me, I know I'm not Kate. And I'm not here to try to replace her. My biggest regret is that I didn't ever meet her."

"Cool." The college-aged woman now finally looked up from her phone. "But I kind of thought your biggest regret might be letting your man-slut of a husband go off on location with the most beautiful actress on the planet." The expression on her face was one of flat disinterest.

"Calandria Gee!" Albert looked appalled at the girl's words.

"Callie," she corrected, looking at me with studied boredom. She was strikingly pretty, with wild dark curls surrounding the impassive face of a Renaissance Madonna. A Renaissance Madonna who kept up on all the gossip blogs, apparently.

This was exactly the sort of conversation I'd fled LA to avoid.

"Is he stupid?" Callie tilted her head and considered me. "Because anyone who knows anything about Priya Sharma knows it won't last."

I hated myself for the surge of ridiculous hope that shot through me, which I immediately squashed. "Look—Callie, is it?" I had some half-formed notion of telling her off, but she continued as if I hadn't spoken.

"Maybe he *is* stupid," she mused. "I mean, Priya Sharma has the brain power of, like, an unripe kumquat, and you've been kind of your husband's unpaid manager or whatever since you gave up writing. So he's kind of an idiot for dumping you for her, right? I mean, aside from him having to hire someone to replace you, you must know tons of stuff that could, like, totally screw him over if you wanted."

I blinked. Albert cleared his throat. Brandon looked between Callie and me like he was waiting for a grenade to explode.

"Ted Bishop is one hundred percent an idiot," I heard Marty say from behind me. He'd come halfway down the stairs again without me noticing. "The least of his crimes is his poor choice in mistresses." Now he looked at me. "You should ruin him professionally and financially, and you should go back to LA to do it." He glanced at Brandon. "Get me a Coke, will you?"

Brandon jumped as if electrocuted and dashed behind the candy counter.

"Callie runs the ticket booth," Albert said, attempting valiantly to get the introductions back on track. "She is also an independent filmmaker."

"Documentaries," she said, still eyeing me like I was a mildly interesting new specimen of something. "I'm studying film at SF State."

I choked out one word. "Right." I figured it was safer than "Who the hell do you think you are to judge me and my marriage based on the self-serving rants of those so-called 'close friends' on the gossip sites, even if you do seem to be weirdly on my side?" Not as satisfying, but safer.

Before anyone had the chance to voice any further opinions on my private life we were interrupted by a metallic screeching sound and an agitated yelp from Brandon. He held an extra-large cup under the ice dispenser, which clanked and shuddered before emitting a thin stream of water that continued to leak down the drain after Brandon took the cup away.

"The icemaker's out again," he informed us.

"Blast," Albert muttered. "We just had it fixed last month." He turned to me. "Never mind, we have a backup ice machine down in the basement. We can bring up buckets as we need them until we get this fixed again."

"Or replaced," Marty said. "I'd replace it. But then I'm not the *manager*." He gave me a look and came the rest of the way down the stairs to the lobby. "I'll haul the ice up. God knows I don't have—"

"No!" I hadn't meant to shout, or to sound as desperate to get away from these people as I felt. "No," I said again. "You all have things to do. I'll go get the ice. It's no problem."

I fled.

I wasn't proud of myself. I'd gotten flustered, and flustered was not strong. I would have given myself a stern talking to if I hadn't been distracted by the realization that I had no idea where the ice machine was.

Downstairs in the basement, I went past the restrooms to the farthest reaches of the maze of hallways, pulling out my phone to call Robbie and noting that, of course, there was no signal down there. I wrote a text instead.

A great staff?!? You said there was a great staff! You didn't say there was a giant Muppet with anger issues who thinks he should have my job and a judgie millennial who knows everything about my personal life! What did you get me into? And where's the damn ice machine!?

It wouldn't send until I got a signal, but I felt a little better after banging it out. I wandered down a few wrong hallways, then followed an electrical humming sound to a room with a barred window high on a wall and a mismatched assortment of ancient machinery, one item of which was an old-fashioned ice maker. It was the kind that used to be in motel parking lots, where you could open the lid, reach in with a scoop and take all you needed. It was the unsanitary kind, and I told myself not to think of probable health code violations, but to focus instead on how fortunate it was that the huge old beast appeared to be plugged in, plumbed in, and operational.

As I approached it I heard the whoosh of my outgoing text, and the chime of an incoming one. The room's window must allow enough of a signal to get through. I would have to remember that for future desperate phone calls to Robbie, of which I was sure there would be many. I glanced at the screen.

Baby. Where are you? I need you.

Not from Robbie. From Ted.

I realized I wasn't breathing. This was a new phone. Only Robbie, my lawyer, and a handful of friends had the number. One of them had given it to Ted.

Ted had wanted to contact me so much that he'd begged someone for my new number.

Ted needed me.

I was blinking up at the light from the window, my mind leaping to a million possibilities, when the phone chimed again.

I can't find the keys to the Bentley.

And once again I realized I was the stupidest woman on the planet. Of course Ted needed me. He needed me to run his life. He needed me to take care of the thousand little things a day that were too unimportant for him to think about until he needed them, at which point they became *crucial*. He needed me to make his excuses, make his decisions, make his breakfast. He needed me in a million different ways, but that hadn't stopped him from leaving me.

"Well, guess what, Teddy," I said out loud. "I don't need *you!*"

I flung back the lid to the ice machine and screamed. Not because of Ted. Because there was a dead man in the ice.

CHAPTER 3

Everyone came pummeling down the stairs to see what had made the new girl scream her head off. After that a certain amount of time was taken up by us all completely freaking out, and then Brandon fainted, so we closed the lid on the dead man and hauled Brandon back up to the lobby. Albert sat down alarmingly suddenly on his ticket-taker's stool, all the color drained from his face, and I reached for my phone to call an ambulance for him.

Callie beat me to it. "911?" she said. "Yeah. We've got one unconscious guy, one possible heart attack guy, and one, like, dead guy. You should probably send everyone."

"I am not having a heart attack," Albert said, with ruffled dignity, as Brandon moaned and came around.

Nevertheless, 911 sent everyone.

"And you'd never seen the victim before?"

I was questioned by a heavyset detective with a hipster goatee and a voice like melted chocolate. He'd told me his name at least three times, but I hadn't registered it. I think I might have been in shock.

I shook my head.

"You're sure?" he persisted.

"I just got here," I said. "I mean, not just to the theater, but to the city. I got here yesterday and I don't know anyone."

He nodded and wrote something down.

"Is there someplace you could wait for a while?" he asked. "Do you have an office or something? We may have more questions later." He glanced around the lobby, which was filled with a cluster of police talking to Marty and Callie, a cluster of EMTs checking out Albert and Brandon, and several other clusters of grim-faced professionals doing the things they do when a dead body turns up in an ice machine.

"Sure," I said, wanting nothing more than a few moments away from everybody. I probably had an office somewhere. I'd just have to find it.

It wasn't my office. It was Kate's office. That much was clear from the second I found it.

It was upstairs on the balcony level in an administrative area hidden behind an unmarked door so camouflaged by the ornate carving of the wall's wooden paneling that I wouldn't have noticed it if Albert hadn't pointed it out on our tour.

The door opened to a hallway which gave access to the projection booth, a tiny restroom, a staff break room, and at the far end against an exposed brick wall, another stairway. The back stairs, I thought. Narrow, iron, and utilitarian.

Halfway down the hall was the closed door to Kate's office. I still had Kate's keys in my jeans pocket, but the door was unlocked. The room was lined with crowded shelves and dominated by an enormous old oak desk and a freestanding blackboard. Both looked like they could have been in the room since Clark Gable was number one at the box office. Shabby furniture cluttered the space, and a window looked out over the top of the marquee to the street below.

The blackboard was covered in cramped handwriting. There were calendar grids for September, October, and November, each with the schedule of films filled in for the month. Clearly nobody had updated it since Kate's death. The slate changed on Tuesdays and Fridays and seemed always to consist of two or three features on a common theme. That added up to a lot of movies.

Robbie had told me the films were ordered many weeks in

advance, and the slate was already booked through the holidays. Still, the prospect of keeping up with the programming and sourcing of films might have seemed a little overwhelming if I hadn't already been overwhelmed by the vivid image of a dead man's frost-glazed face staring at me from a bed of ice.

I sat at the desk in an ancient wooden rolling armchair made somewhat more comfortable by a faded crimson pillow. Kate's desk was cluttered with brochures for film festivals, fliers for special events, and dozens of notes scrawled on pages pulled from a scratch pad next to the telephone.

Telephone. Right. A beige hard-wired multi-line monster, looking like it dated from the Eighties. What about a computer? A quick glance around the place didn't reveal one. A pale blue IBM Selectric typewriter, yes, but no computer.

Seriously?

"I brought you this."

I jumped at the sound of Callie's voice. I had turned away from the door, but now saw her standing in the hallway, looking in. She held my leather backpack by one thin strap. "It was in the balcony. It's yours, right?"

"Oh, right." I must have left it there a thousand years ago at the end of Albert's tour. I looked at my watch. It had been two hours. "Thanks."

"Sooooo..." Callie stepped into the room a little gingerly, looking uncomfortable. She dropped the backpack on the desk. "Are you, like, okay?"

"Absolutely not." I said. "There's body in the ice machine. Are you okay?"

"Probably not." She shrugged, then, "Sorry about all that stuff about Ted Bishop earlier." She gave me a quick glance, then looked away. "Are, like, *we* okay?"

I blew out a breath. "Sure."

"Cool." Her shoulders relaxed a bit. "What are you doing?"

I looked around the room. "At the moment, wondering whether that blackboard is the most advanced technology in this place."

"Oh. No. Kate had a laptop. Marty's been using it to send out the email blasts and update the website and everything." She looked at me with eyebrows raised. "You know he's going to go nuts with this."

Marty seemed pretty nuts to begin with, but I let that thought go unspoken. No, I didn't. "More nuts?"

She grimaced and slumped onto an ancient leather sofa under the window. "He's really not that bad," she said. "He just tends to go from zero to furious in, like, no seconds."

"I noticed." She was the third person to tell me Marty wasn't that bad.

She shot me a look. "He took Kate's death hard. I mean, we all did," she said. "But the rest of us just miss her. We don't think someone killed her. And I heard the cops say that guy has probably been down there for about two weeks, which is right around when Kate died, so you know...What?"

She must have seen what must have been a confused look on my face. "Who thinks someone killed Kate?"

"Marty," she said, her tone implying that I needed to keep up. "He's been going off about it ever since she died."

I stared at her. "How did Kate die?" Robbie had said "accident" and I had automatically filled in "car crash," but I didn't really know.

"She fell," Callie said. "She was walking on the path up Strawberry Hill—at Stowe Lake?" Seeing my baffled expression, she explained. "It's in Golden Gate Park, and it's a totally easy path. I mean, like, people do it with *strollers* and stuff. But she must have slipped or something and..." Her jaw flexed and she looked away from me. "Her neck was broken."

"Oh." I swallowed. "Callie, I'm so sorry."

She waved my words away. "Anyway, that was two weeks ago, and now the cops say this guy downstairs has been dead for like two weeks, sooooo..."

"Marty's going to go nuts," I concluded. And, I reasoned, going nuts might be a perfectly rational reaction. The timing was suspicious.

"Did you know him?" I asked Callie. "I mean, the..." I made a vague gesture toward the basement.

"The dead guy?" she said. "I don't think so. But I didn't really take any lingering looks." She shivered.

Right. Neither had I. But the sight of him was still burned in my brain.

After Callie left, I started sorting the clutter of Kate's desk into organized piles. Because if you can't control unfaithful husbands or bodies turning up in your basement, at least you can control random paperwork, right?

Pamphlets and brochures in one stack; bills (a rather alarming number of them), in another; miscellaneous correspondence; and lastly the handwritten notes, most of them seemingly of ideas for future programming.

I found one that read 'Have / Have,' 'Sleep,' and 'Millionaire' and assumed it referred to *To Have and Have Not* (1944, Lauren Bacall and Humphrey Bogart), *The Big Sleep* (1946, ditto), and *How to Marry a Millionaire* (1953, Bacall, Marilyn Monroe, and Betty Grable). It took me a bit longer to figure out that 'Rain,' 'Charade,' and 'Yankees' probably referred to *Singin' in the Rain* (1952, Gene Kelly and Debbie Reynolds), *Charade* (1963, Cary Grant and Audrey Hepburn), and *Damn Yankees* (1958, Gwen Verdon and Tab Hunter). The connection among those films was the director Stanley Donen. One of my favorites. I would probably want to include *Indiscreet* (1958, Cary Grant and Ingrid Bergman) in any Stanley Donen lineup, but that was just me.

And that was assuming there would still be a Palace to keep showing these movies. I tried not to think about the fact that finding a body in the basement might have cast the slightest bit of doubt on the Palace's future. And on my first day, no less.

Kate's last note was still on the scratch pad. It was longer than the others, and I didn't immediately see the connective thread among "Win," "M," "Lace," "Sorry," and "Gas."

I gave up, stretched, and pressed the heels of my hands to my eyes. I knew I should go back downstairs to ask the detective when they might be finished with their work. There were movies to either show or cancel based on his answer. When I opened my eyes again Marty was standing in the doorway watching me.

"I put a sign in the box office window and told everyone to go home," he said. "The cops won't tell me anything, but it looks like they'll be here for a while, and I know I'm not the *manager* or anything, but I—"

"Thank you." I cut him off before he could launch into a full-blown rant. "I'm sure that was the right call."

He didn't seem to know what to do with that. He shrugged, then came into the room. I saw he was carrying a laptop, which he set none too gently on the desk. "Callie said you were looking for this."

"Right. She told me you've been taking care of everything, and—"

"Someone had to," he said. "Just like someone has to get out the ladder and change the marquee in the morning and someone has to run the projectors and fix them when they break down, and someone has to order the concessions, and—"

"Marty," I said. "I'm trying to thank you."

He gave me a close look, checking for signs of mockery. Then he sniffed and looked away. "The Wi-Fi network is 'PalaceWeb' and the password is Hitchcock, capital 'H' and 'K,' one instead of the 'I.'"

I must have looked baffled because he blew out an exasperated breath, grabbed a pencil, and plucked Kate's last list from the top of the pile. He wrote the password on the back of it, then handed me the paper.

H1tchcocK

"Right," I said. "Thanks." I tucked it into a pocket of my backpack.

"Stop thanking me. It's unnerving."

He looked away again, and I broke what threatened to turn into an awkward silence with a suggestion. "Should we go downstairs to find out what the hell is going on?"

"We should," he said. "Maybe you'll have better luck than I did."

His agreement felt like a small victory. "Did you catch that cop's name? The one who seemed to be in charge?"

"The bear with the voice like liquid heaven?" he said. "I think it's Officer He-Wants-Me-But-He-Doesn't-Know-It-Yet."

I raised my eyebrows. "No, I think it's *Detective* He-Wants-You-But-He-Doesn't-Know-It-Yet."

Marty gave me a look. "Don't," he said. "We're not friends yet."

Noted.

CHAPTER 4

"At least if we're going to start tripping over corpses we're doing it at the right time of year," Marty said as we made our way to the lobby. "Half the people we turned away think this is a Halloween stunt."

"That would be in questionable taste."

"This is San Francisco at Halloween," he told me. "Questionable taste is what we do. And if it were a stunt, it wouldn't be a bad one. I mean, we've got the ghost movies starting tomorrow, so why not stage a murder and then say we have a new ghost?" He seemed to be more thinking out loud than talking to me.

"What do you mean, 'a *new* ghost?'"

He shot me a look. "You know the Palace is haunted, right? I mean, you do know *something* about this place?"

"Hang on, are you saying you believe—"

But whatever he believed about ghosts and haunted theaters would have to wait. Because Detective I-Wish-I-Could-Remember-His-Name was at the bottom of the stairs talking on his phone. He hung up when he saw us.

"I was just coming to find you," he said. "We have an ID on the victim."

"Raul Acosta," I echoed.

The detective had just told us that a wallet found on the body contained a driver's license and credit cards identifying the victim as Raul Acosta, which rang no bells for either Marty or me.

"David Jackson," Marty said, taking the card the detective now held out.

"We'll need to see your records," Jackson said. "Mailing lists, suppliers, anything that could tell us whether Acosta had a legitimate reason for being here."

"Of course," I said. "How much longer—" But the detective's phone rang and he turned away to take it before I had a chance to ask any questions. The answer was clear anyway—they'd be done when they were done.

I'd had enough of hanging out in Kate's office, so Marty and I went upstairs for the laptop and my backpack, then went across the street to a coffee place called Café Madeline. It was late afternoon and I realized I hadn't eaten anything all day. Not that I was hungry. But a double-shot anything seemed like a good idea.

The cafe, modern and clean with high ceilings and free Wi-Fi, was warm and smelled comfortingly of coffee and autumn-spiced baked goods. We scored a table at the window so we could keep an eye on the theater across the street.

Marty downed an extra-large Americano while we scoured the Palace records for any mention of Raul Acosta. We checked the list of people who subscribed to the weekly email blast. We checked the database of frequent filmgoers who were part of the Palace loyalty program. We checked popcorn vendors and film suppliers and former employees going back nine years. We even checked the name of the guy who had last repaired the icemaker. Nothing.

"So how exactly did Raul Acosta wind up in our ice machine?" I asked, as Marty began copying all the files into a folder to email to the detective.

"There's a back door," he said. "It goes out to the alley behind the theater. It's always supposed to be locked, but someone could have left it open."

"Or he could have broken in," I said.

"In an attempt to rob us of our stockpile of Necco Wafers?" Marty scoffed. "Or just to get warm? After which he crawled into the ice machine to commit suicide by freezing?"

"He was bludgeoned," I said.

"What? How do you know that?"

"One of the guys in paper jumpsuits pulled Detective Jackson aside to tell him when he was questioning me earlier. He kept his voice low, but I'm pretty sure he said 'blunt force trauma to the skull,' which means Raul Acosta was bludgeoned, and didn't commit ironic suicide."

"Hrumph." Marty sat back and crossed his arms. "Well, the detective said he had credit cards, right? So he wasn't some homeless guy just wandering in off the street to find a place to sleep."

"Then who was he?" I asked. "And what was he doing in the basement of the theater?"

"And when, exactly, was he killed?" Marty rubbed his eyes, suddenly looking even more exhausted. "Was it before or after Kate? And what's the connection?"

"I thought Kate died in the park," I said.

He gave me a look filled with distain. "Kate was *found* in the park. And what sounds more likely to you—that she died in a freak accident at the same time this completely random murder took place in the basement, or that there's a connection between the two? That maybe the same person who murdered Mister Deep Freeze also murdered Kate?"

"Murdered?! Wait, what?" Robbie's voice over the phone was understandably confused.

"This is why you have to return my texts," I told her. "A lot happened on my first day."

It was almost midnight, and I was back at the guest cottage, having finally been able to lock up the theater after the departing police. The first thing I'd done after walking the six chilly blocks home was raid Robbie's wine rack. I now took a large sip from a large glass of Napa Valley red and told her everything that had happened.

"I'm sure the police will be calling you," I concluded. "You do own the place."

"Co-own," she said. "And they already called. I got a couple messages but they didn't say what it was about. I was on set all day and didn't get a chance to call back—to call anyone back, including you, for which I am so, so sorry, Nora. Are you okay? I mean, this is not exactly the therapeutic escape you signed up for."

I swirled the wine in the glass. "Weirdly, I think I'm okay. I mean, yes, I was having a meltdown when I sent you that text, but finding a murder victim can apparently have a surprising sort of team-building effect." I said it lightly while acknowledging it was true. Callie had apologized for her remarks about my marriage and Marty and I had spent several hours at the coffee shop together without drawing blood once.

"And if nothing else," I told Robbie, "I didn't think of my cheating rat of a husband for hours at a time. So from a distraction perspective, this might actually be working."

"I was hoping it would all be a *pleasant* distraction," Robbie answered. "Not involving heart-attack inducing shocks and visions that will haunt your nightmares."

"Albert didn't have a heart attack," I told her. "He was cleared by the EMTs." After which he'd assured everyone that he'd be right as rain once he went home and had a good strong cup of tea.

I took another good strong sip of wine. "And speaking of haunting my nightmares, what's this about the theater being haunted? Marty said something about a ghost like it was common knowledge."

"It is common knowledge," Robbie said. "Didn't I tell you? Which ghost was he talking about, the showgirl or the usherette?"

I took a moment to take the phone away from my ear and stare at it incredulously before responding. "Are you saying you believe in ghosts?"

"I'm saying I believe in legends surrounding historic movie palaces," she said. "There's one about a showgirl who died during a knife-throwing act, back in the very early days of the theater when they still got the Vaudeville troupes, and there's another about an usherette who was thrown off the balcony some time in the thirties."

"You're kidding."

"No, seriously. They even filmed an episode of one of those ghost hunter reality shows there."

'Reality' may not have been the best description for a show about ghosts, but I let that pass. "I don't suppose they actually captured either of these ghosts on camera," I said.

"Shockingly, no. I think they felt cold in the balcony and saw lights flicker backstage or something."

"Lights are flickering, all right," I told her. "And icemakers are on the fritz, and I think I'm going to have to talk to you about a serious refurbishment budget, but let me see what happens on Day Two before I commit to anything."

"You don't have to stay," Robbie said. "If this was a bad idea just come home tomorrow. Or don't come home. You can still go to Paris or Fiji or wherever you want."

"I know," I said. She was right. I could go just about anywhere. The question was what I would do with myself once I got there. "I'll stick it out here a little longer. I actually want to find out what happened. And besides, I haven't even seen my first movie yet."

After I got off the phone I realized I was starving. Robbie had seen to everything else, so I had no reason not to expect that the same person she'd employed to put fresh sheets on the bed and fresh towels in the bathroom might have put some fresh food in the refrigerator.

I was correct. There were supplies for days, and I made myself a very comforting plate of eggs on toast to go with another glass of wine.

I hadn't explored the compact little house when I'd gotten in the night before, but there really wasn't much to see. A small but well-designed kitchen was outfitted with all the necessities, including the wine rack. It was open to the main room, which contained a deep L-shaped couch, a massive television, and a desk upon which now sat both my laptop and Kate's.

Almost the whole front wall of the house was glass, looking out on Robbie's garden and the back of her three-story main house. She'd wanted me to stay there, but I'd had enough of rattling around in huge empty houses during my marriage. The cottage suited me just fine now.

Behind the main room was the bedroom, separated not by a wall, but by a floor-to ceiling semi-sheer curtain. It contained a king-sized bed and a chair that looked like it was made for reading on rainy afternoons. Off the bedroom was a black-and-white tiled bathroom and a walk-in closet.

I'd opened my suitcase in the closet the night before, and now I stood over it, telling myself that any self-respecting woman would probably do more than just rummage through it when she needed a change of clothes. A self-respecting woman would hang things up and put things in drawers. After a while of not doing any such thing, I realized that I was no longer staring blankly at my jumble of clothes. I was staring blankly at my reflection in the closet's full-length mirror.

I'd avoided mirrors ever since I'd seen the first photo of Ted "canoodling" with Priya Sharma. I hadn't needed a mirror to point out the stark contrast between her voluptuous curves and my lanky athleticism. Between her twenty-six-year-old freshness and my thirty-nine-year-old lack thereof.

My hair, shoulder-length and streaked with mandatory Hollywood highlights, was now in a careless ponytail. I looked forward to the highlights growing out. I looked forward to becoming as pale and invisible as the ghosts of the Palace, while Priya Sharma gloried in her lush dark curls and her smoldering bedroom eyes, and the love of the man who had once promised to forsake all others, keeping only to me.

Okay. Enough of that.

I shook my head, and quoted Cary Grant out loud. "Well, that's no good. That's not even conversation." It's what he said to

Katharine Hepburn in *The Philadelphia Story* (1940, Cary, Kate, and James Stewart), right after she (wrongly) called herself an "unholy mess of a girl."

I, too, felt like an unholy mess of a girl. But I was an unholy mess of a girl with stuff to do. I raised my head defiantly and turned my back on my reflection. I had lots of stuff to do, and the first thing on my list was to google everything that was known about Kate Winslow and her death.

By two a.m. I'd learned enough about Kate to know that the Palace, and the world, was a lesser place without her.

She'd taken over the theater twenty-three years ago, long before Robbie and her partners had bought it. I didn't find out how old she'd been at that time, or what she'd done before taking the job. Her life seemed to begin with the Palace.

What I did learn was that when she showed up in the mid 1990s the building had practically been falling down. It hadn't shown first-run movies since the Summer of Love. After that, it had limped along as a second-run house before finally closing its doors in the early 1980s. Shuttered for years, it had eventually been repurposed for a while as a live stage theater, before being briefly home to a Pentecostal church.

The big turnaround happened when the Palace was bought by two brothers, tech millionaires from Silicon Valley who had dreams of restoring it as a home for classic films. They hired Kate. She poured her heart and soul into it, the brothers poured money into it, and things were just starting to thrive when the dot-com crash of 2001 wiped the brothers out.

After that Kate was faced with the prospect of making the theater actually pay for itself. But she was scrappy and inventive, and somehow managed to keep the place afloat. By hook or by crook, as Albert had said, she kept it going all these years. When Robbie's partners took it over four years ago they didn't even think of replacing Kate.

She was loved and respected. From what I could find in the online newspapers, she was active in the neighborhood merchants association and a frequent volunteer for a variety of causes. She spoke occasionally at local film festivals, but apparently turned down more requests than she accepted. She wasn't married, or in any relationship I could find mention of. She had refused an offer to run for city council. She died in a fall from Strawberry Hill.

I had to believe it was an accident. Who would have killed her? And why? Her life, as far as I could tell, was completely centered on the Palace. In fact, I could see no evidence of a personal life at all. No Facebook page aside from the Palace's. No Twitter, no Instagram, no social media footprint at all.

And no good pictures, either, I realized. The Palace had a Wikipedia page with half a dozen pictures chronicling the building's decline and resurrection. There were pictures of the original architect, the Silicon Valley brothers, and a staff photo from sometime during the Great Depression. But only a few pictures of Kate, all of them in group shots, none of them good. It looked like she'd always turned from the camera as the picture was taken, her face a blur. Even in the loving obituaries I found in everything from the *San Francisco Chronicle* to the newsletter of the local Film Society, the picture they used was grainy and out of focus, the same as one of the group shots, just cropped to show only Kate.

No decent pictures. And no trace of her anywhere online before she took over the Palace. Which left me wondering the same things I'd been wondering at the beginning of all my searching.

What was Kate's story? And was her fall really an accident?

CHAPTER 5

My first thought upon waking the next morning was that I should look through Kate's private email. It wasn't a noble thought, but at least it wasn't a thought about my soon-to-be-ex-husband and his internationally sexy paramour, which had been my first thought upon waking ever since he left me. So I told myself it was a step in the right direction and I showered and dressed with a refreshing sense of purpose.

A hundred possibilities had flickered through my head as I'd tried to go to sleep the night before. What if Kate had been on the run? That would explain her aversion to photos and social media. What if she'd had some sort of criminal past and was living in hiding, using an assumed name, keeping a low profile? She might even have been in witness protection. And what if that past had finally caught up with her? What if that past involved the dead man in the ice machine?

I knew the Palace had an email account that Marty had been keeping up-to-date. But Kate had to have had a personal account as well, right? I opened her laptop with the clear expectation that everything was about to be revealed.

And I found out her email was password protected.

Of course.

Since it was Friday there was a new lineup of movies for the weekend, which explained why I saw Marty high on a ladder changing the marquee when I came around the corner half an hour later.

A milk crate of black block letters balanced on top of the ancient wooden ladder, and he was finalizing the show times of the weekend triple feature.

"Sophisticated spirits," I greeted him, remembering the theme of the films that I'd seen on Kate's blackboard. It was a triple feature of *Blithe Spirit* (1945, Rex Harrison and Constance Cummings), *Topper* (1937, Cary Grant and Constant Bennett), and *Topper Returns* (1941, Roland Young and Joan Blondell).

"Don't stand there," Marty barked. "I could knock this box over and kill you, and I don't need the temptation."

So much for yesterday's truce.

As I went past the ticket booth I noticed that the posters were still of Frankenstein and company and wondered if we had artwork for any of the new slate. If so, they were probably stored somewhere in the basement, and I had no desire to go poking around down there again any time soon.

In the lobby I found Albert and Brandon tidying up the paper coffee cups, candy wrappers, and other assorted detritus that the police had left behind the night before.

When I'd locked up after them, Detective Jackson had told me that the room with the ice machine and the hallway from that room to the outside basement door were still off limits, and clearly marked with crime scene tape. The rest of the Palace was cleared for use.

"Hey you two," I said. "How are you feeling? Are you okay to work today, Albert?"

He looked like a strong breeze could knock him over, but he'd looked that way before I'd found the body yesterday, so I wasn't sure how worried I should be.

He waved my concern away. "I'm absolutely fine. Don't give it another thought."

"I'm sorry about yesterday," Brandon said, blushing furiously. "I've never passed out before in my life!"

He'd probably never seen a corpse on ice before, either, unless I was very wrong about him. "Don't worry about it," I told him. "It was such a shock. I'm just glad you're okay. Are you here all day?" The first movie would show at noon and the last would end only a bit before midnight. I sincerely hoped the Palace wasn't dependent on twelve-hour shifts from high school students and nonagenarians to keep the doors open.

"Mike and Claire will be in for the 6:25," Albert assured me. "I'll introduce you when they get here. And Callie should have been here twenty minutes ago."

"Great." I looked around the lobby. "Now, how can I help?"

I spent the next hour or so attempting to help but largely staying out of their way as they went about the business of readying the Palace for the day. I was surprised to learn that the whole place was usually staffed by only three or four people per shift. One in the projection booth, one selling tickets, and one or maybe two behind the candy counter, depending on the size of the expected crowd. When Albert went home nobody took his place as a dedicated ticket taker.

I viewed this setting-up period as the calm before an expected storm of customers and took advantage of it by poking around while asking questions of Albert and Brandon. The sweeping staircase up to the balcony was on the right side of the lobby, while on the left-side wall was a small accessible restroom, a storage closet containing more gummy bears than I'd ever seen in one place at one time, and a door to the utilitarian back stairwell I'd noticed upstairs. I poked my head in and saw it went both up to the offices and down to the basement, presumably to the back door that was still taped off by the police.

The lobby was just filling with the heady scent of fresh buttered popcorn when I remembered that we still didn't have a solution for the broken icemaker.

"I'll try the yogurt shop next door to see if they'll sell us some ice," I said, almost at the exact moment that Marty arrived, pulling a massive wheeled cooler through the lobby doors.

"I got four bags of ice from the liquor store on Divisidaro," he announced. "That should see us through the first couple of shows."

"You're a genius," I told him.

"I know," he said. "I'll be in the booth." He shoved the cooler in my general direction and took the balcony stairs two at a time.

Callie had sent a text to Albert saying she was running late because her bus broke down, so Brandon went outside to open the ticket booth. That left me polishing the candy counter with someone who had known Kate for over twenty years. Albert had to know something that would shed some light on her death. He had to know something about her past.

"I'm afraid I don't know much about Kate's past." Albert said.

This was in response to the very awkward interest I finally managed to communicate after several uncomfortable false starts. Turns out it's surprisingly difficult to probe for details about someone's beloved dead friend without sounding like a heartless and intrusive monster. I don't think I completely pulled it off, but Albert didn't seem to take offense. He just didn't have anything to say.

"She was a very private person," he told me. "She'd only been here a few years when she hired me, but she never talked about where she'd come from, or how she'd come to be here."

"What about her personal life?" I asked. "I don't want to pry," (I did) "but none of the write-ups after her death mentioned a partner or children..."

"As far as I know, there wasn't anyone," Albert said. "I assumed..." He hesitated. "Well, if I assumed anything, it was that she had been hurt in the past." He gave me a quick look. "There is a way of not talking about yourself that can say much more than if you did talk about yourself. Do you understand?"

"I do," I said. Although, having spent the last decade in Hollywood, I knew very few people who didn't talk about themselves constantly.

He nodded. "I believe Kate had experienced the kind of hurt that you just don't talk about."

The kind of hurt that you changed your whole life to escape? I was stopped from digging any further by Callie's arrival, which prompted Brandon's return to the concession stand and ended my conversation with Albert. But it had given me something to think about.

What if Kate wasn't running from something horrible she'd done? What if she was running from something horrible that had been done to her?

I slipped up to the balcony as the moviegoers started to arrive for the early matinee. There were only a handful, which was a little disappointing, but it meant Brandon, Albert, and Callie didn't need my help. And I'd meant it when I'd told Robbie the night before that I was looking forward to seeing my first movie at the Palace.

I wanted to stake out a front row seat in the balcony, but first I went to the office to drop off my backpack and Kate's laptop. I looked around the room, wondering if there were any clues about what her email password might be. At home that morning I'd tried the name of every actor, director, and movie title I could think of before admitting that random guesswork was probably not going to yield the best results.

And neither would a casual glance around her office, I reasoned. But if Kate had been anything like me, there might be a Post-it tucked away somewhere with all the information I needed. I sat at the desk and slid the pencil drawer open, then jumped about a foot as the clattering drums and booming trumpets of the 20th Century Fox overture announced another day had begun for Marty at the Palace.

I was really going to have to do something to get used to that, I told myself, my hand on my racing heart. The fanfare had seemed even louder in the office than when I'd heard it the day before in the balcony.

My pulse was just beginning to return to normal when a chime sounded on my phone, making me jump again. I pulled the phone out of my backpack and saw there were two texts.

Baby. This is crazy. I know you want to go full Garbo but I need you. James is saying he didn't get the waiver, and the DreamWorks people are screaming their heads off about that contract. You know I don't do conflict. Where are you???

He didn't do conflict. Right. That's why he'd had me for all these years. Good old reliable Nora, making sure everything was smooth and easy for Ted Bishop. Well, it wasn't my job to make anything easy for him ever again.

The second text was from my lawyer.

Nora, I hope you've had some time to think about what you want. Leaving the shared domicile may have been a tactical error. Ted has taken occupancy again, which could hurt you. What about the beach house in Maui and the flat in London? It would do you good to establish residency. But more importantly, I need you to instruct me on how you want to move forward. What do you want?

That's what everyone had been asking ever since the news first broke. What did I want? How should I move forward? Up until this point all I'd wanted was a working time machine that would let me go back six months and keep Ted from ever meeting Priya Sharma. But finding a murdered man and taking over the job of a possibly murdered woman had had an effect on me. Life was short. Sometimes unexpectedly so. Life was too short to keep hoping Ted would change.

I sent the lawyer a text.

I don't want the house. I don't want any of the houses. I don't want Ted's money. I want mine. I want you to figure out what he would have paid a manager and agent all these years. That's what I want.

I turned off the screen and stood, feeling a little lightheaded. I had taken a stand. And now I wanted nothing more than to sit in a dark theater and watch a movie.

There were maybe half a dozen people in the balcony, and roughly twenty more down on the main floor. I knew it was only the early matinee on a Friday, but that seemed light to me. Particularly since, scanning the patrons, I was pretty sure most of them had gotten senior discounts.

Fortunately, ticket sales didn't pay the bills. I'd heard that concession sales and those annoying ads that come on before the show are what keep most theaters solvent. Which reminded me that I should probably take a look at the Palace books. There was a stack of bills on Kate's desk—my desk—that told me I probably shouldn't wait.

I was distracted from this line of thought by a light flickering and buzzing. It was the same one Albert and I had noticed the day before. Even as the house lights dimmed for the previews, that light stayed on, humming and flaring in a way that was sure to ruin the movie for everyone in the balcony.

I got up and made my way to the aisle. An elderly woman gestured at me.

"Are you going to tell the management about that?" She pointed to the sputtering light.

I didn't tell her I was the management. I just nodded and moved along.

Back in the interior hallway, I went up the half flight of steps to the projection booth. I hadn't been inside it yet, and I don't know what I was expecting. What I found was a small room, maybe ten feet by twenty, lined with racks of shelves that were overflowing with equipment. Mixed vintages of projectors, splicers, reels, and platters were all jumbled together on carts and tall tables. The only pieces of gear that didn't look antique were a control board with a Dolby label on it that I assumed worked the sound system and a computer-like thing that was probably a digital projector. Aside from that, the place looked like a storeroom at the Museum of Obsolete Projectors, and Marty was at the center of it.

"What are you doing?" he hissed. "You don't belong in here. Go away."

"That light is on the fritz," I said.

"I know. I saw it." He ran an agitated hand through his already disheveled hair. "I can't leave the projectors until after the changeover to the feature. I'll go fix it then."

"I'm not asking you to fix it," I told him. "I'll do it. Where do you keep the ladder?" This whole conversation was conducted in urgent whispers.

The preview for *Dr. Jekyll and Mr. Hyde* (1941, Spencer Tracey and Ingrid Bergman) ended, and Marty flicked switches on two projectors in quick succession, causing one to stop turning and the other to start. Another preview began playing.

"The ladder you were using outside," I persisted. "Where is it?"

"All right!" Marty said. "But don't use that one. It's too tall. Use the one in the break room. And try not to get electrocuted. They'd probably blame me."

By the time I found the ladder in a utility closet off the break room and hauled it back to the balcony, the opening titles of *Blithe Spirit* had begun. I positioned the ladder, an ancient wooden one that I mentally classified as "rickety," under the offending light. Thank heavens it was located above the aisle, and not in the middle of all the seats. I climbed up and realized I'd burn my hand if I just reached up to unscrew the bulb. So, cursing under my breath, I climbed down and headed back to the break room for something to protect my hand.

The elderly woman was glaring disapprovingly by the time I got back. I didn't blame her. We were a good ten minutes into the movie and the séance scene was about to start. I'd found a dry dishtowel, and I used it to reach up and give the bulb a twist, but it wouldn't budge. I tried for a better grip, afraid of squeezing too hard and breaking the bulb. I twisted again and the whole light fixture seemed to shift.

And that's when everything went dark.

Blithe Spirit
1945

Blithe Spirit was written and produced by Noel Coward, so you can expect wit and sophistication from both the living and the dead.

Charles Condomine (Rex Harrison), a writer, hires a medium to come to his home and conduct a séance as research for a book. His new wife (Constance Cummings) is charmingly tolerant, his friends are charmingly intrigued, and Madame Arcati (Margaret Rutherford) is a fizzy combination of eccentric spiritualist and aging British Girl Guide. (Tip: any movie with Margaret Rutherford is probably worth watching.)

Madame Arcati summons Elvira (Kay Hammond), the ghost of Charles' first wife, and when the séance is over Elvira decides to stick around and make charming and sophisticated mischief for all involved. This gives Rex Harrison a chance to be very Rex Harrison. Nobody can do an exasperated "Look here..." quite as well. If you only know Sexy Rexy as Professor Henry Higgins from *My Fair Lady*, you're in for a treat. (And if you don't know *My Fair Lady*, you're simply not living your fullest life.)

If you believe in ghosts (I don't) you probably won't spend as much time as I did wondering why Elvira can walk through a wall but not fall through a couch when she sits on it. Those sorts of thoughts are useless here. Trust me, you don't have to believe in ghosts. It's enough that you believe in Noel Coward.

What you'll have to get over:
Unfortunate green makeup that makes Elvira look a bit like she's in costume as the Statue of Liberty.

Best line Noel Coward ever gave Rex Harrison:
"You won't die. You're not the dying sort."

Movies My Friends Should Watch
Sally Lee

CHAPTER 6

I woke up on the couch in Kate's office, feeling like I'd been cast in a surreal version of *The Wizard of Oz* (1939, Judy Garland and who cares about anyone else when you've got Judy Garland). I was lying down and the whole cast of characters was gathered around me, but instead of the Scarecrow and the Tin Man, I saw the concerned faces of Marty, Albert, Callie, and a young woman I hadn't yet met.

"She's coming around," Marty said, which is when it first dawned on me that I must have lost consciousness.

"What happened?" I tried to sit up, but Albert gently restrained me.

"There, now, not too fast," he said. "You've had quite a bump."

"Sooooo," Callie drawled. "Am I calling the EMTs or what?" Her omnipresent phone was in her hand.

"No!" I said, this time managing to sit. "We don't need lights and sirens out front for the second day in a row. Who's running the theater? We didn't stop the show, did we?"

Marty gave me a look that almost verged on approving. "No. The people in the balcony are probably the only ones who even noticed anything."

"Good." I cautiously felt the top of my head and located a throbbing lump. "What happened?"

"The whole light fixture fell on you," Albert said. "Luckily Marty was there, and he caught you as you tumbled off the ladder."

"You caught me?" I asked Marty.

"Calm down," he said. "It's not like you fell into my arms. The light came down just as I got out to the balcony, and you sort of slithered down the ladder. I just hoisted you up before you got all the way to the floor."

"Well, thank you anyway." It was just as well that I'd been unconscious for all the slithering and hoisting. If I'd been awake I'd have died of humiliation. Then again, if I'd been awake I wouldn't have needed any hoisting.

"I told you I'd fix it," Marty groused. "If you'd been capable of waiting five minutes this never would have happened."

"Yeah...but if you'd fixed it yesterday this also never would have happened," Callie pointed out.

"Well excuse me for getting all distracted by the dead man in the—"

"That's enough!" Albert held up his hands, causing the bickering colleagues to momentarily back down.

The new woman was watching all this action as if it was the most amusing thing she'd seen in years. She was dressed in costume, in a pale blue uniform of wide-legged pants and a military-looking little jacket with two rows of buttons and epaulettes on her shoulders. She even had on a little brimmed cap with a gold braid. She must have been one of the employees I hadn't met yet, wearing some sort of ye olde movie palace costume for Halloween.

"Hi," I said to her.

At my greeting her expression changed completely. She looked amazed. Thunderstruck. She pointed to herself, her blue eyes growing enormous. "Me?"

"Yeah, hi." What was wrong with this girl?

And just as I completed that thought, she vanished.

I yelped.

"What, what, what?" Albert, Marty, and Callie were all looking at me like I'd lost my wits.

"Did you—?" I pointed to the empty space where the young woman had been, staring wildly at the trio of concerned faces.

"Maybe we *should* call the EMTs," Marty said.

"Nora, are you, like, losing it?" Callie asked.

"No, I'm...did anybody else—"

But my question died on my lips. Nobody else had seen anything because there had been nothing to see. I'd had a serious crack on the head. I'd imagined something. Someone. I wasn't losing my mind, I just had a concussion or something.

Albert was staring at me intently.

"I'm fine," I said, pulling myself together. I'd spent the night before compulsively reading up on the Palace's history. The vision I'd had was just a remnant of something I'd seen in a picture on Wikipedia. "I just need some Aspirin. And coffee. I could really use some coffee."

"I'll send Brandon up with some," Callie said. She glanced at the clock on the wall over the blackboard. "I should get back to the booth. He's alone down there, and—"

"Go," I told her. "I'm fine. All of you please just go back to work. Thank you, but don't worry. It's just a bump on the head." And a hallucination, but I pushed that thought to the very back of my mind.

Marty gave me a doubtful look as Callie left. "You shouldn't be alone after a head injury."

"Are you inviting me to hang out in the projection booth with you?"

The look of horror on his face was almost comical.

"I'm kidding," I told him. "Let me just grab that stack of bills," I nodded to the pile on the desk, then realized what a really bad idea nodding had been. "I'll take them and Kate's laptop down to the candy counter and start sorting things out. That way Albert will be able to keep an eye on me. At least until I'm cleared to go watch a movie."

I *still* hadn't seen a damn movie.

Brandon brought a battered old stool up from the basement, and I installed myself at the far end of the counter in the lobby. It gave me a chance to see the Palace in operation as one feature ended and the crowd came in for the next one. I use the term "crowd" charitably, as it consisted of only a dozen or so more patrons, most of them seniors.

Callie came in from the ticket booth after the rush, such as it was, subsided. Brandon immediately got her a soft drink and turned sixteen shades of pink as he handed it to her. She took it wordlessly and joined me at the counter. Albert had gone upstairs to the break room and I assumed he'd told her to keep an eye on me.

"Heeeyyy..." she said. "You haven't died of a brain bleed. Nice."

"Thanks," I said. "So, what's with you and Brandon?" He was occupied with getting just the right amount of butter on a customer's popcorn, and since the customer was giving loud and exacting instructions, I didn't think he'd hear us talking about him.

"Oh," Callie said. "He's, like, in love with me or something." She shrugged. "He'll get over it."

"Uh huh." I wasn't so sure.

"Sooooo, I have something for you, but I don't want you to get all weird about it." Callie pulled a purple foil packet out of her sweatshirt pocket. She handed it to me and I read that it contained one grape-flavored cannabis lozenge.

I looked at Callie with raised eyebrows. Cannabis is legal in California, and back in LA it seemed like edibles were as commonplace as granola bars. Still, most people don't go around just handing out pot candies to their new managers.

"I don't know if you, like, partake," Callie said. "But I just figured you might need a little help sleeping, what with everything..."

By "everything" I supposed she meant my errant husband and shattered life.

"And if your head still hurts, this might do a better job than Aspirin," she said. "It's like, a low, low dose, but it's really good. I got it at Monica's shop."

"Thanks, Callie," I said. "Maybe later..." I didn't tell her I had already hallucinated once that afternoon without the benefit of psychotropic drugs.

She shrugged. "Cool. Whatever."

I decided to shift the subject. "Who's Monica?"

"Monica Chen. She owns the Potent Flower, down on Divisadero. It's this totally cool, woman-centric, amazing pot shop. She was really good friends with Kate."

"Really?" Now she had my interest.

"You should totally go to her shop. The address is there on the back." She pointed to the lozenge I still held. "Monica knows everything. She can totally figure out, like, the exact right thing to help you."

"Thanks," I said. "I'll look into it."

Monica knows everything, and Monica was really good friends with Kate. Yes, I would go visit her shop. Totally.

I puttered around in the lobby until the last feature ended, and met two more employees, Claire and Mike, when they showed up to relieve Brandon and Callie for the evening shows. They were high school students, brother and sister, but their resemblance was so strong they might have been twins. Both had masses of dark brown curls and freckles like constellations across their faces.

Albert went home when the shift changed. Before he left I asked him whether there was a second projectionist to relieve Marty.

"Nobody else knows the equipment," Albert told me. "Kate used to, but with her gone there's only Marty."

I thought about that as I took over Albert's ticket-taking duties. There was a lot of equipment up in that projection booth, and if Marty was the only one who knew how to work it all, no wonder he was so exhausted and irritable. He must have been working nonstop ever since Kate's death.

The teenagers and I shut down the concession stand and tidied up the lobby while the last feature was playing. Then they went down to the basement to clean the restrooms, and as soon as the movie ended they both grabbed brooms and started sweeping out the theater behind the last of the moviegoers.

Marty came galumphing down the balcony stairs as the last patrons left. He seemed surprised to see me still in the lobby.

"You're here."

"I wasn't supposed to be alone after a head injury, remember?"

"Right. Are you...?" He pointed in the general direction of the lump on my head.

"Fine," I said, reaching up to touch it. "Just a little tender."

"Hrumph." He nodded and moved toward the lobby door. "Have you set the alarm?"

"What alarm?"

He stopped with his hand on the door. "The alarm alarm. The *burglar* alarm." He glared at me and went to the small metal panel in the wall near the door, pulling a key ring out of his pocket.

He opened the panel while talking. "The code is 1927, the year the theater was built. There's a keypad here and on the wall downstairs by the basement door."

I looked over his shoulder. I'd turned off the lights the night before but hadn't set the alarm. Oops.

"Once you see the yellow light flash you have ninety seconds to leave and lock the door behind you. Are you two done?" This last was addressed to Claire and Mike, who had come back into the lobby pulling on jackets and scarves.

They nodded in unison and waved goodbye as they went out the door.

"Do you have your stuff?" Marty asked me, his hand poised above the alarm keypad.

I grabbed my backpack, Kate's laptop, and my sweater from the counter and followed Marty out the door. Once outside, I locked the door behind us.

"Make sure you punch in the code to turn off the alarm if you're the first one in," Marty said. "You've got ninety seconds for that, too." He hesitated. "Are you okay to get home?"

"I'll be fine," I said. "It's only a few blocks."

Which was true, but when we left the shelter of the entryway and the cold wind hit me, it seemed like Robbie's comfy cottage was a million miles away. And home was even farther.

My most urgent thought upon waking the next morning was of coffee. The lump on my head had given me weird dreams that vanished as soon as I tried to remember them and left me feeling unrested and uneasy.

I was too antsy to hang around the house. I decided to go to the theater early and have a real look through Kate's office. I still hoped to find her email password somewhere. Maybe something in her emails would shed some light on why she, and possibly Raul Acosta, had died.

I stopped at Café Madeline for the most caffeinated beverage they offered, then went across the street to open the Palace. After turning off the alarm I went straight upstairs, stopping in the break room to put on a pot of yet more coffee before heading to Kate's office.

When I opened the door, I didn't quite understand what I saw. It was something from the dream I couldn't remember. It had to be. Because what I saw couldn't be real.

The uniformed blonde from my hallucination was sitting behind Kate's desk.

And she was looking at me with something like hope.

CHAPTER 7

She stared at me, a blue-eyed blonde who looked like she just stepped out of the chorus line in a Busby Berkeley musical. "Can you see me?"

I nodded. I could see her, but was she real?

"And hear me?"

I barely noticed as the backpack and laptop bag slipped off my shoulder to the floor. "Yes." My voice sounded strangled. What was happening?

She had the arched penciled brows and cupids-bow lips of a Jean Harlow wannabe. She pursed those lips now and gave a low whistle. "Well, if that don't beat..."

"Who are you?" I asked.

She looked as amazed as I felt. "Eighty years," she said. "More than that, I think? What year is it?" She looked confused for a moment, then focused on me again.

"All that time and nobody's ever seen me. I mean, some people thought they saw something, maybe out of the corner of their eye, a flash of light or something. I was holding a flashlight when it happened, you know." Her hand fluttered up to her forehead. "Well, no, you don't know. How would you know? You weren't born yet." She shook her head and then beamed at me. "But now you're here." She made a delighted sound that was half laugh and half gasp. "You can really see me? I haven't finally gone crazy?"

If one of us was crazy it probably wasn't the hallucination. It was probably the person having the hallucination. I groped my way to the couch and sat down hard as my legs gave out. This is what a mental breakdown felt like.

"Say, are you all right?" She stood, and I held up my hands. I didn't want her coming any closer to me.

"Don't be scared," her face crumpled in concern. "Honey, please don't be scared. I promise I'm not that kind of ghost. I'm just so darned glad you can see me. You don't know how lonely I've been."

One word of that declaration stood out to me. I had a hard time repeating it.

"Ghost?"

She nodded, curls bouncing. "Ghost, spirit, apparition, specter...I don't mind what you call me." She came around the desk—not through it, thank heavens—and sat on the couch, at the far end, away from me. I scooted back. "But, gee, I'd like it if you called me by my name. Nobody's said my name in all these years. It's Trixie—Beatrix, really, Beatrix George, but everyone calls me Trixie. Or at least, everyone did." She shrugged and smiled encouragingly.

"Trixie," I repeated faintly.

She sighed. "Boy, that sounds good. It makes me feel like I'm really *here* again. What's your name?"

"Nora," I said. I was having a conversation with a ghost named Trixie. That's all. Just a normal, everyday conversation with a ghost named Trixie. Happens all the time. To crazy people.

"Nora," she repeated, then grinned. "If you tell me your husband's name is Nick, I'm going to think you're pulling my leg."

A ghost who made jokes about the Thin Man movies. That sounded about right. That's just the kind of ghost I'd hallucinate when I lost my mind. Sure.

"Now, tell me, Nora—"

But whatever the ghost was going to ask was interrupted by the boom and thunder of Marty blaring the 20th Century Fox fanfare. I jumped and yelped. Trixie gasped and vanished.

One minute she was sitting there at the end of the couch, little blue cap on her head and look of delighted anticipation on her face, and the next minute she was gone.

"Trixie?" I felt like an idiot.

There was no response.

Of course there was no response.

"Trixie, are you there?"

"Who's Trixie?"

I may have screamed the tiniest little bit at the sound of Marty's voice. I jumped to my feet and turned to the door. "Did you do that?"

He crossed his arms. "I told you I require an overture to start my day."

I waved my hands. "Not the music. Did you..." But the look on his face had turned from defensiveness to bafflement. And how could he have made Trixie appear? I'd seen state-of-the-art holograms in Hollywood, but they'd been nothing like as realistic as the ghost I'd just been chatting with.

"Nothing," I said. "Never mind."

His eyes narrowed. "Who's Trixie?"

"I'm writing a screenplay." The lie surprised both of us. "I was just trying out some dialog."

He looked at me suspiciously, and I really couldn't blame him, but he let it go. "Whatever. I just wanted to tell you that there are doughnuts in the break room." He gave me one last look, then shrugged and left.

I sat down, shaking, and looked wildly around every inch of the room.

"Trixie?" I whispered.

Nothing.

There was no way I was going to sit in that office alone after that. I bolted.

I found Marty in the break room, pouring a cup of coffee. A box of doughnuts was open on the table next to the latest issue of *Classic Monsters of the Movies*.

I almost didn't go in, but I figured even grumpy Marty was going to be better than solitude in my current state. He may have been a lot of things, but at least he was undisputedly human.

"Finished writing?" he said in a way that implied he didn't believe for a minute that I'd been writing a screenplay and not talking to myself like a crazy person.

"Thanks for the doughnuts," I non-answered, perching on a chair at the table.

"I didn't bring them. Monica did. She'll be back up after she's had a look in the basement. She wanted to meet you."

"Monica?" I repeated. "Wait, who's in the basement?"

"Monica." He put the pot back on the warmer and turned to the table, piling three doughnuts on the magazine before picking it up to go. "She was a friend of Kate's."

"The Monica who runs the pot shop?"

He stopped on his way to the door, looking surprised. "How do you know that?"

"Callie mentioned her. What's she doing in the basement? There's still crime scene tape—"

"I know. I told her not to go back there. But she's looking for a pair of earrings she loaned Kate for a lobby display a while ago." At my look of utter confusion Marty sighed heavily, put the magazine back down, and sat. "Kate staged displays in the lobby for some features. A few months ago we showed *Jezebel*, and she put up a mannequin in a red ball gown. She got a wig from a costume shop, and Monica loaned her these old earrings she had. Now she wants them back, so she's looking down in the prop room for them." He raised his eyebrows. "Satisfied?"

"I didn't know we had a prop room."

"If you saw it on your first day you probably assumed it was a junk room." He took a huge bite of a jelly doughnut and wiped the red filling off his chin with the back of his hand.

"Should we put a display together for the mad scientists?" The movie lineup would change on Tuesday, and we would be showing a double feature of *Dr. Jekyll* and *The Mad Ghoul* (1943, Turhan

Bey and Evelyn Ankers). "Maybe something with lab coats and beakers?" Anything to avoid going back to Kate's office and facing the fact that I was losing my mind.

Marty finished the doughnut in one more bite. "That's a management call," he said when he'd swallowed. Then he raised his eyes to something behind me.

I turned, half expecting to see my bubbly delusion waving from the doorway. What I saw instead was a fortyish-looking Asian woman in workout clothes. "You must be Nora," she said.

I stood. "And you must be Monica. I've heard so much about you."

She looked surprised. "Really? Did you know Kate? I thought—" She glanced nervously at Marty.

He stood, gathering up coffee, magazine, and doughnuts. "I have things to do," he said. "I *always* have things to do." He gave me a pointed look before leaving me alone with Monica.

She still hovered near the door. "Um, did Kate mention me?"

"Oh," I said. "No. I never met Kate. Callie told me about your shop. She said I should go see you."

"Oh, right." She seemed weirdly relieved. "Yes, please do. I hear you're going through a challenging time. I'm sure I have something that could help."

I'd been going through a challenging time yesterday, when I'd only had to contend with the public humiliation of a divorce and one, or possibly two, murders. Now I was losing my mind on top of it. I didn't think pot candies were the best of all possible ideas.

Nevertheless, "Thank you. And I'm so sorry for your loss. I know you and Kate were close."

She nodded and moved into the room. "It's been hard. It isn't easy to make new friends as an adult. Everyone already has their own lives, their own interests..." She sat, and I found myself joining her at the table. "But Kate and I clicked from the beginning. Both of us were running neighborhood businesses, and she'd started her life over again when she came here all those years ago, too."

And suddenly I forgot all about the morning's hallucination.

This was the source of information about Kate's past that I'd been looking for.

I gave Monica a very genuine smile. "Can I get you some coffee?"

CHAPTER 8

Monica couldn't stay. She had to get to her shop, which was unfortunate because for about two minutes the thought of quizzing her about Kate had distracted me from the whole losing-my-mind-and-seeing-ghosts thing.

"Stop by the shop any time," she said as I walked down to the lobby with her. "I can give you some tips on the neighborhood."

"I'd like that," I said. "Hey, did you find your earrings?"

"Oh! No." She flushed for some reason. "But don't worry about it. I'm sure they'll turn up. And they weren't expensive, so it really doesn't matter."

"I'll still keep an eye out," I told her.

We said goodbye at the doors and I watched her go down past the ticket booth to the sidewalk, where she met Albert on his way in. They hugged and chatted for a moment and I tried not to feel completely nosy for watching them.

Monica had seemed friendly, but there was a weird nervousness about her. I was willing to bet she knew more about Kate's life than anyone else. She might even know where Raul Acosta had fit in.

Albert came in with a blast of chilly air.

"Good morning, Nora. Are you fully recovered?" He gestured toward his head.

"I'm fine," I told him. Aside from a slight case of psychosis. "I take it you know Monica."

He nodded, taking off his coat. "She's a lovely girl. I haven't seen her much since Kate passed. What brought her by?"

"Lost earrings," I told him. "She was looking for them in the prop room."

Albert frowned. "I hope our thief didn't strike again."

"Thief? What thief? I thought we only had a murderer."

He grimaced. "We showed a Richard Widmark double feature last spring, including the one where he pushes the old woman down the stairs in her wheelchair."

"*Kiss of Death*," I said automatically (1947, Widmark and Victor Mature).

"Right. Well, Kate got her hands on an old wheelchair and she tipped it over at the bottom of the lobby stairs with a shawl across it." He grinned.

Once again I regretted never meeting Kate.

"Unfortunately," Albert continued. "The wheelchair went missing from the prop room after we stowed it away. We couldn't find it last week when we were going to use it for *Whatever Happened to Baby Jane?*"

"Oh." Bette Davis had famously terrorized the wheelchair-bound Joan Crawford in *Baby Jane* (1962, Davis, Crawford, and a very unappetizing rat). "And you think someone stole it?"

"Well, if they did, they must have needed it more than we do," he said philosophically.

He'd walked past me and now stood at the bottom of the lobby stairs.

"When—" I wanted to ask him exactly when this had all happened, but I was distracted by someone at the top of the stairs. Someone wearing a vintage usherette uniform and waving cheerily at me.

"Nora! Hey, Nora! Can you still see me?"

I froze, staring at the apparition. Albert looked from me to the top of the stairs and back to me again. "Are you all right?" he asked. He glanced up again. "Is something there?"

I blinked. This could not be happening. Again.

"Nora?" Albert said.

"Excuse me, Albert." I dashed past him up the stairs, much to Trixie's delight.

"Oh, you *can* still see me! I'm so—"

"Not here," I muttered under my breath as I went past her. If I was going to have a full-scale breakdown it wasn't going to be in front of the nicest old man in the world.

I went to the office and Trixie followed me.

"I'm so sorry I went *poof* like that," she said. "It happens when I'm startled or scared or something. I wish I could control it, but—"

I went to Kate's office and slammed the door behind us. Behind myself. There was no us. There was just me and a manifestation of the massive stress I'd been under since Ted left.

"Look," I turned on the manifestation, intending to tell her in no uncertain terms to go away and leave me alone, and was confronted by big blue innocent eyes and a radiantly thrilled smile.

"You have to tell me everything, Nora," she said. "What's it like out in the world these days? I haven't left the theater in all this time." She perched on a wooden chair and looked up at me, all eyelashes and hope. "At first I could watch the pictures to figure out what was going on, but when they stopped showing new ones I started to lose track of things a little." A shadow passed across her face. "Sometimes I went away for I don't know how long, and every time I came back things were so different." She shook her head, shaking the momentary gloom away. "But now you're here and I feel, well, not quite alive again, but not so much like a ghost anymore either." She beamed. "So, tell me, what's happened in the world? Is everything better? I know we won the war, but there was another one, wasn't there? Tell me that was the last one. I hope everybody's safe now and there's peace and everybody has a job and there's a chicken in every pot and everyone just learned to get along with each other. Is that what it's like?" She gazed up at me.

Was that the utopia a woman of the 1930s would have dreamed of? I must have thought so, because I was the one hallucinating her. Even so, I was not about to shatter the optimistic illusions of a figment of my own imagination. Instead, against my better judgment, I asked her a question of my own.

"What do you mean when you said you went away? Where did

you go?"

"Oh." She sat back, her features clouding. "Just...away.
Nowhere. Or if I do go somewhere I don't remember it when I get
back here."

I sat on the couch opposite her, intrigued despite myself.
Maybe, if she was some sort of avatar conjured up by my own
imagination, I might be able to learn something from her—
something my subconscious was trying to tell my conscious self.
And maybe when I figured it out she would go away for good.

"Why are you here?" I asked her.

She blinked. "Because I loved Eddie Wheeler more than was
good for me."

It was not the answer I was looking for. I wanted to know what
Trixie—figment of my deranged mind—needed me to realize. What
I got was why Trixie—self-described ghost—was haunting the
Palace.

"Gee," she said, her voice filled with wonder. "I never thought
about it like that before. All these years, if I thought about why I
was still here, I thought it was just because I missed my chance. But
when you put me on the spot like that..." She blinked. "I think it
really was because of Eddie."

I couldn't help myself. "Who's Eddie?" I asked. "What
happened?"

"I was an usherette," Trixie told me. "I got the job when I was still
in school, and gee, it was swell. I got to see all the pictures before
anyone else did. You should have seen the Palace back then—why,
it was just about the most elegant spot in the world. Certainly the
most elegant spot I'd ever seen, except for in the pictures.

"All the kids from school came here, and I felt so grand in my
uniform." She straightened her spine and ran a hand along the line
of gleaming buttons on her jacket. "I may not have been able to get
a second look from Eddie Wheeler in Mrs. Brocken's American
History class, but boy, when I was here and all dressed up..." She

nodded and gave me a look. "He noticed."

"I'll bet he did," I said. She was, after all, an imaginary bombshell in a gold-embroidered cap.

She sighed deeply. "After I graduated they made me Head Usherette. There were eight of us then, so I had seven other girls under me. I never thought I'd have that kind of responsibility. But it was different, because the Head Usherette is the one who has to shush people and shine her flashlight on couples playing hanky-panky in the balcony." She grimaced. "And sometimes Eddie Wheeler and his girl were one of those couples."

"Oh." I thought I knew where this was going.

She nodded. "Sure, he came to the pictures every Saturday night. He was a big man after graduation. He got a good job and rode the streetcar to the Financial District every day in a clean shirt and a tie." She glanced at me. "And good jobs weren't easy to come by then. We were in a Depression, you know?"

I nodded.

"The awful thing was, Eddie always had some girl on his arm. Different girls all the time." She sighed. "But he still talked to me. Every Saturday night when he'd come in he'd say, 'Hiya Trixie, how's show business?' and we'd talk a little, and sometimes he'd buy me some licorice or something, even though he had another girl with him. And sometimes they got pretty steamed, too." She raised a penciled eyebrow.

"You really liked him," I said.

"Boy, I sure did," she sighed. "And he liked me too. I know he did. He'd have gotten those other girls out of his system after a while, and then he'd have realized I was right there, all the time. The one for him. Just like in the pictures." She stared off into the distance, looking wistful and longing and tragic and brave.

I knew she was just a hallucination, but she was kind of breaking my heart.

"Then something happened," I said.

Her gaze returned to me. "We were showing *The Awful Truth*," she said. "And Rivka—she was another usherette and my best friend in the world—she came and found me and said there was trouble in the balcony. So I went up and I saw that it was Eddie and some other guy, someone I didn't know. This guy was in the front row, and Eddie and his girl were in the row behind him, and they were arguing. Not shouting or anything, but it was loud enough that all the other people around them were shushing them and looking angry. So I shine my light on them and tell them to quiet down or take it outside. Eddie looks really surprised, like he didn't expect me to be like that, but what else could I do? They do quiet down, and I think everything's going to be all right, and then Eddie's girl says 'Are you going to let him get away with talking to me like that?' and the other guy turns around and says to Eddie 'Your dime-a-dance gal has quite a mouth on her.' And Eddie stands up and so does the other guy and I go over to stop things, because I can tell they're both plenty mad, and then the other guy says something else that I don't catch, but it must have been something terrible, because Eddie just hauls back and pops him one."

Trixie's eyes were huge, but they weren't seeing anything in the room around us. They were seeing a dark balcony more than eighty years ago.

"The guy doesn't see it coming. He falls back, and crashes into me, and I...I go right over the balcony, right over the side, and I drop my flashlight, and I remember thinking that it would break, and they'd take it out of my paycheck, and then before you know it I'm down in the seats below the balcony, looking back up at Eddie looking down on me. And for a minute that's all I see, just Eddie, looking at me."

Trixie's eyes fluttered. She seemed almost to flicker in front of me.

"Then I hear the screaming, and I look around, and the lights have gone up and they stopped the show and everyone in the seats around me is yelling and pointing at me, or covering their eyes and looking away, and it takes me a minute." She cleared her throat. "It takes me a minute to realize what they're seeing. And it isn't me standing there looking up at Eddie. It's me...broken. It's me laying across the seats and staring up at nothing because my eyes don't work anymore. It's me dead."

I held my breath.

"And then everything happens at once. First, it's the oddest thing. I see a gentleman on a horse, just as plain as day, come riding down the aisle. He's all dressed up in old-fashioned clothes and wearing a top hat." There was wonder in her voice. "And he's looking right at me—not at the broken me, but at me—and he's holding the lead to another horse, a beautiful white one, and he holds it out to me, like I'm supposed to get on the horse or something. And then I hear the yelling from the balcony, and I look up, and a couple of guys have grabbed Eddie, and they're saying he pushed me. They're saying he killed me and they're calling for the cops."

She looked at me, desperation in her eyes.

"And then the gentleman on the horse says 'Beatrix, I've come for you,' but I don't want to go. They all think Eddie killed me and he didn't, and I've got to make them understand that it was an accident, that he didn't mean to hurt me. And then the gentleman says, 'Beatrix, it's time,' but I barely even hear him. I run right past him up the aisle, and I practically fly up the balcony stairs to Eddie, but nobody can see me. Nobody can hear me yelling that Eddie didn't mean to hurt me. And then I look down, and the gentleman is looking up at me, and I can hear what he says, even over all the shouting, and he says 'Beatrix, please dear, it's now or never,' and I can see he's starting to fade a little, and I want to go to him, and I feel myself being sort of pulled to him, sort of floating, and then I hear Eddie yell 'Trixie!' and I stop myself. I stop myself from going to the gentleman and I look over at Eddie and he isn't looking at me, he's looking down at the broken thing and calling my name, and I go to him, but I can't make him see, I can't make him understand that I know he didn't mean to hurt me." Tears were rolling down her cheeks. "And when I looked for the gentleman again, he was gone."

She looked at me, and despite myself I wanted nothing more than to put my arms around this girl and comfort her.

The instant I moved toward her she disappeared.

Poof.

CHAPTER 9

Okay, I admit that after-midnight online searches for ghosts on blustery October nights were arguably not the best thing for my mental health, but I couldn't *not* look up Trixie when I went home that night. And the sanity-restoring news was that I found her.

Beatrix George was a real person.

My first stop was the Wikipedia page for the Palace that I'd found before. I zoomed in as far as I could on the photo of the Depression-era staff. There were a couple dozen employees, all wearing uniforms that were heavy on buttons and braid. They stood in rows on the sweeping lobby stairs and faced the future like they had no idea what it was about to do to them. Trixie was in the third row from the top. That blond hair stood out like a beacon.

Good. I had seen her photo before I conjured her up. Good.

Next I tried to search the online archives of the *San Francisco Chronicle* and the *Examiner*, but neither of them went back far enough. I could probably go to the library and scroll through microfilm, but in the end I didn't need to. Because the guys who had made that TV show about the haunted Palace had done all the work for me.

From the *Evidence Found!* website:

> Beatrix "Trixie" George was a 21-year-old usherette at San Francisco's Palace theatre in December of 1937. One night, during a movie, she was pushed from the balcony and died instantly.
>
> Edward Wheeler was a popular young man from a good family, but was also known as a troublemaker in the

neighborhood. Wheeler was in the balcony that night and several eyewitnesses swore they saw him push the beautiful young usherette to her death.

Wheeler was charged with murder. The charges were later reduced to involuntary manslaughter as it emerged that Trixie was accidentally pushed as she tried to stop a fistfight between Wheeler and another man. Wheeler pled guilty and served two years at San Quentin. The ghost of the usherette Trixie haunts the balcony to this day.

It went on to list numerous sightings and strange occurrences in the theatre over the course of the next eighty-some years, some more preposterous than others. I refused to believe that Trixie could be heard moaning the name "Edward" in the balcony on the anniversary of her death. I scoffed, and then realized I was scoffing because I knew Trixie called him "Eddie," which I didn't really *know*, I reminded myself, because Trixie was a figment of my imagination and not a ghost.

Still. Trixie's story checked out. Which meant that I had probably read something about it when I was researching Kate and the Palace the night before I got bumped on the head. That's all. That's what I kept telling myself. The story was missing some of the detail my imagination had supplied, like the film that was showing, but that was to be expected. Trixie—my hallucination—had said it had been *The Awful Truth*. That made total sense. *The Awful Truth* is about a divorcing couple, and it had probably crept into my subconscious simply because divorce was never long off my mind these days. Simple.

I shook my head and focused back on the Wikipedia page, staring at the photo, looking at the faces of people who had all presumably died long ago. Then I stopped looking at the picture, just the slightest bit afraid that I'd see myself staring back at me from under a jaunty little gold-embroidered cap. I had no intention of turning into Jack Nicholson at the end of *The Shining* (1980, Nicholson, Shelly Duvall, and a couple of very creepy little girl ghosts).

I shut down my laptop and then glanced at Kate's. I had made no progress in finding her email password, looking for the piece of "ah ha!" information in her emails that would tell me whether she'd been murdered and what, if anything, she'd had to do with Raul Acosta's chilly death.

Was my vision of Trixie related to the investigation? It had to be. There must be something that I'd noticed on some subconscious level, and I'd simply conjured Trixie up to tell me what it was.

And then it hit me. If I really had noticed something, and if the hallucinated Trixie really was trying to tell me what it was, maybe the simplest thing in the world would be to ask her. What if I just asked Trixie what she'd seen on the day Kate died? Or the day Raul Acosta was murdered?

Okay. That sounded like a plan. In the morning I would interrogate the figment of my imagination and with her answers both solve the murders and get rid of the ghost.

That's assuming she would appear to me again.

"Good morning, Nora! What did you do last night? Did you go out? Are there still nightclubs? Gee, I always wanted to go to a nightclub—you know, the kind of nightclub with a floor show and dancing and everything. But I never had the right kind of fella to take me. Do you have a fella, Nora? I bet you do, and I bet he's a wonderful dancer. Do you like dancing?"

Trixie greeted me with this as soon as I opened the lobby door the next morning. It was early on a Sunday, so I expected the theater to be empty. Which it was, except for one bouncy hallucination.

She peppered me with questions as I turned off the alarm and danced around me as I went up the balcony stairs, humming something that might have been Cole Porter's "You're the Top" as I opened Kate's office and deposited laptop and backpack on the desk.

"Trixie, we need to talk."

"Oh, goody!" She sat on the desk and put her feet on the chair in front of it. "I can't believe I finally have someone to talk to. It's so exciting! What do you want to talk about?" She hugged her knees and looked at me with the thrilled anticipation of a kid on the countdown to Christmas. "What kind of music do you like? Who's your favorite singer? Mine's Bing Crosby. Gee, he's swell. Do people still listen to Bing Crosby?"

"Some of them," I answered. "But, Trixie, I want to ask you about Kate."

She gasped in excitement. "Oh! Kate! Can you tell her about me? I've tried everything to get her to see me, but she never has. When she first came here I was always knocking things over and moving things—you have no idea how hard it is to knock things over or move things when you're a ghost—but she never realized I was here. But now if you tell her—What's wrong, Nora?"

Trixie didn't know. How could she not know? And how could I tell her?

I swallowed. I hesitated. Then I just had to say it. "Trixie, Kate died."

She blinked rapidly several times. "No." She shook her head. "No, I just saw her." She looked confused. "When did I see her? I saw her just the other day. Or maybe it was longer than that. Did I go away before you came here?" Confusion was turning to panic. "How long was I gone? Is Kate really—When? How?"

"What happened the last time you saw her?" I asked. "Think very hard. It's important."

Trixie turned her huge blue eyes to me. "It was...I don't know exactly when it was, but it was the first day *Random Harvest* was playing. I know because my friend Rivka's daughter brought her granddaughter—she would have been Rivka's great-granddaughter—to see it." Her brow furrowed in concentration. "The previews were playing, and there was nobody in the lobby but Kate, and then this man came in." She looked up at me. "He talked to her, and I wondered who he was, because Kate knew him right away. Is that important?"

"It could be," I told her. "What did the man look like?"

She shook her head. "I don't know. I only saw him from behind."

"Was he dark, fair, tall, short?"

"Tall, I think, but then everybody seems tall now compared to me. And dark hair..." She nodded. "I'm sure it was dark hair."

Dark hair like Raul Acosta?

"What happened?" I pressed. "What did Kate and this man talk about?"

Trixie's face crumpled. "I don't know. I didn't stay. On any other day I would have, but I heard *Random Harvest* starting, and I just love that picture, and I wanted to watch Rivka's great-granddaughter getting to see it for the first time." A look of horror came over her. "Kate and the man went up the stairs and I went into the theater. But she shouldn't have gone up the stairs with him and left the lobby unattended, should she? So something must have been wrong." She wrung her hands. "Something was wrong and I didn't see it and now Kate's dead and I should have—"

"No, Trixie, this isn't your fault," I told her. "There was nothing you could have done." Her eyes brimmed with tears, and I caught myself before reaching out to hold the hand of a hallucination.

"What am I doing?" I muttered. "This is not real. She is not real. What am I trying to tell myself?"

Trixie straightened, wiping her eyes. "What's not real? Who's not real?"

"You're not," I told her bluntly. "You're a figment of my imagination. You're my subconscious trying to tell me something that I already know about Kate's death. Or Raul Acosta's. I'm not even sure anymore." I slumped onto the couch and closed my eyes.

Maybe this whole San Francisco experiment had been a bad idea. Maybe I needed to check into a nice, quiet sanitarium somewhere. Did they still have sanitariums anymore? The one Bette Davis went to in *Now, Voyager* (1942, Davis and Claude

Rains) seemed quite nice. Woodsy, if I remembered correctly.

"Well!" Trixie said. I opened my eyes, and what I saw was a very indignant usherette. "Not real? Well, I like that. I'm standing right here!" Anger simmered in her eyes. "You've got some nerve, telling me I'm not real. I'm just as real as you are! Why, I'm—"

But whatever she was would have to wait. Because just as she was working up a good head of steam the door to the office opened, and in the doorway stood a tall dark stranger.

The Awful Truth
1937

Jerry (Cary Grant) and Lucy (Irene Dunn) are getting a divorce. All they need is the final decree and they can move on and marry other people. And if you believe that...

This is one of those rich-people's-problems movies that were so essential during the Great Depression. They may be dressed in gowns and top hats, but they squabble and love and break up just like the rest of us. Except with better dialogue.

The story begins with the assumption that both Grant and Dunn are having affairs. Each suspects the other is up to something, which leads to hurt feelings and brilliant lines like "You've come home and caught me in a truth."

Another stellar line: "The road to Reno is paved with suspicions." (For all you kids out there, people—usually wives—used to go to Reno for six weeks to establish residency for a divorce. There was a whole industry of dude ranches for divorcing women. Don't believe me? Watch *The Women*. Even if you do believe me, watch *The Women*, it's amazing. But I digress...)

So they split, with Dunn seeing a new guy (Ralph Bellamy) and Grant pausing for a brief dalliance with a showgirl on his way to an engagement to a stuffy heiress (Molly Lamont). But separated is not divorced, and the awful truth of the title is that Grant and Dunn still love each other. Of course they do! They're perfect for each other.

Grant and Dunn are so good in this movie. There's an ease to their performances, and they play off each other gorgeously. Just take a look at the interplay between the two as Grant's showgirl performs a cheesy nightclub act involving a wind machine blowing her clothes off. The look Dunn gives Grant is priceless, his reaction perfect.

This might be the first film where we see that signature Cary Grant thing where he's operating on two levels. We see how he's interacting with the other people in the scene, but we also see what he's thinking about them. And what he's generally thinking is "isn't this amusing?" Why, yes, Cary, it is.

And let's just take a moment to appreciate Ralph Bellamy, who made a career out of never getting the girl—or at least the lead. He's always likable and decent. He's just never Cary Grant.

Fashion thoughts:
While I bitterly regret that women rarely have the occasion to wear gloves indoors anymore, it must be a lot easier to get away with hiding an inconvenient lover in your apartment now that men's hats have gone out of style. Fashion is a double-edged sword.
Speaking of fashion, take a moment to soak in the sequins, the sequins, the sequins on Irene Dunn's gowns.

Things you'll have to overlook:
The opening scene's "what wives don't know won't hurt them" attitude of male entitlement to infidelity. Harrumph.

Most Cary Grant delivery of an annoyed line:
"Why don't you go...on with what you were doing."

Parting thought:
Does Cary Grant not realize that he'll always go back to his first wife? Has he not seen *The Philadelphia Story*? Or *His Girl Friday*? Or *My Favorite Wife*? Really?

Movies My Friends Should Watch
Sally Lee

CHAPTER 10

"I'm sorry." The man smiled enquiringly, glancing around the office. "I called out from the lobby but nobody was around. I came up here looking for the new manager."

I'd jumped to my feet, completely freaked out. "Who are you? How did you get in?"

I knew I'd turned off the alarm that morning, and I was sure I hadn't left the lobby door unlocked. There was no need to since all the senior staff had their own keys. And they wouldn't show up for hours anyway.

He held up both hands and backed up a step. "Whoa...it's okay. I'm not—" But I wasn't waiting to hear his explanation. I had already made it to the desk and picked up the phone.

"Hang on," he said. "Look, I didn't mean to scare you. The lobby door was open and I really did yell 'hello' a few times from downstairs, but I guess you didn't hear me." He turned his still-upraised hands. "I'm Todd Randall?" He said it questioningly, as if testing to see if I recognized it. When it was clear I didn't, he went on. "I have a film blog. I was working with Kate on putting together a film noir festival." He flashed a quick smile. "We'd been emailing about it for the past few months."

This made me slightly less inclined to call 911. Slightly. Had I left the lobby door unlocked? Trixie had been waiting for me. Had her chatter distracted me from closing it properly behind me?

"I came upstairs because I thought I heard someone," he went on. "And I followed the sound of your voice..." He lowered his hands. "Who were you talking to?"

I was talking to the still-fuming usherette who was standing right next to him, but I thought it best not to say so.

"No one," I replied.

"Well, I like that!" Trixie snorted.

"So," Todd gave me another smile. "Are you the new manager?"

"Nora Paige." I didn't smile back, but there was something engaging about the guy that made me want to. He looked to be in his early fifties and had that comfortably-broken-in-yet-still-quite-fit thing going on that some lucky men can pull off.

"Nora Paige," Trixie mimicked in a sing-song voice. "Nora Paige, who doesn't believe her own eyes when someone is standing right in front of her." She stamped a petite foot.

"Sorry," I said—to Todd, not to Trixie. "I haven't had a chance to come up to speed on everything Kate was working on."

"Oh, of course. Don't worry about it," he said. "I was sorry to hear about Kate. She was...something else."

There was a slightly awkward silence after that. More of a silence for Todd, probably, because he didn't hear the indignant protest from Trixie.

"The nerve of some people, calling other people imaginary!"

"Um," I said. "You mentioned something about a film festival?"

"Right." He took a step into the room, then paused, as if waiting for permission. I relented and made a "come in" gesture, still keeping a wary distance from him as he entered. "We were thinking of this spring. It's coming up on the ninetieth anniversary of the publication of *The Maltese Falcon*, and San Francisco is such a great town for noir." He sat easily in one of the guest chairs by the blackboard. "It just seemed like a natural connection. I hope you'll agree."

"Most of what I know about San Francisco comes from the movies," I admitted.

Trixie snorted. "Sure. Like you know anything about anything." She circled the intruder, regarding him appraisingly. He was dressed in dark jeans, a button-down shirt and a thick knit cardigan. The outfit, along with wavy salt-and-pepper hair and Clark Kent glasses, gave him the look of a liberal-arts professor on sabbatical.

"What's your blog?" I asked him, doing my best to ignore Trixie.

"It's called *Real on Reel*," he said, taking a card out of his pocket. "But do me a favor and hold off on looking at it this week. I just changed web hosting services and everything's a little messed up." He grinned wryly. "Computers, right?"

Trixie now stood behind his chair. "So I'm a hallucination, am I? Well, could a hallucination do this?" She stuck her tongue out at me.

"Yes," I said. Then, to Todd, "I know what you mean." I took the card.

"Could a hallucination do this?" She reached for yesterday's coffee mug on Kate's desk. I thought she was going to sweep it to the floor, but her hand went right through it.

Her hand went right through it.

"Darn it!" She stamped a foot again and screwed up her face in concentration.

I tried to concentrate on my non-imaginary visitor.

"What other movies were you thinking of?" I asked.

"Oh, we hadn't gotten very far in the planning." He crossed his legs, looking like he was settling in for a nice cozy chat. It occurred to me that if I wasn't primarily occupied with ignoring a ticked-off apparition, I might find him attractive. Which was a complicated and terrifying thought.

But the ticked-off apparition was hard to ignore. She was trying again for the coffee mug, this time using both hands. She compressed her lips and brought her eyebrows together in focused intensity.

The mug didn't move. Of course.

"Maybe we should have lunch some time this week," Todd suggested. "I know I just barged in here this morning, but I'd love to get your thoughts on the project. And get to know you." Another friendly smile. Maybe a little more than friendly. There was a gleam both warm and speculative in his eye. At which point my internal alarm system started flashing red lights. My marriage might have been over, but I was in no way ready for some guy to start flirting with me. Even an attractive one. Especially an attractive one.

"Oh. Ah, look..."

"Great. It's a date."

Wait. It's a what?

Which is when the mug went crashing to the floor.

Todd jumped to his feet, brushing at the cold coffee that had splashed onto his sweater. "What the—"

"Hooray!" Trixie yelled triumphantly. "Could a hallucination do that?"

"No," I said, staring at her.

She pantomimed casually buffing her nails. "I expect you'd like to apologize to me now." Cool as a ghostly cucumber.

I blinked. "I'm afraid I'm going to have to ask you to leave."

I was still staring at Trixie, but we both knew I was talking to Todd. He was looking around in confusion, not knowing how he had just wound up with a damp sleeve and a broken mug at his feet.

"Was that an earthquake?" he asked.

"Maybe. Look, I'm sorry, but I really do have a lot to do today." I practically dragged him to the door. "I'm sure you can find your own way out."

"Sure, but—"

"I'll call you about the...thing," I said absently, closing the door behind him.

I stood, my hand still on the knob, until I heard his footsteps retreat down the hallway. I took a very deep breath. And another. Then I turned to Trixie.

"You're real," I said.

She grinned. "Well, for heaven's sake. What do you think I've been trying to tell you?"

"You're a real ghost."

She curtsied.

"How..."

"I told you how. It was on account of Eddie Wheeler and missing my chance." She tilted her head. "Are you okay? You don't look so good."

I put a hand to my forehead. "Either I'm not crazy or I'm a lot crazier than I thought I was."

"If I were you I'd try 'not crazy,'" she said encouragingly. "Just see how it feels."

I nodded. "It feels like I'll have to rethink a few basic assumptions about the universe and reality and...everything." I sat on the couch without realizing I'd walked across the room.

"You do that, honey." Now that she'd made her point, Trixie was getting downright solicitous. "How about we go down the hall to get you a cup of tea and then we can have a nice long talk? Would you like that?"

I looked at her. At the real ghost of a real usherette who had really died in this theater in 1937. I stopped fighting it. I believed. And with that belief came a fizzing rush of energy I hadn't felt in a while. Energy and a mad curiosity.

"Yes, I'd like that," I said.

But that's not what happened. Instead, the office door flew open, I shrieked, Trixie vanished in fright, and Callie burst into the room.

"Nora! Are you all right—Oh!" She screeched to a halt as she saw me on the couch. "Oh. You're okay. I thought—" She pointed behind her. "I saw some random guy coming down the stairs, and, I mean, after the guy in the basement..." She leaned over, hands on her knees, shaking with unspent adrenalin.

"I'm fine." I got up and put an arm around her, guiding her to a chair. "Everything's fine. Just breathe." A minute ago I'd been the one on the verge of passing out.

She let out a shaky breath. "Nobody was supposed to be here this early," she said. "I just wanted to play the rough cut of my film on the big screen."

"It's okay," I said. "Of course you were startled to see a

stranger wandering around."

She gave me a look. "Startled? Try freaked AF." She moaned and closed her eyes. "I hid behind the candy counter until he left. How's that for being a warrior woman?" Her eyes flew open "You *cannot* tell anyone I hid."

"I don't have to tell anyone anything," I assured her. "And, by the way, hiding was the smartest thing you could have done. That guy could have been anyone, and he probably outweighs you by a hundred pounds. Unless you've got some pepper spray or the world's smallest gun in your pocket, you made the right call."

Her head flopped back into the cushion. "I have a media stick in my pocket. With my film on it."

"Right. Which probably wouldn't have helped much if he *had* been a homicidal maniac."

"No," she agreed. "So who was he?"

"Todd..." I had to fish his card out of my pocket to recall his last name. "Randall. He's a film blogger. He wants to do a noir festival."

She snorted. "Oh, great. Another one."

"Have we done one before?"

"Guys always think film noir is the be-all and end-all of classic movies," she said, scowling. "I mean, like, how about screwball comedies? How about honoring the great classic film editors, all of whom were women? How about women at war, or women in westerns, or anything other than private dicks and the dangerous dames they fall for?"

I laughed. Not because what she said was particularly funny, but because I was so surprised to see the ultra-cool student completely fired up by what was clearly her passion.

She gave me a dark look.

"Those are all great ideas," I hastened to tell her. "And we should do every single one of them."

"Seriously?"

"Absolutely," I told her. "I haven't even started to think about programming for after the holidays, but I'm going to have to, and soon. I'd love your help."

Did that mean I was staying? Staying in the haunted theater?

"Cool," Callie said.

Okay. My heart rate had just about gone back to normal. Trixie hadn't returned, but I knew she would eventually. Because she was real. A real ghost.

"Soooo..." Callie gave me a sidelong look. "Do you want to, like, watch my film or something? It's still really rough, but, like, maybe you could give me notes or something?"

"I'd love to." I blinked, surprised that it was true. I did want to see her film, and I did want to get to know her better. And I wanted to crack Marty's cranky exterior and hear more of Albert's stories. And maybe even figure out if it was Raul Acosta that Trixie saw Kate take upstairs on the day she died.

And, most of all, Trixie.

I wanted to know everything about Trixie.

CHAPTER 11

Trixie didn't come back all day.

I kept expecting to see her around every corner, but she stayed "away," wherever that was. Maybe she had to rest up after her big morning of knocking over a coffee cup and shifting the foundation of everything I thought I knew.

So I watched Callie's film with her from the projection booth.

"I thought Marty was the only one who knew how to use the equipment," I said as we entered his sanctum.

"He's the only one who knows how to use the, like, old stuff," Callie said, moving cautiously past a table with disassembled pieces of equipment arranged in neat rows. "But any idiot can use a new projector. You just turn it on and plug the stick in." She did so.

"This is what the multiplexes use, so they can hire one untrained teenager to run everything on twenty screens. Or some of them don't even do that anymore, they just beam everything in from the mother ship." She nodded toward a massive carton on a shelf on the far wall. It had a picture of a projector on it, a matte black box with a lens, and text that proclaimed the contents to be a 20,000-lumen 4K RB Laser Projector, which sounded both modern and expensive. "We got that like six months ago. We haven't used it yet. Marty calls it 'Hal.'"

Marty would. I looked at the carton. How the heck did Kate afford new equipment like this when the Palace seemed to be sustaining business on the strength of a handful of elderly regulars? Popcorn and advertisement revenue could only stretch so far. I made up my mind to have a good hard look at the books, and soon.

Callie was biting her lip. "Um, it's okay with Marty that I use the brain-dead equipment for my work, but I don't know how he'd feel about you being in here when he's, like, not."

"Don't worry," I said. "I'll tell him it was all my idea." I was, after all, his boss. Something I should probably keep in mind when I was around him.

She looked doubtful. "Just don't touch anything."

Callie's film was everything you might expect a rough cut of a student's documentary to be—both incredibly awkward and incredibly heartfelt. I praised what worked and gave her notes on what could be improved. She took it all in and then gave me a rare unguarded smile.

"Thanks, Nora. It means a lot to have someone of, like, your era get what I'm trying to do."

My *era*? At thirty-nine I was maybe fourteen years older than her. But I was spared a response by the now-familiar bombast of Marty's arrival music. I was getting more used to it. I only jumped a few inches out of my seat.

"How does he do that?" I asked. I'd always assumed he played it from the projection booth.

"He set up his phone to connect to the wireless speaker system," Callie said, grabbing her media stick and looking around to make sure we hadn't disturbed anything. "We should probably, like, bounce."

I agreed. I had no problem with telling Marty that I'd watched the film with Callie from his booth, but I was no fool. It could wait until he'd had some coffee.

The rest of the day got away from me, what with running a haunted theater and everything. There were staff schedules to figure out, and vendor orders to review. I lost a good couple of hours just searching for the warrantee on the soft drink machine. Turns out we were no longer covered. So with all that going on it wasn't until the next day that I got a chance to take a look at the Palace books. On the bright side, it was Monday, and the theater was closed on

Mondays, so I figured I'd have the whole place to myself.

Aside from the ghost of a chatty usherette.

"Trixie!" I called her name as I carefully made sure the lobby door was locked behind me before turning the alarm off and the stairway lights on.

"Trixie!" I felt like an idiot, calling to her softly as I went up the stairs. "It's Nora. Are you here?"

She wasn't. At least not on any spiritual plane I could see.

I fully intended to come up to speed on the Palace's finances, but after an hour and a half of looking at spreadsheets and QuickBooks files I had a better idea. I'd get a professional to do it. Because what I was seeing simply didn't add up. Kate had made some massive purchases in the past year. The digital projector I'd seen the day before cost almost a hundred thousand dollars. How could she possibly have paid for that, and why, since it had never even been taken out of the box?

I thought about it. Had she been planning to change the Palace? To turn it into a modern theater, showing a steady stream of CGI superheroes fighting each other while cities exploded spectacularly around them? That was a depressing thought. But what if she had? Would someone have wanted to stop her? Wanted to enough to kill her?

And the projector wasn't her only extravagant expense. There had been a steady stream of smaller but significant equipment purchases. A ten thousand dollar large-format laser printer. A twelve thousand dollar professional-grade espresso maker. And as far as I could tell, none of it had been installed. I didn't even know where it all was. And why would she have made those sorts of elaborate investments anyway when she had a soft drink machine with a broken icemaker, faulty lighting, and a to-do list for her once-a-month handyman that stretched to three pages?

No, I wasn't up to this kind of financial analysis. Income versus outgo I understood. But this kind of thing called for a professional accountant. I sent a text to Robbie.

Hey you. Call me when you get a chance. I've been digging into the Palace books and I've got some questions.

I'd only just gone back to the laptop when my phone pinged with a response.

If it's about money, talk to <u>Naveen</u>. He's the best. How are you doing? Settling in? Feeling better?

I was, actually. Both settling in and feeling better. Possibly because I had the many puzzles of the Palace to solve, and possibly because, in light of what I'd learned about the existence of ghosts in general and Trixie in particular, the entire world had suddenly taken on new and fascinating dimensions. That strange fizzing sense of renewed energy hadn't left me. But it would probably be best not to mention that to Robbie. At least, not in a text. And possibly not ever.

Yep, you were right. Keeping busy is the best medicine. That, and not looking at the gossip blogs.

Her reply told me she'd bought it.

So glad. I'll call tonight.
xxoo

I clicked the link to Naveen, recalling him as Robbie's longtime financial manager. I'd met him at the housewarming party for her first place, a bungalow in Hancock Park that she'd since traded up for her Hollywood Hills mansion. I wasn't sure Naveen would remember me, but a basic doctrine of the Hollywood religion is that you never admit to not knowing someone, so I figured I'd at least get a response to a text.

I sent it and quickly closed my app before I caved in and looked at the seventeen texts Ted had sent. Whatever he had to say,

I didn't want to hear it.

Okay, that much was done. And I was alone in Kate's office, so it was arguably the perfect time to ransack it looking for her email password. Not only did I still want to see if there were any clues about Raul Acosta, I now also wanted to make sure Todd Randall's story about the film festival checked out.

I stood and surveyed the room. Where would I hide a Post-it, or a pad of paper, or a notebook that I used to write down my passwords?

The room's clutter seemed to mock me. And then I had an idea. What if someone had seen Kate stash a password somewhere? Or, better yet, what if someone had stood over her shoulder when she typed her password in? Someone who had been hovering around her for years trying to be noticed? A lonesome ghost, perhaps?

"Trixie?" I tried again. "Are you there?"

Nope. She was real, but I had the feeling she wasn't going to be predictable.

I decided to mentally section off the office and search it in pieces, the way my granny had taught me to clean my room when I was a kid. First, the desk. No, first clean up the broken mug that still lay in pieces on the floor. I grabbed a pamphlet and used it to brush the ceramic shards into a wastebasket. When I stood I bumped into the blackboard, getting chalk dust on my shoulder and smudging the writing for the September lineup.

The September lineup. Wastebasket in one hand and pamphlet in the other, I stared at the programming Kate had organized for the month before October's Halloween horror movies began. September had begun with two weeks of back-to-school features, starting with the silent classic *The Freshman* (1925, Harold Lloyd), before moving chronologically through everything from *Good News* (1947, June Allyson and Peter Lawford) to *Teacher's Pet* (1958, Doris Day and Clark Gable), and ending, of course, with *The Graduate* (1967, Dustin Hoffman and Anne Bancroft). The next week was screwball comedies, and the month ended with a "Falling in love with Fall" theme. And there, on the last weekend of the month, was *Random Harvest* (1942, Greer Garson and Ronald Colman), the movie Trixie had watched with Rivka's great-granddaughter on the day she'd seen Kate go upstairs with a strange man.

It had opened on the day Kate died.

Random Harvest
1942

You guys...*Random Harvest*. I mean, I know it's preposterous and completely impossible, but come on! It's so good! You may see it listed as a "drama" or maybe a "romance," but this, my friends, is a tearjerker. A good old-fashioned two-hankie affair that will break your heart in a million places and then fill it back up again.

We begin in a mental hospital at the end of World War I. Ronald Colman, whose gently mussed hair and slight stammer tell us he's in Great Emotional Pain, is a patient named "Smith" who suffered a head injury in the trenches and has lost his memory.

In the nearby town, Greer Garson is a singer/showgirl who wears the most adorable little shorty kilt onstage and has a knack for making wayward amnesiacs feel good about themselves. She meets Colman in the street during the armistice celebration, calls him Smithy, and takes him in when he collapses with fever. When he recovers she leaves her troupe and the two of them head to a storybook cottage in the countryside, "the end of the world, lonely and lovely" so he can regain his strength.

A modern viewer will undoubtedly raise an eyebrow at her willingness to give up her entire career and way of life for a guy she's known five minutes. Maybe that was expected of a woman in 1918? Or, more importantly, in 1942 when the film was made? Never mind. She gives up her whole life for him. It will not be the last time.

In the country, their happiness blooms like the soundstage cherry trees beside their white picket fence. They're in love, and they build a lovely life together. He starts earning money by writing (adding to the fairytale aspect of things) and even though he hasn't recovered his memory, everything is lovely. Until, well, it isn't.

Colman is in an accident, and the knock on his head knocks his memory back. His original, pre-war memory. And while in another movie this might be cause for some celebration, it also knocks all memory of his life with Garson away. Heartbreak! Grab that hankie now, because he remembers his name, and it isn't Smithy.

Colman goes back to his old life, which includes a family manor (Random Hall), a family business (making lots of money), and Kitty (Susan Peters) a niece-by-marriage who goes from fifteen to twenty-two while crushing hard on him. Maybe it isn't supposed to be icky because she isn't really his niece, but it is. Because she's twenty-two and he's fiftyish and I know, but really.

In any case, watching her grow up we see that years have passed. Years with no Greer Garson. The only hint Colman has of his missing years is the key to their humble cottage, which he carries with him always. Clueless.

And then...THEN...we have a scene where Colman the businessman sits contemplative in his office. His secretary enters, and yes! It's her! Greer Garson has found him and is working as his secretary! There's no dialogue for a moment because everyone in the theater must have been losing their minds. Greer!! Sitting there serenely and calling him "Mr. Rainier" while he has no idea he used to love her! I can't take it.

The look on her face as she watches him tells us everything we need to know about her. She still totally loves him. Once again she's given up everything to be near him. And then the look on her face when he says he's marrying the youngster Kitty—I can't even.

I won't say more. I won't. You have to watch this movie. If you're the type who believes in destiny and "the one," you'll be delirious. If you're not (and I'm not) you'll wish, just briefly, that you were. And although good taste and my lawyers prohibit me from endorsing a strategy of hitting your lover over the head to get him to snap out of it and remember you, you will be tempted. God knows I have been.

Random thoughts:
Check out the frothy frothy lace Garson wears at her collars and cuffs when she first meets Colman. So soft and feminine. Then her whole look changes to sleek sophistication when she becomes his long-faithful secretary.

Garson and Colman have two of the poshest voices ever to be recorded on film. I could just go on listening.

They made a lot of movies back then. This came out the same year as *Mrs. Miniver*, probably Greer Garson's definitive role, for which she won the Oscar. Consider yourself encouraged to go watch that next. And bring another hankie.

Movies My Friends Should Watch
Sally Lee

CHAPTER 12

An unknown man had come to see Kate on the day she died. Trixie had seen him go up the balcony stairs with her.

Was he Raul Acosta? I tried to imagine a set of circumstances that started with Kate and Raul going up the stairs and ended with both of them dead, him on ice in the basement and her at the bottom of a hill in Golden Gate Park.

Did she kill him for some reason? And hide his body? Then kill herself in a fit of remorse by throwing herself off a hill?

That seemed doubtful.

Why would she have killed him? Who was he to her anyway? Trixie said it had seemed like Kate knew the man who came to the theater that day. If it had been Raul, what was their connection? And even if she had killed him, for whatever reason, why would she then kill herself? And in such a weird way? But the alternative was that she'd murdered him, then gone for a walk in the park and met with a highly unlikely accident. None of it made sense.

Which brought me back to what answers might be lurking in Kate's email account. Maybe I should forget about finding her password written down somewhere and just get a hacker to break into it.

Wouldn't it be great if I just happened to know a hacker? But my social circle tended more toward the out-of-work screenwriter set. And even they were in LA. The only people I knew in San Francisco were at the Palace. And one of them wasn't even alive.

My phone pinged and I reached for it. Naveen had gotten back to me quickly.

Hey Nora. Long time! I'd be happy to take a look at the numbers for you and Robbie. Send the files anytime.

Okay. At least one piece of the puzzle might get some traction. I went back to the laptop, zipped up the files, and sent them to Naveen. Then I stared at the icon for Kate's email some more. It taunted me.

I was still staring at it when I heard Marty's overture.

Oh, good. Company.

"What was Kate's favorite movie?"

I'd given Marty a chance to settle in before going to look for him, and I now hovered in the doorway to the projection booth. Marty sat on a stool at the table I'd seen yesterday with the disassembled equipment spread out on it. He was methodically examining and cleaning each piece. If he was surprised that I was at the theater on a dark Monday, he didn't show it.

"She had a hundred favorite movies. That's a ridiculous question."

"It's not a ridiculous question." I came into the room and perched on the stool opposite him. "It's the kind of question that keeps dinner party conversations going even in the toughest of times."

He gave me a stony look. "I don't go to a lot of dinner parties."

This did not come as a surprise.

"From what I've seen, you don't go to a lot of dinners," I told him. "You're always here."

"Someone has to be."

"Even on your day off?"

"There are no days off."

"Right." I hadn't intended to have this particular conversation right then, but since he'd opened the door, and since we weren't likely to be interrupted, I went for it. "That's why I think we need to hire some backup for you."

"Backup?" He stared at me. "You think you can just *hire* someone who knows how to..." he gestured to the pieces of equipment in front of him, then more broadly to the piles of gear on the shelves and the multitude of projectors and paraphernalia all over the room. "Good luck."

"No, I don't think I can just hire someone who already knows everything," I said. "But I do think I can hire someone that you can train on some of it. Someone who can take a few shifts for you, once you're comfortable that they know what they're doing. Someone who can let you have a day off once in a while. I know Kate used to be able to help, but I—"

"You're not Kate."

I ignored his accusatory tone. "I'm not, and I'm not saying you should train me. But you should train someone."

He placed the gear he'd been polishing on the tabletop, then crossed his arms and regarded me. "You do realize that would just add to my workload."

"Temporarily," I said. "Until they can actually help out with your workload."

"Or leave," he said. "Just about everyone who applies for a job here is a student. I can just see myself spending months training someone who'll up and leave the minute they graduate."

"Okay, let's not hire a student," I said. "Maybe someone who's retired, like Albert."

The look he gave me was scornful. "Alberts don't just grow on trees. And don't go getting any ideas. Albert himself does a lot around here. I don't want him to overdo it with anything more."

I put my elbows on the table and regarded Marty. He looked genuinely concerned that I might exploit the ancient Albert. "I have a theory about you."

"I'm sure you do. I have one about you, too."

"I think you're a great big softie."

He rolled his eyes. "Why did you ask me what Kate's favorite movie was?"

I sat back. "Okay, sure. Let's change the subject. But we'll come back to it." I gave him a look. "I asked because I'm trying to open her email." I held up a hand to ward off his inevitable protest. "I know, it's a terrible invasion of her privacy. But, among other things, I want to know if she'd had any contact with Raul Acosta."

Marty stared at me. He didn't protest.

"Also," I went on. "Some guy showed up yesterday claiming that he'd been working on a film festival with her. He said they'd emailed about it. I want to see if that's true."

Marty's eyebrows lowered. "What guy? Kate wouldn't have planned anything without letting me know about it."

"Todd Randall," I said. "He's got a blog."

Marty snorted.

"I know, I know, everybody and his uncle has a blog. But this guy got into the theater yesterday morning—maybe because I left the door unlocked and maybe not—and he knew where Kate's office was, and I just want to make sure he checks out. Have you ever heard of him? Or the *Real on Reel* website? He said it's down right now, but—"

"You left the door unlocked!?"

I waved my hands. "Maybe. Not the point. Do you know this guy?"

Marty stood. "I only read one film blog." He started to pace, as best he could in the overstuffed room. "And it isn't *Real on Reel*, whatever that is."

I resisted the urge to ask him what that one blog was. "Okay, so, if Kate never mentioned him to you, it's possible this guy isn't who he says he is. One way of verifying that would be to look at her email."

Marty stopped and glared me. Then he sighed and said one word.

"*Summertime.*"

Summertime (1955, Katharine Hepburn and Rossano Brazzi) is about an American spinster opening her heart to romance in

Venice. It's a gorgeous film and I love it. I don't know if I'd call it my favorite movie, but, according to Marty, it had been Kate's.

He followed me back to the office, muttering. I took a seat at the desk and opened Kate's laptop. I clicked the email icon and hoped for the best.

summertime
Nope.

Summertime
Nothing.

Summertime1955
No.

SummertimeHepburn
Uh-uh.

I tried every variation on the movie name that I could think of, then tried a few Marty came up with, including Kate's favorite quote from the movie: "Eat the ravioli." Nothing worked.

Eventually Marty stopped hovering over my shoulder and slumped into the chair opposite the desk. "It isn't the movie."

My fingers still hovered over the keys. "I don't suppose you could introduce me to an obliging hacker, could you?"

He shrugged. "We could always put an ad on Craigslist."

I leaned back in the chair. "It may come to that."

We sat for a moment in despondent silence, then Marty spoke. "Were you serious?"

I blinked. "About what?"

"About hiring someone else." He cleared his throat. "Someone to...help."

"Of course I'm serious! Let's start looking." I was surprised but relieved that he'd apparently decided to be reasonable about this.

"Because I was thinking..." he said.

Oh. Something in his voice told me not to be too glad just yet.

"Maybe the reason Robbie sent you here instead of making me manager is that she knew it would be hard to backfill for me. I mean, aside from you being her bestie who's having a breakdown and everything." He shifted in his seat. "Maybe she and the other owners don't see how they could replace me as projectionist. But if I can get someone else in, and at least partially train them, maybe when you leave she'll see that she can promote me after all."

I opened my mouth, then closed it. There was so much to object to in what he'd just said, but I focused on the most insulting bit.

"Her *bestie* who's having a *breakdown*?" I said. "I mean…I'll grant you that Robbie did me a huge favor by sending me up here, but being her friend is hardly my only qualification—"

I was interrupted by Marty's snort of derision.

Okay. That did it. I'd had just about enough. "Do you think you know me?" I demanded. "Because of what you've seen on the gossip sites? Because you think you know my husband? You think you know my story? Well, you don't, and the sooner you figure that out, the better."

"Look, I was only saying—"

"And furthermore," I stood. "What makes you think I'm going to be leaving anytime soon? What makes you think I won't fall in love with this place and stay for—"

"Oh, please," he interrupted. "You're not staying, and we both know it."

"We both know *what*?"

"We both know you're only here for the duration of this midlife crisis divorce drama. By the end of the third act you'll be back to swilling green drinks in Malibu with the rest of the LA narcissists, writing rom-coms that have any suggestion of originality focus-grouped out of them. And I'll be the one still here, because I'm the one who goddamn loves this place."

He spoke with heat and with certainty, as if no one could possibly disagree with him.

I was flabbergasted, hurt, and angry in equal parts. "That's what you really think?"

He seemed to suddenly realize the epic inappropriateness of his remarks and had the very small grace to look uncomfortable. He cleared his throat. "Okay, maybe you won't start writing rom-coms," he allowed.

"Probably not," I said icily. "But if I did they would be spectacular. Anything else?"

He sat again, not exactly squirming but close. "Well, maybe you're not a complete LA narcissist," he said grudgingly. "I mean, a complete LA narcissist probably wouldn't get so invested in trying to figure out who killed Kate."

"Thank you," I said, sitting. "And maybe you're not a defensive jerk, but I haven't seen much evidence to the contrary." I didn't give him a chance to respond. "And I know you goddamn love this place."

He gave me a wary look.

"I also know that you're exhausted, and you're threatened by me being here, and you're grieving Kate. And I think the only emotion you allow yourself to show is anger. And I'll admit it, the truth is I don't know how long I'm going to be here. But I'll make you a deal: if I do decide to move on, I promise you'll be the first to know."

At this he looked interested.

"But don't think that means you'd automatically get this job," I warned him. "For one thing, it wouldn't be up to me."

He crossed his arms. "And for another thing?"

I blew out a breath. "Has anyone ever told you that you're not exactly a people person?"

Which is when something stunning happened. It wasn't exactly on the scale of finding out that ghosts were real, but it was still something of a shocker.

Because that was when Marty laughed.

CHAPTER 13

"So, one employee thinks I'm so old I'm from another *era*, and another thinks it's just a waiting game until I abandon ship and leave him to his rightful place as manager."

I was on the phone with Robbie, sunk deep into the cushions of the couch in her guest house. And yes, I was drinking her wine.

"Okay, one," she responded. "Millennials think anyone who didn't grow up worshiping *Hannah Montana* is ancient. Just ask my beloved daughter. For all practical purposes, you are from another era. So am I. And I'm assuming you're talking about the bitter projectionist wanting to be manager?"

"I think of him more as the hostile projectionist," I said. "And to think, earlier in the day I called him a big old softie."

"To his face? You're a braver woman than I am," she laughed. "But you're right. Plus he'd do anything for the Palace and knows literally everything about it. If he weren't so completely antisocial he might make a decent manager. He loves the place. If the ghost of a showgirl really were running around, he'd probably want to marry her."

I didn't know about the ghost of a showgirl. I only knew about the ghost of an usherette. And I didn't think Marty was Trixie's type. Or vice versa.

"On paper you two should be friends," Robbie said. "He knows almost as much about classic films as I do, which means he knows maybe half as much as you do. Why don't you just stick to talking about movies for a while?"

"He doesn't think I know anything about movies," I told her. "Classic or otherwise."

There was a pause. "Okay, that's hilarious. Does he know who you *are*?"

"He thinks he does." I drained my glass. "That's the problem. Hey, Robbie, tell me something. Were you and your partners ever thinking of turning the Palace into a first-run theater again?"

"Of course not. Why would we do that?"

"It was just a thought. I'm trying to figure out why Kate bought some of the equipment she did."

"Oh! That reminds me, Naveen called this afternoon. He said there was something off with the books."

I sat up. "Did he say what?"

"No. It was just a voicemail. I'll call him back tomorrow."

"Who actually managed the Palace finances?" I asked. "Did Kate have an accountant or a tax person that we should call in?"

"She handled everything herself," Robbie said. "I guess that's something else we need to take care of. I've got a conference call with the other owners set up for next week."

"How often do you all talk?"

"Hardly ever. Most everything is over email. There are three other investors, but I haven't even met the newest. We've all got crazy schedules, and none of us are involved in the day-to-day of running the theater. Speaking for myself, I just collect my quarterly profits and enjoy the free popcorn whenever I'm up in San Francisco. Kate took care of all the actual work."

Once again I realized what an enormous void her death had left.

"And the other owners are all that hands-off too? How can you be in partnership with someone you've never met?"

"It's just sort of worked out that way. The ownership is split into four equal parts. I bought my fourth a couple years ago when one of the original guys needed cash to finance some project. Then about a year ago another of the owners decided to retire and sold his fourth to a woman up there in the Bay Area. There's been an owner's meeting since, over video conference, but I was off on location at the time so Jason covered it for me." Jason was Robbie's ninja-like assistant. "I suppose we'd all have gone to Kate's funeral, but she'd left instructions that she didn't want one."

"Didn't you have to clear it with them when you sent me up here?"

"I sent them all an email floating the idea before I said anything to you. They were just happy to have someone step in, even if it's only temporary."

Was it only temporary? Of course it was. Just until I felt like myself again. Still, I felt a weird pang when she said so.

Robbie was still talking. "I think, when we meet next week, I'll recommend hiring Naveen to take over the financial stuff. That's once he figures out where we stand."

"Let me know what he thinks," I said. "Maybe Kate had some weird system I don't understand, but the numbers just didn't make sense to me."

"Sure. And, um..." Robbie became uncharacteristically hesitant. "Naveen wasn't the only person I heard from today." She took a breath. "I got a call from Ted."

I poured another glass of wine, hating the jolt of electricity that shot through my system.

"He asked me to tell you he misses you."

"Misses me or misses the hundred thousand things a day I did for him?" I kept my voice dry as my traitorous pulse pounded.

"'Atta girl," Robbie said, sounding relieved. "Stay strong."

"Of course I will," I told her. "I have very few other options."

The next day I met Albert outside the theater. He was chatting with Marty, who was once again up on the ladder changing the marquee to the new lineup.

"Mad scientists," I said by way of general greeting.

"Oh, Nora!" Albert was typically warm in his welcome. "I was just telling Marty that I seem to recall a poster for *Dr. Jekyll* in the archive. Perhaps it's time to switch out Karloff and friends?" He nodded toward the *Frankenstein* and other monster posters currently lining the tiled walkway to the lobby doors.

"Great idea. I'll help," I said. "Morning, Marty," I called up to him.

"Sure," he said.

So, that went well.

After dropping our things upstairs in the office (where Trixie was not in residence—at least not visibly) Albert and I took the back stairs all the way down to the basement. The stairwell couldn't have been more different from the sweeping grandeur of the lobby stairs. The walls were exposed brick, the railing was iron with a layer of peeling green paint, and the stairs themselves were bare concrete.

We clattered to the bottom and I saw that we were just a short distance away from the equipment room and alley door, both still sealed off with crime scene tape.

"I should call that detective," I said. "And ask him when they're going to be finished with the room." I could also ask him if he'd found a connection between Raul and Kate, and if they'd figured out exactly when Raul had gone on ice, and any number of other things that he undoubtedly wouldn't tell me.

"The prop room is this way," Albert said, leading me around a corner, then around several more, and down a long hallway to a room I barely remembered from my first day tour.

It was large and windowless, and if I'd kept my bearings correctly, it was directly underneath the stage upstairs.

Miscellaneous piles of junk revealed themselves to be not entirely miscellaneous on a second look. A rack of shabby costumes was in one corner, surrounded by accessories ranging from tap shoes to umbrellas. Another area had furniture—beat-up chairs and tables stacked with random odds and ends.

Albert went straight to the only new-looking piece of furniture in the place, and even that looked like it had been scavenged from some office in the eighties. It was a tall gray metal file cabinet with very wide, very shallow drawers. I'd seen cabinets like it in art departments. Albert pulled out one of the drawers, labeled "D–G" and sighed.

"Gorgeous."

I peeked over his shoulder. He was regarding a sultry Rita Hayworth trailing cigarette smoke as *Gilda* (1946, Hayworth and Glenn Ford) and whether he was talking about the actress or the poster itself, I had to agree. Gorgeous.

"Is that an original?" It certainly looked like one to me. But it also looked brand new. There were no pin holes in the corners or other signs of the rough usage it would have seen when the movie was first in theaters.

"No, but Kate found a supplier that does amazing reproductions. You should see some of these. Careful."

He slid Rita down a bit to reveal a sheet of archival paper covering the next poster. *Gaslight* (1944, Ingrid Bergman and Charles Boyer). Again, the quality of the reproduction was extraordinary.

"Should we bring that one up?" I suggested. "It's part of the 'Ladykillers' slate that starts Friday."

"Good idea," Albert said, pulling it carefully from the stack and holding it by the top corners. "Oh. Could you..." he nodded to a nearby desktop. I quickly moved everything on it to one corner. "There's paper in the top drawer," Albert said. I opened the drawer to find sheets of poster-sized archival paper in a neat stack. I took one and placed it on the table. Albert put *Gaslight* on top of it.

"It's probably silly to take such care, but Kate was very particular about the posters. When she started acquiring the high-quality reproductions she made sure everyone handled them as respectfully as if they'd been originals—that's when we handled them at all. She preferred to take care of them herself. She even switched to magnets in the display frames, instead of pushpins, to avoid damage."

"I wonder how much an original *Gaslight* would be worth," I said.

"Probably more than I am," Albert grinned.

"You're wrong there, Albert," I told him, carefully looking through the rest of the stack. "I have the feeling you're priceless."

"Oh," he said. "Yes. Well. We'll see if you still think that when you know me better." He gave me a sly grin and came back to the "D-G" drawer. "*Dr. Jekyll* should be near the bottom."

It was, and so was *Dial M for Murder* (1954, Grace Kelly and Ray Milland) which was also part of the 'Ladykillers' lineup. There were four display frames in the walkway to the lobby doors, but we didn't have posters for any of the other upcoming films, so we decided to use the three we'd found and leave *Frankenstein* where he was until after Halloween.

I spotted a notebook in the top drawer next to the archival paper. "That's the catalogue," Albert said when he saw me pick it up. "Obviously we don't have art for every film we show, but we have well over a hundred posters. You'll find the ledger has them listed alphabetically, along with where they were sourced and when we've displayed them. Kate started the system when she found her new printer. We'd better jot down that we're putting these up and taking three of the Universal monsters down."

"Right," I agreed, holding the book. "I think I'll take this up to the office with me. I'd like to see what other treasures are hidden away in these drawers." I was getting a tingly feeling. It started when Albert said, "new printer." I knew he meant the new supplier Kate had found for the reproductions, but what if there hadn't been a new supplier? What if there had really been a new *printer*? Kate had bought a large-format high-end laser printer a while ago. It was a crazy half-formed thought, but I couldn't help being excited by it. What if forged movie posters had been the source of the inexplicable money Kate had been spending?

"Oh, the treasures of the Palace," Albert's teasing voice brought me back from my fevered speculation. "Once you start looking you'll find they're all around you."

"I have no doubt of it." I took another look around the room as Albert carefully closed the last drawer. This time I glanced up at the ceiling. "Are those trap doors?"

"Yes! There used to be magic acts back in the Vaudeville days," Albert said, his face lighting up. "There was a time when this room was filled with stage sets and backgrounds and all kinds of wonderful things. Back when she first started, Kate arranged an auction and one of the old magician's cabinets turned out to be quite valuable. I believe she used the money to restore the lobby chandelier." He looked at the piles of junk fondly.

"Isn't there a story about a showgirl from back in those days?" I asked. "A knife thrower's assistant who was killed onstage? Isn't she one of the Palace's ghosts?" I kept my eye out for Trixie, thinking a conversation about ghosts might conjure her somehow. I was starting to get worried about her. Can something happen to a ghost?

Albert gave me a considering look. "There was a showgirl who died, but not onstage. She choked on a chicken sandwich between shows and was rushed to the hospital. She died there, not here, and no, she isn't one of the Palace's ghosts."

"Oh." I felt a little bit let down. "I guess getting killed onstage by a knife thrower is a better story than choking on a chicken sandwich."

Albert smiled. "Yes. And what is the Palace about, if not telling stories?"

Right. Although there was one ghost story that I knew to be true.

"Although there is one ghost story that I know to be true," Albert said, uncannily.

I stared at him.

"An usherette died here in 1937," he said.

I blinked. "I heard about that." I cleared my throat. "Do you think that one's true?"

"Oh, I know it is," he said. "I was there that night. And what's more, I've seen her ghost."

CHAPTER 14

"I was ten years old."

I had insisted that Albert tell me everything right there and then. We'd pulled two chairs together in the vast basement prop room, and I was now on the edge of my seat as he told me about the night Trixie died.

"The film that night was *The Awful Truth*," he told me. "Which wasn't exactly made for ten-year-old boys, but my father worked nights, and my mother often took me to the movies—the pictures, she called them—just to get out of the house in the evenings."

"Sure," I said, wanting him to get to the next part. The Trixie part.

"We were in the balcony that night, about halfway back, and I was perhaps more interested in watching the audience than in watching the movie. I was also hoping to catch a glimpse of the head usherette." He looked at me, eyebrows raised. "Her name was Trixie and she was just about the most glamorous girl I'd ever seen, in all my ten long years." He grinned.

"I can imagine," I said, although I didn't have to.

"I don't know what started it," he went on. "But there was some sort of argument down front. Two men were raising their voices, and the people around them started shushing, and pretty soon Trixie came upstairs to see what the fuss was all about."

"You saw her?"

"I did," he nodded. "The object of my boyhood affections. She had this blonde hair, and the curls bounced when she walked, and she was so very kind to all of us who came every week to the kiddie matinees." He sighed. "My friends and I all agreed—you can keep your Jean Harlows and your Carole Lombards—Trixie was the most beautiful blonde in the world."

"I'll bet she was."

A shadow crossed Albert's face. "What happened next was terrible," he said. "Trixie got caught up in the fight, and then the men started throwing punches, and—I can see it like it happened yesterday. One minute Trixie was there, trying to get them to calm down, and the next she was gone."

I held my breath.

"I couldn't believe it. I truly couldn't believe what I had just seen. It made no sense. It couldn't have happened—that one minute she'd be right there, and the next...Then people downstairs started screaming, and the lights came on, and...it was true." More than eighty years later, his face was still bereft.

I took his bony hand in mine. "Albert. I'm so sorry."

He shook his head, bringing himself back to the present. "Well. It was all a very long time ago." He gave my hand a squeeze before letting go.

"You said you'd seen her," I prompted. "I mean..."

"Her ghost," he nodded. "Many times. The first was when I was back from the army. It was Christmastime and I took my parents to see *The Bishop's Wife*. That would have been..."

"1947," I said without thinking (Cary Grant, David Niven, and Loretta Young).

"Yes. 1947. And there she was. We were sitting in the balcony. I glanced over toward the aisle, and I saw her standing there plain as day, wearing the same uniform I remembered, and carrying her flashlight like she was just about to scold someone."

"What happened?"

"She disappeared," he said. "I looked over to my mother, to see if she could see her as well, and when I looked back she was gone."

"But you've seen her since," I said. "Have you ever spoken to her?"

His smile was tinged with sadness. "No, never. But I saw her several times over the years before the Palace closed."

"And since it reopened?" I asked. "Since you came back to work here?"

He nodded. "Here and there," he said. "Never for more than an instant. But you can take my word for it. Trixie is still at the Palace." He sat back, waiting for my reaction. Then I heard a familiar voice from behind me. A familiar usherette's voice.

"Well, if that don't beat all."

CHAPTER 15

"Nora, he's *seen* me!" Trixie said.

"Right," I said softly. It had taken all my self-possession not to turn around and talk to the ghost as soon as I heard her speak. Albert was still watching me expectantly.

"Why doesn't he see me now?" Trixie moved from behind me to put herself squarely in front of the elderly man. She leaned down and waved a manicured hand in front of his face to no apparent effect. "Hello! Hi there!"

Albert cleared his throat. "Of course I don't expect you to believe me," he said. "But maybe one of these days you'll see her yourself." He tilted his head and peered at me from behind his thick round glasses.

"It wouldn't surprise me," I told him.

Trixie turned to me, hands on hips, her face a study in exasperation. "Why, I'm here just as plain as the nose on his face!"

"All right, then." He stood. "I should get these posters up, don't you think?"

Back upstairs in the office, I put the ledger on the desk and tried to calm a pacing Trixie.

"I don't understand!" she said. "If he could see me once, why can't he see me all the time?"

"I don't know," I told her.

"And why can *you* see me when he can't?"

"I don't know."

"For heaven's sake! If anyone can see me and talk to me, I'd suppose it would be a person I knew when I was alive, don't you think?"

"I don't know."

"Will you please stop saying 'I don't know?' I know you don't know!" She threw herself into a chair and tossed her head to move a stray lock of hair off her face.

"I think," I said hesitantly. "I'm not sure, but I think it may have something to do with getting conked on the head by that light fixture."

She stared at me. "You think that's why you can see me?"

"It only started after I woke up," I said. "You were right there in the room with everyone else when I came to."

She sat up, pointing at me. "*Random Harvest!*" she declared. "You're just like Ronald Colman!"

"Except that was amnesia," I said. "But I see what you're getting at."

"Oh, Nora." Her eyes widened in alarm. "Whatever you do, don't get conked on the head again."

"I'll try not to," I assured her.

"Hmm," something seemed to occur to her. "I wonder what would happen if Albert got conked on the head."

"Trixie! He's a ninety-year-old man!"

"Older than that, if he was ten when I died," she mused.

I gave her a look.

"All right, fine. I promise I won't conk him." She sighed. "But, gee it would be wonderful to talk to someone about the old days."

"I know," I said. "Do you remember him?"

She thought about it. "There were so many kids running around all the time. You know that kiddie matinee he mentioned? Every Saturday we'd show two serials, then cartoons, then some B-movie monster picture or gangster picture or something, and then a feature, or even a double feature. The neighborhood kids would be here all day long." She smiled, then seemed to think of something. "Say, I wonder who his mother was. He said she came to the pictures all the time, and I might remember her more than a little boy."

"I'll ask him her name," I promised.

She nodded, chewing her lower lip in thought.

"Trixie," I said. "There's so much I don't understand about how this works."

"You mean about being a ghost? That makes two of us."

"I know you said you can't help it when you go away," I said.

She nodded. "It just happens. *Poof.*"

"Right. When you're startled or frightened. But you didn't go *poof* when Todd Randall showed up yesterday. I think I was more startled than you were."

"Gee, that's true," she said. She tilted her head. "I wonder if it was because I was so darn mad at you."

"Oh!" I hadn't thought of that. "Maybe you were too mad to be scared?"

"Maybe. I was plenty steamed."

I cleared my throat. "About that. I'm sorry I hurt your feelings. It just honestly never occurred to me that you could be real."

"Oh, honey, that's okay," she said. "It seemed less crazy to think you were crazy, right?"

"It did seem to be the more logical explanation."

"Logic is for the birds," she said.

"In this case," I agreed. "Here's another question: Who do you think the guy on the horse was?"

"You mean the gentleman who came for me when I died?"

I nodded.

"I don't know. He was nobody I knew, that's for sure."

"Do you think he comes for everybody?"

"No," she said, drawing her brows together. "Different people come for different people. I have a notion that it may be someone from your family who comes. You know, to sort of welcome you, and take you to...well, that's another thing I don't know. Would he have taken me to heaven, do you think?" She looked wistful.

I swallowed. "Knowing you, I'm sure of it," I said.

"Aw." She smiled. "Thanks, Nora. That's nice of you to say."

"Could he have been someone from your family?"

"I don't know," she said. "My mother and father were both still alive, so I've wondered if he might have been my grandfather. My mother always said what a refined gentleman he was."

"Did he keep horses?" I asked.

"Didn't everyone, back then?"

That was a point. Then something caught up with me. "Trixie, you said different people come for different people. How do you know that?"

"Oh," she said. "Because of that fella who died in the basement. Someone different came for him."

I think my heart stopped.

"*What?*"

CHAPTER 16

"Didn't I tell you?" Trixie looked confused. "I know I lose track of things sometimes, but I thought I told you about that."

"I think I would have remembered." I sat on the couch next to her, forcing my voice to remain calm. The last thing I needed was to startle her into going *poof* again. "Tell me now. Please."

"Oh. Sure." She sat up straight, as if she were about to recite her lessons in some strict Depression-era classroom. "Well, it was..." She blinked a few times, then shook her head. "I think it wasn't too long ago, but I can't really remember. I think I'd been away." She thought about it and I tried not to scream in impatience. "Yes, I'm certain I was. I was away, and then I was down in the basement." She smiled but it was shaky, as if she were still a little uncertain.

"And then what?" I urged.

"Well, gee, it's hard to explain, but I just sort of knew something was happening." She thought about it, a tiny line appearing between her perfectly plucked eyebrows. "It was just...electric or something." She glanced at me.

I nodded. "Electric," I encouraged.

"And then, I don't know why, but I *knew* I had to look in the ice machine. I was just sort of drawn to it, as if that's where the electric feeling was coming from. So I looked. I couldn't open it, you understand, so I just flitted inside."

"You can do that?"

"Well, naturally," she said, as if it were the most obvious thing in the world.

"Okay, sorry." I told myself we'd circle back to her ghostly superpowers later. "What happened next?"

"Well, when I first saw him in there, I thought 'How silly. He better not stay in here or he'll catch his death.'" She grimaced. "So I tried to wake him up. He was asleep or unconscious or something. I tried to move him but I couldn't." A pained look flashed across her face. "You just don't know how awful it is not to be able to talk to people, or move things, or help somebody when he really needs help and there's no one else around."

"I can't imagine," I said, truthfully.

"So I flitted out again, and I was trying to figure out how I could get Kate or Albert or someone to come down and help the poor fella out, and that's when it happened." Her face took on an expression of wonder. "All of a sudden he was just standing there, in front of the ice machine."

I held my breath.

"So he looks at me, and I can tell he's confused, but *he looks at me*." She paused to make sure I understood the significance of this. "He can see me. And I just about go out of my mind I'm so happy— finally! And he starts to say something, and then..." Her expression clouded. "Then the lady came."

"What lady?" I was ready to jump out of my skin.

"She was so pretty in this sweet yellow dress that was all summery. She looked over at me, and it was a sad sort of look, but then she went right to him. There were tears in her eyes, and he backed up when he first saw her, but then she said something and he stopped, and he seemed more confused at first, but she kept talking and then he seemed to understand, and he was...happy. He hugged her and he started crying too." She looked at me, her own eyes full.

"What did she say?" I asked, breathless.

Trixie shook her head. "I don't know. It was in Spanish, I think. One word I know she kept saying was 'me-ho.' Do you know what that means? Is it Spanish?"

"*Mijo*," I told her. "It means 'my son.' I swallowed. "'My dear son.'"

Her hand flew to her mouth. "Oh. She was his mother. I thought it was something like that."

"What happened next?" I asked.

"She took his hand," Trixie said. "And then this line of light just appeared behind them, and it got longer, all the way from the floor to the ceiling, and it got brighter, and wider, and I had to close my eyes because it was too bright, and I couldn't look anymore."

The look of loss on her face, the devastation, was almost more than I could take. I didn't press her for anything more. I thought I knew what had happened next.

"When I opened my eyes they were gone."

Trixie needed a break after that, and I didn't blame her. She didn't go *poof*, but she said she needed to rest. She walked out of the room, already fading as she left.

I paced in the confines of the office, trying to process everything I'd learned that eventful morning. Albert knew about Trixie. Trixie had met Raul Acosta's ghost. Raul Acosta's mother had led him to...somewhere. Which meant there was a somewhere. Somewhere after.

It was a lot to process.

But revelations about an afterlife aside, if I understood what Trixie had just told me it meant that Raul had been alive when he was put in the ice machine. Alive, but probably unconscious from his head wound. Had whoever killed him intended to come back for him? Had that person been Kate? And had she been prevented from coming back because she herself had been killed? Or met with an accident? It still didn't make any sense.

Feeling stir crazy, I grabbed my backpack and was about to go out for a walk, or possibly a drink, when Callie appeared at the door.

"Ummmm, Nora? There's somebody here who wants to talk to

you."

The way she gazed at the man who entered the room with her made it clear that poor Brandon might have some serious competition for Callie's affections. But I can't say I blamed her. The man, fortyish and wearing a rumpled suit, was easily the most chiseled manifestation of male good looks I'd seen since I last visited my gym in Hollywood. But that wasn't what I found interesting about him. What was interesting was that he bore an uncanny resemblance to the icy Raul Acosta.

"Ms. Paige?" He advanced into the room, holding out a hand. "My name is Hector Acosta. I believe you...the police told me you..."

I shook his hand, finishing his introduction for him. "You're Raul Acosta's brother."

We went across the street to Café Madeline. Not only because I was getting claustrophobic in Kate's office, but because Callie had shown no sign of voluntarily leaving Hector's presence.

So now I sat sipping a latte with Raul Acosta's brother.

"Please excuse me for coming to see you like this," he began. "But when the police told me how my brother was found..." He fixed me with a look. "I have many questions."

He spoke with a barely noticeable Spanish accent, and everything about him, aside from his obvious emotional pain, gave the impression of a cultured, moneyed man. His suit, although rumpled, was cut to perfection. His hair was groomed to within an inch of its life. His white shirt was open at the collar, no tie. If I'd met him in Hollywood I would have pegged him as a mid-level agent or, more likely, a real-estate developer.

"I've come to take my brother's body home," he said. "To Bogota. My family has an estate in the hills above El Poblado. We have a small chapel and a family crypt. It is where Raul belongs."

Bogota. As in Columbia. Raul Acosta had been Columbian. Warning bells, fueled by everything from *Green Fire* (1954, Stewart Granger and Grace Kelly) to *Romancing the Stone* (1984, Michael

Douglas and Kathleen Turner) went off in my head. In the movies, Columbia is a land of emeralds and drugs, and the people who are ready to kill for them.

"I see a question in your eyes and I will spare you the embarrassment of asking it," Hector said. "There is a certain stereotype about wealthy Columbian families. In this case that stereotype has truth. My family," he continued, speaking carefully, "has been very successful in some very lucrative enterprises. Not all of which were entirely legal."

"Oh." I wasn't sure if I thought it or said it out loud. Was he telling me he was part of some Columbian mafia? Was Raul?

I realized Hector was looking at me, clearly expecting a further reaction. I tried not to look as freaked out as I felt, and I focused on the only question that really mattered. "What do your family's enterprises have to do with my movie theater?"

I startled myself with that proprietary "my." But it was how I'd already started to feel about the Palace.

Hector sat forward in his chair, keeping his voice low in the café. There was nobody at the table next to us, but the rest of the long narrow room was filled with people. His body language was saying you couldn't be too careful. "That is what I would very much like to find out."

I leaned toward him. "You do know that the manager of the Palace, Kate Winslow, also died recently?"

"On the same day as my brother," he nodded.

I blinked. I hadn't been sure about the timing. "Did the police tell you that?"

"Yes. They're investigating the deaths as related crimes."

Ah ha! It sure would have been nice if Detective Jackson had mentioned that to me.

"But the police," Hector's mouth twisted, showing frustration. "They hear the name Acosta and they think, of course, this must involve criminal activities. This must involve drugs, or gambling, or worse."

I didn't think I wanted to know what "worse" was. I also didn't want to think about the fact that I was apparently having coffee with a criminal overlord.

"What they don't know, or won't believe, is that my brother and I have entirely dismantled that part of the family business. That is our history, not our future."

"Okay." So, I was having coffee with a *retired* criminal overlord?

"And you don't believe me either," he observed. "But it's true. My mother died four years ago, and after her death my father could no longer go on. He went to live out his days in Santa Marta, looking at the sea and contemplating his many sins." Hector stared into his coffee. "When he left, Raul and I vowed we would end everything that was illegal. We would take what remained and build a legal business."

"You wanted to go legit," I said. "Like Michael Corleone." I couldn't stop myself from referencing *The Godfather* (1972, Al Pacino and Marlon Brando).

He winced slightly. I was probably not the first to make the comparison. "Raul has been here," he continued,   "in San Francisco, for the past three months, looking into opportunities opened up by the legalization of recreational marijuana."

"*Oh,*" I said again, things beginning to fall into place.

"No," he said. "We have nothing to do with the product. Not cultivation or production or distribution. That isn't what interested us."

I blinked. "What else is there?"

He took a deep breath. "There is another enormous piece of the business which no one has yet been able to figure out." He gave me a shrewd look. "There is banking."

Here's the thing: Pot may be legal at the state level, in several states, but it's still very much illegal at the federal level. So those people involved in the aforementioned cultivation, production, and distribution may very well make a bundle, but no federally-insured bank will touch it.

This is the problem, Hector informed me, that he and his brother had planned to solve.

Again I asked the obvious question. "How?"

"Starting here, in California, with a state-only bank," he said. "One that is rock-solid and as trustworthy as any federally-insured financial institution in the country."

That raised a thousand other questions, but only one concerned the Palace. Only one concerned Kate. "Right," I said. "I'll ask you again: What does any of this have to do with my movie theater?"

I spoke to Hector until our coffee went cold, but neither of us could come up with a reasonable answer to my question. There was no obvious reason why Raul Acosta had been killed at the Palace. And no obvious connection between Raul and Kate.

The screenwriter part of my brain immediately began concocting theories about the excess income on the Palace books and possible ties to Columbian crime families, but Kate had been overspending for at least a year and Raul had only been in town for three months, so I didn't want to get carried away. Still, there had to be a connection.

"Could they have been involved?" I asked at one point. "I mean, romantically?"

"I very much doubt that," Hector said drily.

I bristled on behalf of all women who didn't look like international movie stars. "Well, I mean, Kate was a bit older than Raul, but..."

"My brother was gay," Hector explained. "He was in a relationship with a professor of economics who lives in Berkeley. Who has a very good alibi," he added, guessing I was about to ask that very question.

"Okay, so he probably wasn't dating Kate," I relented.

"No."

I gave up on logical connections. "What if it was just a horrible coincidence?" I asked. "Suppose he was just there to see a movie? And suppose someone followed him in to kill him? And suppose Kate saw something, and they chased her out of the theater and killed her in the park?"

"That's a lot of supposing," Hector said, making me think of the "suppose" scene from *Double Indemnity* (1944, Barbara Stanwyck and Fred MacMurray) because that's how my brain works even when I'm discussing a real murder with a real person.

"But I suppose it's possible," Hector continued. "What movie was playing?"

"*Random Harvest*," I told him. Which I believed any gay man over a certain age would be contractually obligated to love. But. "Oh, wait. Never mind. Raul didn't go into the auditorium anyway. He met Kate in the lobby and they went upstairs."

Hector stared at me. "What? How do you know that?"

Whoops. I couldn't exactly tell him that my one eyewitness was a ghost. "Someone saw them," I said.

"Who? I need to talk to them." He pushed away from the table, as if he planned to hunt the witness down right that minute.

"No!" I put my hand on his arm.

He looked at me, frustration written on his face. "Nora, what you've just told me confirms that my brother and Kate Winslow knew each other. I have to know what else this person saw."

"That was all," I told him. "And she didn't even get a good look at the man Kate met. I'm just assuming it was your brother." That actually hadn't occurred to me before. I had just been assuming the stranger Trixie had seen from behind was Raul. Probably because it would have been too confusing to assume anything else. "But besides," I said quickly, hoping to divert his attention from this mystery witness. "The real question is who would have followed him into the theater to kill him? What enemies had he made here in San Francisco, or who could have followed him from Columbia?"

Hector ran a hand across the dark stubble on his face. "That's exactly what I've been trying to figure out."

I let out a breath. Trixie was safe from discovery for the moment.

I mean, she was probably safer than any of us, what with a murderer still running around.

Double Indemnity
1944

This is a movie about trust. Yes, it's also about murder and scheming and sex and insurance, but it's mainly about trust. Dissatisfied wife Barbara Stanwyck has to trust insurance salesman Fred MacMurray, right from the time she asks him if she can get an accident policy on her husband without him knowing about it. This is not the kind of question anyone trustworthy would ask, but Stanwyck is the definition of a femme fatale, and we wouldn't have a movie if MacMurray chose to walk the straight and narrow.

They pretty much spell out their future relationship right at the beginning.

Him: "What a dope you must think I am."
Her: "I think you're rotten."
Him: "I think you're swell, as long as I'm not your husband."

But I'm getting ahead of myself. Everything begins at night, of course, with something very wrong with MacMurray. How wrong, and how it got so wrong, is the totally noir tale he'll tell his Dictaphone.

In flashback, MacMurray meets Stanwyck on a sales call at her gorgeous Spanish-style LA home. She's wrapped in a towel, looking at him appraisingly from the top of the stairs. The spark between them is immediate. This is classic noir stuff. She's bad and he knows it, but he can't look away. And BTW, he's no prince himself.

They're sniffing each other out from the first. Does he handle accident insurance? You bet he does. And that's not all he'd like to handle. MacMurray is full-on sleazy in his role, which was a departure for him. I wonder if his heavy-handed come-ons and his leering obsession with her ankle bracelet seemed quite as gross in 1944. Or would the sexually-provocative Stanwyck have been "asking for it"? I mean, there is that ankle bracelet...

In any case, innuendo gets poured all over everything, and then MacMurray heads back to his office, where we meet his boss, played by Edward G. Robinson looking so much like my Grandpa John that it's eerie. Robinson is our only moral actor in this piece, and he has a sixth sense about insurance fraud. This will be significant.

MacMurray knows full well what Stanwyck wants of him. He put it to her in unvarnished tough-guy terms: "Look, baby, you can't get away with it. You want to knock him off, don't ya?" She does.

Later, MacMurray confesses to the Dictaphone. "I knew I had hold of a red-hot poker and the time to drop it was before it burned my hand off." But knowing and doing are different things. The next time he sees her it gets steamy quick, and then it's all "I'm crazy about you, baby" and tales of accident policies and widows winding up in jail. The good news is, he's seen it all so he knows what mistakes to avoid. He has a plan. Right.

Back at the office, Robinson sums up the difficulty in trusting a partner in crime. "It's not like taking a trolley ride together where they can get off at different stops. They're stuck with each other and they've got to ride all the way to the end of the line, and the last stop is the cemetery." This is eerily similar to the promise Stanwyck repeatedly makes to MacMurray. "It's straight down the line for both of us."

And where will that line lead? I'll just say that in these matters you should always listen to Edward G. Robinson.

Killer lines:

This movie is so full of killer lines! MacMurray's voiceover defines the tough-guy 40's image, everything tossed off with nonchalant swagger. And Stanwyck gives us fast-talking dame for the ages.

"Yes, I killed him. I killed him for money. For a woman. I didn't get the money and I didn't get the woman. Pretty, isn't it?"

"We were talking about automobile insurance, only you were thinking about murder. I was thinking about that anklet."

And this has to be the best sexually charged exchange ever between two people who've known each other less than five minutes:

Her, knowingly: "There's a speed limit in this state Mr. Neff. Forty-five miles an hour."
Him, with a sly grin: "How fast was I going, officer?"
Her: "I'd say around ninety."
Him: "Suppose you get down off your motorcycle and give me a ticket?"
Her: "Suppose I let you off with a warning this time?"
Him: "Suppose it doesn't take?"
Her: "Suppose I have to whack you over the knuckles?"
Him: "Suppose I bust out crying and put my head on your

shoulder?"

Her, steely: "Suppose you try putting it on my husband's shoulder?"

Him, smiling: "That tears it."

Movies My Friends Should Watch
Sally Lee

CHAPTER 17

"Trixie!" I was so relieved to see her in the office the next morning I could have hugged her, assuming that was even possible.

"Nora! I'm so glad you're here! How long was I away? It can't have been too long because the same pictures are on the marquee. That's how I know, sometimes, when I come back. I see if the same pictures are playing. If they are, I know I was just away for a little bit, but if they're different I have to check the board to see what I've missed." She nodded to the blackboard, her curls bouncing. "That's if I can remember what was playing before I went away." A shadow passed over her face, then she shook it off and brightened again.

"What did I miss? Have you told Albert that you can see me? Have you thought of a way for him to see me, too? I can't believe he's been looking for me all these years. Imagine that! And I think I might just remember him. Can you ask him if he wore glasses back then? There was this serious little boy who wore glasses who was just the sweetest thing. I wonder if it was him. Do you think—"

"Trixie," I interrupted. "I have to ask you something. It's important."

"Oh!" She sat on the edge of the desk and put her tiny feet on the chair in front of it. "What is it, honey? What's happened?" She leaned forward, elbows on her knees.

"I found something out," I told her. "About the man you saw in the basement. I met his brother yesterday."

"Oh." Her expression became concerned. "Did you tell him that his brother is all right? That his mother came for him, and…everything?"

I sank onto the couch. "Well, that's a little awkward, you

know? Without telling him how I know it?" That had hit me when I was with Hector yesterday. Telling him I knew Raul had gone to a better place, that he was with their mother, would sound like empty platitudes without citing my spectral source. And citing my spectral source was the first step on a path that was likely to get me locked away in a nice, quiet psych ward somewhere.

"Oh." She deflated. "I suppose that's true."

"What I wanted to ask you," I began. "I found out that Raul was..." how to put it in the sort of 1930s terms she would understand? "He was kind of a gangster."

Her eyes widened.

"He was trying to go straight," I added. "But I think that must have had something to do with why he was killed."

"Sure," she nodded.

"But I still don't understand why he was killed *here*. And how Kate was involved."

Trixie's forehead creased in concentration. She held up a finger, as if she were about to say something, then stopped herself. She tilted her head, frowning, then opened her mouth but closed it again before speaking. She bit her lip, then chewed a fingernail, then sighed in exasperation.

"I don't understand it either," she said.

I'd been holding my breath throughout her entire visible thought process. Now I let it out, disappointed.

I tried another angle. "Trixie, I've found out one more thing. Kate died on the same day that Raul did."

The perfectly painted mouth formed an O.

"I want you to think very hard. You got a feeling when Raul was about to die, right? You felt it like electricity."

She nodded.

"Did you feel anything like that any other time that day? Did you feel it when Kate died?"

Trixie's expression shifted. Her gaze went to a faraway place. When she came back she looked certain. "No."

"You're sure?" I pressed.

She shook her head. "If I felt a stranger like that, surely I would have felt Kate. Wouldn't I?"

"I think so," I agreed. Which meant that Kate probably *had* died in the park. Which just made things that much more confusing.

I looked over to Trixie, who was sitting on the desk next to Kate's laptop, contemplating the situation with her chin in her hands.

"Trixie, I keep forgetting to ask you," I said. "In all the times you were around Kate, and she was working on her laptop, did you ever notice what she entered as her password? Or if she wrote her password down someplace and hid it? Did you ever see anything like that?"

She smiled quizzically. "What's a laptop?"

So, technology wasn't exactly Trixie's strong suit. Fair enough. After a bit more pointless speculation she left to go watch *Dr. Jekyll,* because "That Spencer Tracy is just dreamy," and once again I contemplated the email situation.

I'd had it. I did what I probably should have done in the first place. I placed an ad for a hacker on Craigslist. I didn't actually say "Wanted: Nerd of dubious morals to hack a dead woman's email," but the posting in the Gigs | Computer section pretty much summed up the need. Without violating the site's terms of use.

After hitting the Submit button I stared at Kate's computer desktop. And then I realized I'd totally forgotten to pester Robbie about what Naveen had said about the Palace's finances. I used my phone to send her a quick text asking her to call me when she got a chance.

Then I stared at the laptop screen some more. Finally I took a deep, strengthening breath and clicked on the only folder I hadn't yet explored. The folder I'd been avoiding, afraid of what it would contain. It was titled "Repairs."

There were yearly spreadsheets going back five years, which is probably how old the laptop was. Each had a list of repairs to the Palace, along with what they had cost. Unfinished repairs from one year were carried over to the next. When I opened the current spreadsheet I saw that the list was long, and even though it was October, the tasks were barely a quarter complete. And there were some significantly big-ticket items—electrical and plumbing to name a couple—that were still glaringly not checked off.

Why in the world had Kate been spending money on pricy equipment that she didn't use when she had a list like this of things that really needed to be done?

I thought I found the answer when I clicked on a subfolder titled "Renovation."

Kate had been planning something big.

I studied the plans for a while, and then I went looking for Marty. I couldn't imagine that Kate had been planning the kind of massive remodel she'd itemized in that folder without talking it over with her second-in-command.

He wasn't in the projection booth.

"Hi, Nora," Brandon greeted me in a cheerful whisper.

"Hey." I hadn't seen the teenager in a few days, as he hadn't worked the weekend shifts. "I'm looking for Marty."

"He said he had to run an errand, so Callie's watching the concession stand while I watch things up here." Brandon said. "He'll be back before the movie ends, which is..." he glanced at the large clock above the window through which the film was projected. "In fifty-three minutes."

I glanced at the screen through the window. Things were getting pretty complicated for Spencer Tracy, what with keeping a mind-bending secret of vast metaphysical implications and everything. I could relate.

"Marty left you in charge?" I asked Brandon. I hadn't thought Marty ever left the booth when a film was playing.

Brandon nodded. "He put the whole film together on a platter, so it doesn't need to be switched from one machine to the other between reels," he explained. "I'm just here in case anything goes wrong. But it won't." He tapped his forehead. "Knock on wood. Should I tell Marty you were looking for him?"

"Sure." I left him in the dimly-lit booth. I was thinking about alibis and wondering if *Random Harvest* had also been set up on a platter. Would that mean Marty would have been free to roam around the building when Raul and Kate were getting murdered?

I went down the stairs to the lobby slowly, thinking. What if Kate had been planning to turn the Palace into a first-run theater after all? Marty certainly would have been opposed to that.

Violently opposed?

My increasingly wild thoughts were interrupted by a man's voice.

"Nora."

"Todd." The film blogger. Better looking than I'd remembered and regarding me in a way that said he knew it. He lounged at the concession stand, one elbow on the counter, where he had apparently been in conversation with Callie.

"It's so good to see you again." He left the counter and grinned engagingly as he approached. "I was just asking this young lady where I might find you."

Callie shot me one perfect "I'm so bored" look, then picked up her phone. There were no other customers in the lobby.

"You're looking gorgeous today," he told me. This was, objectively, a lie. I was wearing sneakers, jeans, and a sweatshirt advertising the 2015 Telluride Film Festival. I couldn't even say for sure if I'd showered that morning.

"Thanks. Sorry I haven't called." I couldn't actually remember if I'd promised to.

"Please," he held up his hands. "No worries. I was just in the neighborhood and thought I might be lucky enough to find you free for coffee." He tilted his head invitingly. "Or a late lunch? Or an early drink?"

"Um..." I was thrown. And there was no good reason to be thrown by a perfectly nice guy asking me out for a perfectly innocent coffee. Or even a not so innocent coffee. Yes, I'd been married for the past ten years, but I hadn't been mummified. Men had flirted with me on a fairly routine basis in Hollywood. Was I thrown by this guy just because for the first time in a long time I might be available?

He was still waiting for an answer.

"I'm sort of in the middle of something."

He lowered his head, giving me a fair approximation of puppy dog eyes from behind his sexy professor glasses. "Please. You have to eat."

Which I realized I hadn't done in a while. But despite the eyes and the obvious interest, or maybe because of them, my instinct was to reject the idea. Rationally, I told myself it was because I still hadn't managed to check out his story about working with Kate on the film noir project. But irrationally, there was just something about him. Sure, with all of his charm he was the tiniest bit Cary Grant-ish. But, I realized with a jolt, it was the Cary Grant from *Suspicion* (1941, Grant and Joan Fontaine).

I stood a little taller. "Some other time," I told him. "I promise. But right now I'm afraid I have..." I glanced around the lobby. "...Things to do."

It wasn't a strong finish, but he accepted it, holding his hands up again in mock surrender. "That's what I get for dropping in on such a busy woman," he smiled. "Next time I'll call."

"You do that." I didn't offer my number.

He nodded, giving me one last look. It was a good look. Maybe I should have gone for coffee with him.

I watched him walk out the lobby door, wondering if this sort of thing was going to happen a lot post-divorce. I was exhausted just thinking about it. If Ted hadn't been such a cheating narcissist of a bastard I might have preferred to stay married to him.

"Soooo..." Callie said as the door closed. "He's thirsty."

I gave her a look. "Is that what the kids are calling it these days?" I was still stung from her "your era" comment about my advanced age. "He's just a blogger," I told her.

"Uh huh," she nodded. "I guess that's why he's acting like he's Rick and you're Ilsa and you just ran into each other at a cute little bar in Casablanca."

I had to give her points for the reference. Still. "He just wants to use the theater."

"Uh huh. So, are you going to, like, *have coffee* with him?"

"There is no *having coffee* with him," I said. "He just wants to put on a film festival." Even I didn't believe that anymore.

"Uh huh. If you say so. But, like, that guy's totally not interested in a film festival." She raised her eyebrows. "Just saying."

I frowned at her. "He probably just googled me and now he thinks I can help him get his screenplay made."

"He has a screenplay?"

"Everyone has a screenplay." I leaned my elbows on the counter. "My head hurts."

"Mine would too."

I grimaced. "Tell me again where I can find Monica's pot shop."

CHAPTER 18

The Potent Flower was four blocks down and three blocks over from the Palace on a busy section of Divisadero Street. I showed my driver's license to the guard outside the door and walked into what looked like an upscale boutique.

The shelves were light glossy wood, and the walls were a soothing gray-green. There were a few free-standing display cases with glass tops, and the overall vibe was of the kind of place you'd find in Malibu selling hundred-dollar candles endorsed by Gwyneth Paltrow. Except it was much more crowded.

And there were no candles. Instead, the shelves on the right side of the shop held a multitude of small jars containing buds of every possible shade of green. Each strain was labeled, and available for purchase au natural or already rolled. The other side of the store had more shelves, these containing beautifully packaged chocolates, caramels, teas, ointments, and other goodies, presumably all made with THC. The whole place reeked of stoner chic. It also, to a lesser extent, reeked of weed.

I looked for Monica.

She was behind the sales counter that ran along the back wall, helping out three employees who were busy at three cash registers. She spotted me at about the same time I saw her, and an expression I couldn't identify flashed across her face before she smiled hugely in greeting.

"Nora!" She came out from behind the counter as I approached and gave me a quick hug. "I'm so glad you came! What can I do for you? Tell me what you need."

I needed answers about Kate and Raul Acosta, but it seemed a little hasty to just plunge right in without a few polite preliminaries.

"This place is gorgeous," I told her.

She glanced around the store, which was brimming with customers. Most of them women, and most of them my age or older. "It fills a need," she said, straightening a row of little bottles. "I can't tell you how tired I get of the stoner dude culture in this business. I wanted to create a safe, welcoming space for people to explore all the beautiful possibilities provided by one of nature's most perfect plants." She beamed at me.

"I think you've done it," I said. "Um, Monica, I can see you're busy, but I was hoping we could talk. Is this a really bad time?"

Again, that something flickered across her face and was almost instantly replaced by a smile. "No!" she said. "This is a perfect time. I don't think the lounge is busy. Let's go have a nice quiet cup of tea."

"Thank you," I said. Then, "Plain tea?"

She laughed. "Well there might be some caffeine in it, would that be a problem?"

"The more the better," I said, and followed her past the cash registers, through a doorway that led to a windowless space almost the size of the shop out front. This room was painted a darker gray. A comfortable-looking leather bench ran the length of one wall, scattered with pillows. Small tables were arranged down the length of it. Two more tables, large enough to seat six or eight, were in the center of the room. I'd been expecting a Hollywood version of an opium den. Instead it looked like the dimly-lit common room of a very nice college dorm.

"Have a seat," Monica said. "I'll go get that tea."

A huge TV was mounted on the far wall, playing a nature documentary at low volume. There was only one person in the room, a fortyish woman, who was ignoring the TV and working on a laptop, earphones connecting her to the computer. I watched the documentary until a snake showed up—as they always seem to do in nature documentaries—then I turned away and tried to come up with the perfect movie to watch in this space.

I had just settled on *Sunset Boulevard* (1950, William Holden and Gloria Swanson) when Monica came back, bearing a tray with tea and cookies. "Plain cookies," she assured me with a grin.

I'd chosen a spot in the corner away from the other customer, where I didn't think anyone who happened to walk through the lounge to the employee-only area beyond it would be able to overhear us.

"Now." Monica sat, pushing up the sleeves of her jacket. She was once again wearing workout clothes, the kind of trim, put-together outfit that yoga types seem to live in. "How are you? Are you settling in to your new life?"

She looked at me, really looked at me, with eyes that were filled with compassion. And although I'd intended to ask her what she knew about Kate and her possible connection to a diversifying Columbian crime lord, I found myself answering her with something quite different.

How was I? "I don't know," I heard myself say. I was alarmed to feel tears welling. "I can't bring myself to look at the texts my husband is sending me, I haven't returned any of the messages from my lawyers, and I don't really feel like I'm settling into any sort of new life as much as I'm running away screaming from my old one."

She placed her hand on mine, which was suddenly shaking. I didn't know where the burst of emotion had come from, but it was clear that everything I'd been doing my best to ignore was simmering much closer to the surface than I'd thought. One kind word from a virtual stranger was all it took to have me spilling my guts.

She squeezed my hand. "You poor thing."

Which is what I realized I'd been wanting someone to say to me ever since Ted's face had first been plastered across the tabloids.

At which point I didn't interrogate the pot dealer about Kate's possible criminal connections. Instead I sobbed in her arms.

* * *

"Okay. There it is. Let it out."

The woman at her laptop took no notice of my breakdown. It's possible that scenes like this happened all the time in the cannabis lounge. She typed away while Monica gave me the kind of comfort I hadn't known I needed.

Eventually I sniffed hugely and wiped my eyes. "I'm so sorry."

"What in the world for?" Monica said. "Everybody needs a good cry now and then." She handed me a napkin from the tea tray. "All kinds of terrible happens if you don't let it all out once in a while."

I blew my nose. "Are you some sort of witch?" I asked her. "It feels like you're putting a spell on me."

She laughed and made a woo-woo hand gesture toward me. "You *will* get your groove back," she intoned.

"I don't know if I ever had a groove."

"Then you'll find one," she said simply. And, for whatever reason, I believed her.

"I lost it," I told Robbie. "I mean, I really lost it, right there in the smoking lounge of a pot shop."

I'd used an app to call for a ride-share car when I left Monica's shop. Robbie had called just as I was telling the driver where to take me.

"Well, if you're going to lose it, that's probably as good a place as any," she now said.

"I feel like an idiot."

"Okay, but do you feel better?"

I took a deep breath. "Oddly, I think I do."

"There's nothing odd about it. Everyone needs to lose it sometimes, and you've kept it together far too well for far too long. It was almost getting weird."

"Well, then consider me normal," I told her. "Painfully so."

"I consider you my best friend," she said. "I'm just sorry I wasn't the shoulder you cried on."

"You're the shoulder I lean on for everything else," I reminded her. "Remember, I'm working in your theater and living in your house."

"Only my guest house," she said dismissively. "And it's not like you don't have several houses of your own."

I winced, watching the scenery of San Francisco pass me by. "Maybe I do. I really should look at all the emails the lawyers have been sending me."

"You really should," she said. "But maybe not right this minute."

"Maybe I'll think about it tomorrow," I suggested.

"That's a good little Scarlett O'Hara," she agreed. Then, "Um..."

Robbie never hesitated without good reason. "Um what?" I asked. "Tell me."

She blew out a breath. "I wasn't sure if I should say anything, but Ted dropped by last night."

Every muscle in my body clenched. I didn't trust myself to speak, so I didn't.

"I'll spare you the blow-by-blow recap," Robbie said. "All I'll say is that never in my life have I ever met anyone more self-centered than that man. And you know the list of divas I've worked with."

I did. It was a long list.

Robbie's voice changed. "Nora, I have to ask you this, and if you don't want to answer that's fine, but I had the feeling that, over the last few months—I mean before this insanity all started—I had the feeling you were getting pretty fed up with Ted. Am I wrong?"

I blinked. Had I been?

"I've been frustrated," I admitted. "I mean, it just seemed like every single inch of space I had in my head, in my life, had been taken over by taking care of Ted. It's like he was the Blob, and his needs just kept expanding and expanding, and sometimes..."

"I get it." Robbie sounded relieved. "And I just hope you remember that, as he's putting you through all this hell. The way I see it, if Ted hadn't run off with that woman—" she knew better than to utter the name Priya Sharma in my hearing "—you might very well have left him."

That thought hit me like a revelation. It was a totally new way of looking at things.

"Do you think he knew?" I asked. "Do you think, on some level, that he wanted to pull the ripcord before I did?"

"Well," Robbie considered. "If he did sense your frustration, it would be totally in keeping with his narcissist character to run away from you rather than doing something crazy like asking how he could make things better."

I blinked, thinking of the implications. I'm ashamed to say that my first reaction to this line of thought was a self-hating *Ah ha! So I am to blame for him walking out on me!* But in Robbie's careful silence, I had another thought. One that gave me much more comfort. *No matter what I did or might ever do, Ted is always going to be a hopelessly self-centered shit.*

I decided to go with that.

"I don't think I was ready to leave him," I finally told Robbie. "But I think I was ready for him to completely change several fundamental aspects of his personality and magically turn into the man I wanted him to be."

"Show me anyone who's married who isn't ready for that."

I laughed.

"Now *that* sounds good," she said. "Hey, I have to go. But I wanted to tell you that I'm still playing phone tag with Naveen. I'm going to try to set up a conference call for tomorrow so the three of us can figure out what the hell has been happening with the Palace books."

"Oh, great," I said. "Let me know when."

"I love you, you normal person," she said.

"You too, you weirdo."

We hung up just as the car pulled up at my destination.

Golden Gate Park. Stowe Lake. Strawberry Hill.
The place where Kate had died.

CHAPTER 19

By the time I got to the top of Strawberry Hill I had realized two things. One, that it had been far too long since my last spin class. And two, that there were any number of places along the path where a person could plunge over and break her neck.

Especially if she was pushed.

The hill was on an island in the middle of the man-made Stowe Lake. And "lake" may have been overstating it. It reminded me more of a moat surrounding the hill. The shallow water was spanned by two arched bridges on opposite sides of the hill, one old, stone, and gothic looking, and the other a newer concrete version. There was a boathouse that was pretty lively, even on a somewhat blustery weekday afternoon. Row boats and paddle boats were available for rental, and hot dogs and t-shirts for sale.

The whole perimeter of the lake was less than a mile around. Walkers, joggers, and moms watching their kids feed the ducks occupied the path around it. On the island, another path circled the hill and wound gently up to the top.

Callie had said the walk was so easy you could push a stroller, and she was right. I hadn't seen any strollers, but I did see a nurse pushing a wheelchair and he seemed to be having no difficulty. The path was paved for a bit, then gravel packed with dirt. And it was the width of a single-lane road, not the sort of trail where one misstep could send you tumbling over. I'd read on a helpful park sign that the stone bridge and the path had been designed in the Gilded Age so San Francisco's gold rush kings and railroad barons could drive their carriages up to the top to enjoy a picnic with a spectacular view. That's why it was called Strawberry Hill. No rich man's picnic was complete without strawberries.

In this less-gilded age, the path was overgrown with cypress and redwoods, but the view was still spectacular with the Golden Gate bridge peaking over the trees in one direction and houses stretching all the way to the ocean in another. It was impossible for me to see the city laid out like that and not have scenes from San Francisco-set movies pop into my head. There were dozens of them.

San Francisco, of course (1936, Spencer Tracy and Clark Gable), *Vertigo* (1958, Jimmy Stewart and Kim Novak), and *The Maltese Falcon* (1941, Humphrey Bogart and every bad-guy contract actor on the Warner Brothers lot) were just three from my top-ten list. Oh, and *Pal Joey* (1957, Frank Sinatra, Rita Hayworth, and Kim Novak again). So make that four. Or I could have a whole different list for San Francisco musicals.

I took a moment to ponder the cinematic history of my new city, then got down to the business of figuring out how I would kill someone by pushing them off Strawberry Hill.

When I'd first started thinking about it, I'd wondered doubtfully whether Kate's fall had been suicide, and now that I saw the landscape I was more than doubtful. In a city full of tall buildings, why would you throw yourself off a wooded hillside? And the suicide theory assumed she was remorseful for having killed Raul Acosta. But why would she have killed him in the first place?

So if not suicide, what about an accident? I couldn't see that either. Even if she'd fallen, she wouldn't have had the momentum to fall very far. Unless she was moving pretty fast. Running, maybe? Running from someone?

But from whom? And why? The obvious answer was that she was running from the person who had killed Raul. But what in the world would have made her run to the park? Which was, by the way, a good four miles from the theater. Even in my wildest imaginings I couldn't see that happening.

The only thing that made any sense was that she'd been

pushed. And the only person I could imagine pushing her was the person who had killed Raul that day. But as to *why* the killer had dragged or chased her here to push her off a hill, I was out of theories.

Could the killer have pushed her to her death? On the one hand, it seemed possible. There were several spots, including from the picnic grounds at the top of the hill, where it was almost a straight drop down. On the other hand, Kate would have to have been incredibly unlucky to fall far enough to break her neck. There was a ton of undergrowth and branches and fallen tree trunks that she could have grabbed to stop herself from being killed. In theory, at least.

I shivered in my sweatshirt and sat on a rock near the hilltop picnic grounds, stumped. I had hoped that seeing the place where Kate had died would send everything clicking into place. Or at least send something clicking somewhere. But no.

A group of maybe fifteen birders had set up cameras and telescopes on tripods near the picnic tables at the top of the hill. I watched them for a while, envying their obliviousness to everything but the black-crowned night heron that their leader was pointing out in hushed reverence. The bird moved and cameras went off like a fusillade. I felt a little sick at the sound. It reminded me of the paparazzi.

I stood to go, and then it hit me. Cameras. There were cameras all over the place. People taking pictures of birds, of their kids, of the rowboats and the trees and the bridges.

Had someone taken a picture of Kate that day? Was some tourist, or some random birder, walking around with the evidence of who had killed her on their camera?

I waited until the heron had flown and the crowd was milling around in search of new sightings, then I approached the elderly woman who seemed to be in charge of the group. She had frizzy gray hair and wore the kind of hat that said she took sun protection seriously, even on an October afternoon.

"Excuse me," I said. "Hi. Do you lead these tours often?"

"Every Wednesday," she said cheerily. "Are you interested in our feathered brethren?"

"I am," I lied. "But I'm hoping there's a group that meets on Fridays." Because Kate had been killed on a Friday.

"Oh, that would be Kelly," she said, and began rummaging around in her fanny pack. She withdrew a business card and brandished it with a clear sense of triumph. "We're both with the same Meetup group. She's wonderful. You'll love her talks."

She handed me the card and I thanked her from the bottom of my heart. Would Kelly's group be willing to share the photos they'd taken on the last Friday of September? I could only hope.

But I could do that really well. I could hope.

I made my way back down to the boathouse and summoned another ride-share to take me back. While I was waiting for it I sat at one of the picnic tables and looked for the other business card that I'd gotten recently. Detective Jackson's.

My backpack was so organized that I could never find anything. Made of incredibly soft leather, it had zippers upon pockets upon compartments. I had to dig around in most of them before I found the detective's card tucked away in the smallest exterior pocket. I pulled it out along with a folded piece of notepaper. I called.

"Detective Jackson." Of course I got his voicemail. "This is Nora Paige from the Palace theater. I'm calling because I'd like an update on the investigation, and also because I've had an idea. There's a group of birdwatchers that meets at Stowe Lake on Fridays..."

The message I left was probably too long, and definitely too complicated, but I think I got the point across. The police should look at what was on those birder's cameras. With any luck, they'd find Kate in the background somewhere, accompanied by her killer.

Satisfied, I did some people-watching while I waited for the car. The line at the boathouse snack bar moved slowly, and there were only a few hearty souls in rented rowboats on the water. Still, I was willing to bet every single one of them had a camera phone.

What would be the most efficient way to ask anyone who had been at the lake on that Friday to check their phones for pictures of Kate? I could put a flyer up at the boathouse. That might get some of the regulars. But the tourists? The ones most likely to have taken lots of pictures? They were probably long gone by now.

I shuffled the two business cards and folded notepaper while I thought about it, wondering how effective social media might be in getting a request out. Eventually I found myself glancing at the notepaper. It was the page from Kate's notepad that Marty had torn off on my first day. He'd written the theater's Wi-Fi password on the back of one of Kate's programming lists.

I unfolded the paper, looking at what had presumably been Kate's last list.

"Win," "M," "Lace," "Sorry," and "Gas."

It occurred to me that it would be a nice gesture to use Kate's last list to program my first slate of films. Sort of a nod of respect at the changing of the guard. That was, if I could figure out what movies she was talking about in that random list of five words.

Not random, I corrected myself. Kate's lists always seemed to have some theme.

My phone alerted me that the car had arrived and as I stashed the paper and cards back in my bag a question popped into my mind. Why five films? The theater usually showed only two or three at a time.

But of all the odd things I needed to figure out, that was pretty far down on the list.

Callie was in the ticket booth when the car dropped me off outside the Palace, in anticipation of the crowds that were expected for the 4:45 show. And by "crowds" I mean roughly nineteen people. At best. She glanced up from her phone as I approached.

"Feeling better?"

When I'd last seen her I'd left her with the impression that I was about to go stock up on pot. "You know, I think I am," I told her. Mostly because of a good cry and a brisk walk in the fresh air, but I didn't want to blow my street cred by telling her that.

The look she gave me assured me that I had no street cred. "Marty was looking for you." She went back to her phone. "I think he's in the break room."

"Thanks."

I waved to Brandon as I came in the lobby door and just about collided with Albert at the top of the balcony stairs.

"Oh, Nora. There you are. Marty was asking about you."

"Thanks. He's in the break room?"

"Yes." Albert peered at me a little more closely. "Hello. You've got some roses in your cheeks." He stepped back and grinned approvingly. "Whatever you've been doing, keep it up."

I'd been wandering around a hilltop trying to get into the mind of a murderer. And I probably would keep it up, at least until I'd figured out who had killed Kate and Raul, and what any of it had to do with the Palace.

"Thanks, Albert."

Marty was doubtless looking for me because I'd told Brandon I was looking for him earlier. I'd wanted to ask him what he knew about Kate's plans for renovating the theater. So I was just the teensiest bit blindsided when I strolled into the break room and he asked me the question I'd been meaning to ask him. Although he asked it in his own inimitable way.

"What the hell was Kate planning? And why the hell didn't she tell me about it?" He practically attacked me the minute I appeared in the doorway. Then he crossed the room to stand too close, towering above me. It took all my strength of will not to back up into the hallway. He glared at me for a moment, then turned away and ran both hands through his already-disheveled hair.

"Nora," he wailed. "What the hell is going on?"

CHAPTER 20

Here's what happened: The handyman had finally come to fix the ice machine. And when Marty had asked him—or more likely yelled at him—about why the Palace's routine maintenance had fallen so far behind schedule, the handyman had told him that Kate had instructed him to defer anything that wasn't an emergency because she was going to change everything anyway in the massive remodel she was planning.

I got this backstory out of Marty in pieces, sandwiched in between his accusations of duplicity, treachery, and general awfulness. I finally got him to listen long enough to convince him I wasn't any of those things—at least in this case—and that I hadn't been keeping anything from him.

"Seriously, I just found out about the renovation plans this afternoon," I told him. "And the first thing I did was come looking for you." Partially because it had crossed my mind that he might have killed Kate in a fury over her plans, but his obvious distress now pretty much convinced me that he hadn't known a thing about them.

The truth finally seemed to sink in for him, and he dropped into a chair at the break room table, all the fight gone out of him.

"Why wouldn't Kate have told me about it?"

Now, instead of being angry and accusatory, he was just hurt.

"Do you think..." I was about to say something that might get him all worked up again, so I accompanied the question with a box of cookies that I grabbed from the counter and poured onto a paper plate in front of him, on the theory that a spoonful of sugar, etc.

"Do you think," I sat opposite him and started again, "maybe she was planning something she knew you wouldn't like?"

He stared at me, munching furiously on snickerdoodles. "What wouldn't I like?"

Right. Because he was so open-minded. "Maybe," I suggested, "modernizing?"

"Why wouldn't I like that? We've been talking about new carpets and upholstery for years. And the screen could stand an upgrade, and you've experienced the state of the light fixtures."

"Sure," I said. "But that's not what I mean. What if she wasn't just thinking of modernizing the building? What if she was thinking of modernizing what you show? Turning the Palace back into a first-run house?"

Marty stopped munching. He swallowed painfully and looked me in the eye. "Never."

I sat back, and he must have seen the doubt on my face.

"You don't get it," he said. "This isn't in your blood. But this theater, these movies, they were her *life*. She saw this place as more than important. It was...*sacred* to her." He looked at me searchingly, desperately wanting me to understand something he didn't think I could. "People like us, in places like this, we keep these films alive. It isn't the same to see them on your living room couch. It isn't the same to stream them to your phone. To see them on a real screen, in a theater—this kind of a theater, that was literally made for them—to see them in the company of other people, laughing together and *feeling* together—that's more than a movie. That's an experience. Kate would never, *never* have given that up. She'd have died first."

I caught my breath, both of us realizing the implication of his last statement.

"I understand," I told him. "I know you don't think I do, but I get it."

"Then you see how ridiculous it is to think that she'd have wanted to show 3D IMAX bullshit action flicks in one of the last bastions of classic film."

I saw. But. "Why did she buy that projector?" I asked him.

"The 4K laser extravaganza that's in a box on a shelf in your projection booth?"

He snorted. "She didn't buy it. She won it at a trade show she went to last spring. And it's still in a box because she was trying to sell it to raise money to keep the Palace going."

Oh.

Still. "That was a pretty expensive prize." When I'd looked it up it had been in the range of a hundred thousand dollars.

Marty shrugged. He probably hadn't looked it up. And he was still obsessing. "None of this makes sense," he said. "If she was planning to restore the theater, she knows I would have been on board. One hundred percent. She would have talked to me about it. She would have asked me what we needed." He looked at me. "When we upgraded the sound to the new Dolby equipment three years ago she asked me to design everything. Why wouldn't she talk to me this time?"

"Maybe it was going to be a surprise?" I suggested, knowing how lame that sounded.

He didn't even acknowledge the idea. "And how was she going to pay for it?" he went on. "Is there some new investor I don't know about?"

That hadn't occurred to me. Was the extra money that was apparently pouring into the theater an investment from some silent partner? Someone Robbie didn't even know about?

"That would be pretty strange." I reached for a cookie. "Marty, how much are you usually involved in the Palace finances?" A casual question, no big deal.

"Not at all," he said. Then he looked at me sharply. "Why? What's going on with the finances?"

"Just some bookkeeping I don't understand," I said, minimizing the situation. "Robbie has a guy figuring it out."

Marty's expression returned to hostility. "I hope you're not suggesting that Kate was up to anything—"

"No, no, no," I said quickly. Although I didn't have any other explanations. "I just didn't understand some things. I'm not an accountant. I can barely balance my checkbook."

"How long has it been since you had to?" Marty scoffed.

Fair point. Being married to a hugely successful movie star had had major financial perks. I felt a pang, knowing how many unread emails my lawyers had sent me on just that subject.

"In any case," I evaded. "I'll let you know what the finance guy says. Maybe he can clear everything up."

"Fine," Marty said, unconvincingly. "And speaking of you not knowing what you're doing—"

"We weren't—"

"I looked up that guy who's been hanging around. His blog is bullshit."

This piece of news distracted me from defending myself.

"What blog? You mean Todd Randall?"

He snorted. "Todd Randall. That's probably not even his real name. That Real on Reel website? He's got about ten movies on it, and his descriptions of them are lifted straight out of IMDB."

IMDB is the Internet Movie Database, and it's an incredible source of useful information—and useless information, which can be more fun.

"What do you mean? He just copied and pasted?"

"It looks like he put that site together in half an hour. If he's a real blogger—and the bar for being a real blogger is incredibly low—I'm a Goldwyn Girl."

"Please don't make me visualize that," I said, sincerely not wanting to imagine him as a rhinestone-studded chorus girl. What I did visualize was the guy who had gotten into the theater on Sunday morning when I was now suddenly *sure* I'd locked the door. "What the hell is he up to?"

Marty shot me a look. "According to Callie, he's up to hitting on you."

"And I suppose Callie's an expert?" Actually, she probably was. "In any case, he was hanging around before that. He said he was working on a film festival with Kate before I ever got here."

"He *said*," Marty emphasized.

"Well, at least we should be able to check out that part of his story. I advertised for a hacker this morning. With a little luck we should be able to get into Kate's email and see if she really was in contact with him. Meanwhile, let's tell everyone to let one of us know if Todd Randall shows up here again. I don't want him wandering around the building."

"We should tell everyone to throw his ass out on the basis of that so-called blog alone," Marty said. "I mean, for God's sake, all anybody does in those movie blogs is regurgitate the same set of facts that they lift from Turner Classic or IMDB or the *one* movie star's biography they may have read. But at least most of them do it with a minor *attempt* at creativity. This guy just flat out stole."

"How could he think he'd get away with something like that?" I wondered. "Especially with me?" I opened my eyes wide as I remembered something. "He did ask me not to judge him by the site. He said it was under construction or something."

"Especially with *you*?" Marty's tone dripped with mockery.

"Not everyone thinks I'm an idiot," I told him.

"It looks like Todd Randall does," he countered.

Which could have sent us spinning into another argument, but I was distracted by the sight of a vintage usherette in the doorway.

"Nora! Where did you go? I came back after the picture, but you were gone. I heard Callie tell Albert you went out." Trixie came into the room and perched on the counter behind Marty. "Gee, I miss going out. Did you have fun?"

I did my best not to look at her, speaking to Marty. "Um...Don't you have a projection booth to run?" Because it was hard enough having a conversation with him without Trixie in the room.

Marty looked startled, then disappointed. He'd probably been looking forward to another round of I-know-more-about-movies-than-you-ever-will.

He stood and made a point of looking down on me from on high. "That's right. *I* have essential things to do around here."

He was just about out the door when I threw caution to the

wind and stopped him.

"Hey, I know you hate movie blogs, but the other day you said there was one you read. What is it?"

He hesitated in the doorway. "You'll never have heard of it. It's called *Movies My Friends Should Watch*." He turned. "It isn't exhaustive and it isn't updated as regularly as it should be, but at least it has an honest-to-God point of view."

Interesting.

He left, and I turned back to Trixie, who tilted her head and looked at me curiously.

"Hey Trixie," I said.

"Hey Nora," she grinned. "What's a blog?"

CHAPTER 21

"I just can't get over these computer things," Trixie said, following me down the hall to the office. "You say just anyone can write their own newspaper articles?"

I'd said something like that. It wasn't easy to explain the Internet to someone who hadn't ever used a telephone without a switchboard operator to connect her call.

"People can write their own articles," I told her. "And record their own music, and even make their own movies and put them on the computer so everyone else can see them."

She stared at me. "Why, that's just...unnatural."

"Maybe," I said. "But it's also pretty egalitarian. Back in your day you'd have to convince one of the handful of old white men running the major studios that your idea was good enough to turn into a movie. Now you don't have to."

She wrinkled her brow. "Then how do you know it is good enough?"

Wow. Times had *really* changed.

"I guess you just have to believe it yourself." I told her. I sat at the desk as she curled up in a corner of the couch. "Does that make sense? What do you think?"

She gave the laptop a suspicious look. "I think there must be a lot of terrible pictures on that contraption."

I laughed. "Oh, there are. But some pretty good ones too. And even some of the great ones, from your day."

Her eyes widened. "You mean like with Clark Gable? And everybody? Right there in that thingy?"

"More or less," I said, not having any desire to get into the specifics of cloud-based content servers with a hundred-year-old ghost.

"Gee," she marveled. "Clark Gable. Right there whenever you want to see him." She shook her head in wonder. "Well, that's different. Just imagine." She looked at me. "It kind of makes you think anything is possible, doesn't it?"

It hadn't, until I saw it from her perspective. But now..."It kind of does," I agreed.

The next morning I woke to the sound of an incoming text from Robbie.

Happy week anniversary. I'll call with Naveen at 2.

Good. At least one part of the Palace puzzle might be revealed by her financial expert. I sank back onto the pillow, having a hard time believing I'd only been in San Francisco for a week. One week, two murders, and a ghost. *Two Murders and a Ghost.* That sounded like the title of a movie Jack Benny might have made. Or maybe Bob Hope and Bing Crosby. It would be a comic thriller. I'd want Ann Sheridan as the fast-talking female lead and we'd set it in a castle in Scotland with Gale Sondergaard as the sinister housekeeper.

This is how I usually spent my sleepless hours. Casting imaginary movies or thinking up ways to adapt my favorite classics for a modern audience without ruining them. At least that's how I'd spent my sleepless hours before they'd become filled by the hideous imaginings of what inventive new ways Ted would find to enjoy the many delights of Priya Sharma. Maybe it was a good sign that I was casting imaginary movies again.

I looked at the clock. Five a.m. Robbie must have had an early call. I told myself it was way too early to get up and go to the theater.

Then I got up and went to the theater.

*   *   *

There was a light on in the office. I noticed it as soon as I turned the corner in the hallway. It was too dim to be the ceiling light. Probably the desk lamp. I'd probably forgotten to turn it off when I'd left after closing up the night before.

That's how clueless I was. It never occurred to me to be alarmed about a light in an empty office. It never dawned on me to be afraid. Not until I breezed into the room and saw Todd Randall going through the desk drawers.

I froze. He'd spilled the contents of a drawer onto the desk and was running his hand along the underside of it, as if looking for a secret compartment. He froze too when he saw me.

I had a flash of primal certainty that I had to be the one to unfreeze first.

I spun around and started for the lobby stairs.

"Nora! Come back! I can explain!" I heard him pounding after me and knew he'd catch up before I got downstairs and out to the street. So instead I flung myself into the break room and slammed the door behind me. I flipped the lock, just a flimsy button on the doorknob, and threw my weight against the door.

"Nora," Todd said through the door. "I'm so sorry I startled you." He was breathless but reasonable, apologetic, his voice overly patient. "Please. Come out. Let me explain." He paused. "I didn't want to say anything to you before, because I honor Kate's memory, but the truth is she owed me money."

I half listened while I dropped the laptop bag to the floor and ransacked my backpack for my phone, glad that he was arrogant enough to think he could reason with me instead of kicking down the door with one try.

"You see, I'd given her a down payment for the film festival," he said.

Where was my phone?

"And I found out she'd spent it on something else. An investment, she called it. She said it would triple my money."

My fingers hit the blessed rectangular shape and I pulled the phone out, my hand shaking so badly it took three tries to unlock it.

"But then she died, and I just want my down payment back," Todd was saying. "I don't know what she bought, but she used my money, and I need it to get my website up and running. You understand, don't you? I should have told you, but I didn't want to damage Kate's legacy." His voice was plaintive, and if I had been the trusting sort I might have fallen for his story.

But two people had been killed in this theater, and that meant I was no longer the trusting sort. So I dialed 911 and backed away from the door, speaking loudly enough for Todd to hear me.

"My name is Nora Paige and I'm at the Palace Theater on Sacramento street. There's an intruder and I need you to send the police. The intruder's name is—"

With that the door came crashing open. I screamed, and the operator said something, but then Todd grabbed the phone out of my hand and threw it against the wall. He turned to me, the imploring look on his face in direct opposition to the violence he'd just exhibited.

"You didn't have to do that. We could have settled this between us."

I swallowed and backed up until I felt the counter behind me. "The police are on their way."

He advanced on me. He expression was still pleading, but there was something simmering underneath it. Then I heard a cry behind me and Trixie appeared, rushing at Todd. "You keep away from her!" she yelled.

She was amazing, and completely ineffective. Todd was oblivious to her presence as she swished right through him, her fists flailing. I grabbed the only thing handy, the empty coffee pot, and raised it like a club. "You've got about two minutes until the cops show up, Todd. Is this really how you want to spend it?"

"Nora, you're overreacting." His voice was calm and infuriatingly patronizing. "I really want what's best for you. What's best for the Palace and Kate's memory." Then he hesitated, noticing the laptop bag on the floor between us. His glance shot from it back to me, and recognition dawned. "Is that Kate's computer?"

"No." I lowered the coffee pot.

"It is." He made a grab for it as I dropped the pot and did the same. Glass shattered. He swept the bag into his grasp and backed away from me, toward the door, his eyes locking on mine.

"No," I repeated, my shoe crunching on glass as I took a step toward him.

"Trust me, Nora. This is what Kate would have wanted." And he was gone.

I'd reached the door in pursuit when Trixie's voice, sounding dazed, stopped me.

"Nora?" She was on the floor where she had fallen after heroically throwing herself at—through—Todd. "I don't feel so well."

I turned back to her.

"I think..." she said.

Then her eyes fluttered and I found out that ghosts can faint.

CHAPTER 22

How do you revive someone who's fainted? If that someone is a ghost, you can't exactly rub their wrists or wave smelling salts under their nose. Not that I had any smelling salts handy. I was just considering whether I should try splashing some water on Trixie's face when she moaned and came around.

"Are you okay?" I knelt on the floor beside her.

She blinked a few times, seeming disoriented. Then she looked at me and I could see it all came rushing back to her.

"Oh, Nora, he was so angry. I thought he was going to conk you on the head," she said. "I was so scared he would, and then you wouldn't be able to see me anymore." Her lower lip trembled. "I can't go back to being alone, Nora. I just can't."

"Oh, sweetie—" Which is when I learned that you can't hug a ghost. My arms went right through her, which was cold and awkward for both of us. "You were so brave," I told her as she reconstituted herself.

"I was so scared," she said.

"But you didn't go *poof*," I pointed out. "You stood up to him."

"Gee, I suppose I did," she said. "I must have been more scared about losing you than scared of him."

"You're not going to lose me," I said, which is when we both heard police sirens on approach. "But for now, do you think you should, um..."

She nodded. "I could use a rest." She began to fade, and then came back into focus, a stern look on her face. "Don't you go getting conked, you hear me?"

"Yes, ma'am," I said.

She gave me a quick nod and vanished.

I went downstairs to greet the police.

An hour later the squad car was just pulling away from the curb in front of the theater when Marty came around the corner from the opposite direction. I waited for him outside the ticket booth.

He glanced at the retreating car. "What did they say? Did they take down the crime scene tape?"

"I wish," I said.

His eyes narrowed. "What?" he accused. "What have you done now?"

I stopped myself from flaring at him with a "Me? How dare you imply..." sort of response. Because I'm the bigger person.

"Todd Randall," I told him instead. "He broke in and was searching Kate's office for something when I got in this morning."

Alarm flashed across his features. "Are you okay?"

I was surprised that his first response wasn't to accuse me of being in cahoots somehow. "I'm fine," I said. "But he took Kate's laptop."

"Is that what he was looking for?"

"No. Maybe. I don't know." I rubbed my forehead. "He had some story about how he'd given Kate a deposit for that film festival, but she'd spent it on something, and he just wanted his money back."

"I one hundred percent don't believe that," Marty said. "How much money?"

"He didn't go into detail, as he was on the other side of a locked door and I was calling 911," I said. "Oh, and we'll need to fix the break room door."

Marty looked at me closely, and I can't imagine what he saw. I only knew how I felt and, despite my brisk words, I felt like I was just about ready to shatter into a million pieces.

"Okay," he said. "You're going to need to tell me the whole story, from the beginning. But you're going to need to do it while drinking a very strong cup of tea. And maybe while wrapped up in a blanket or something."

Whereupon he led me into the theater, and—I have a hard time believing this myself—did his gruff best to take care of me.

"Do you suppose there's a tiny grain of truth anywhere in his story?" I asked Marty.

I was under an ancient plaid blanket on the couch in the office. I'd sipped hot sugary tea and told Marty everything while he'd put the contents of Kate's drawer back in place and rummaged through the desk looking for signs of anything else that Todd Randall had disturbed.

"You mean about the deposit?" he asked. "No. If things had gotten that far with an actual film festival Kate would have told us all about it. And if he'd paid her any money she'd have given him a receipt. That whole story is bogus. What did the police say?"

"That we need to change the alarm code and fix the lock on the back door."

Marty looked at me sharply. "He had the code to the alarm?"

"They asked me how long since we changed it."

Marty grimaced. "Probably two or three years."

"Right. That's what they figured. And with as many people as have worked here in that time..."

"Okay, but they're looking for him, right? For Randall?"

"I gave them his name, which they told me might not be real, and his description, which boils down to 'tall white guy around fifty.'" I shrugged. "I got the impression that they wouldn't have gotten all excited over a stolen laptop, but with Kate and Raul...we should expect a call from Detective Jackson later."

Marty's jaw tightened as he scanned the bookshelves for anything out of place. With all the clutter, I didn't know how he'd be able to tell.

"One part of Randall's story makes sense," he said. "He was looking for something. I don't believe it was anything Kate owed him, but there must be something he knew she had. Something valuable."

"Whatever it is," I said, "I don't think it's on the laptop. Or if it is, it isn't anything obvious like a password to a Swiss bank account or a stash of Bitcoin. I think I've opened every single file on the hard drive," I said. "Everything except the emails, and now we won't be able to get to them, even assuming any of the hackers who answered the Craigslist ad could get in." Several dozen had responded by the time I'd checked the night before.

"Of course," I said, more to myself than to Marty, "there could be all kinds of passwords to Swiss bank accounts or Bitcoin stashes in her emails."

"Who said anything about Swiss bank accounts or Bitcoin?" Marty asked.

"They're just 'for instance,'" I said. "All we know is that Todd Randall was looking for something. Something valuable. We don't know what it is, why Kate had it, or how Randall found out about it, but there's something. And even though he started his search in this room, realistically it could be anywhere in the theater. And I hope it is. I hope it's an actual physical thing and it's hidden in the Palace. Because if it isn't, if it's just a piece of information that's on the laptop, Randall already has it."

Marty dropped into the desk chair. "Something hidden somewhere. That narrows it down."

"Have you got any idea," I asked him. "*Any* idea what it could be?"

"Not a clue." He shook his head, then looked at me. "It's the MacGuffin."

I nodded, realizing he was right. The MacGuffin is a term used by screenwriters. It means the thing that drives the plot—the thing the good guy has and the bad guy wants, or the bad guy has and the good guy has to get. It's the Maltese Falcon or the Queen's diamond studs. It doesn't really matter what the MacGuffin is. The story is driven by people trying to get it.

And people willing to kill for it.

* * *

My phone was blessedly unbroken. I mean, aside from a spectacularly cracked screen. But when I eventually left Marty in the office and went looking for it in the break room, it still worked. Seeing that almost made me feel like a whole person again. Then I saw a text from a number I didn't know.

I have your laptop. Please meet me across the street in the cafe. Come alone. HA

What? Was Todd Randal sitting across the street and mocking me? *Laughing* at me? I stormed down to the lobby and was halfway across the street before I realized how stupid I was being. Then I saw who was sitting in the window of the Café Madeline and I felt stupid in a wholly different way.

HA. Not as in "ha, ha, ha." As in the initials H.A.

Hector Acosta stood to greet me as I entered the café. He was dressed less formally today, but his gray-green sweater was cashmere and his jeans fit in ways that would have made the designers at Balmain very pleased. A leather jacket was flung over the back of one of the chairs. Kate's laptop bag was on the table.

"*What*? How?" I looked from the bag up to his stubbled face. Was he working with Todd Randall?

The look he gave me was wary. "Please don't be alarmed."

"*Alarmed*?" I said, probably more loudly than I should have, as several people looked up from their screens.

He pulled out a chair. "Please. Sit. Can I get you something? A coffee?"

I gave him a look that I hoped spoke volumes. "You can tell me what the hell is going on." I sat.

He nodded and took a seat opposite me, the laptop between us. "There is something that I must confess to you."

"Damn right there is."

"I have been watching your theater."

I stared at him, a dozen questions racing through my mind. How long had he been watching? And why? Didn't he trust the police investigation? Didn't he trust the people at the Palace? People like me?

Of all of those, the only question I asked him was the final and perhaps most pressing one. "What have you seen?"

A fraction of the tension seemed to leave his body. Apparently I wasn't going to cause a scene over his blatant invasion of my privacy. At least not yet.

"Nothing until this morning," he said. "But at five forty this morning a man entered the theater by way of the back door in the alley."

Five forty. That meant Todd had probably been in the office for only a few minutes before I'd gotten there. And it meant that the police's assessment had been right. He'd come in the basement door, near the bottom of the back stairs and the room where Raul's body had been found on ice.

Hector gave me a moment for everything to register before going on.

"The break-in was observed by my associate, who was watching the back of the theater from a parked van. My plan was to follow the intruder into the theater and observe his actions, in hopes that he would somehow incriminate himself in my brother's murder."

"What—?" I began, but Hector was on a roll.

"That plan was changed when I saw you approaching the building. I attempted to get your attention, but you were—"

"Listening to a podcast," I realized. "I had my ear buds in. Where *were* you?" I may have been catching up on NPR on my walk to the theater, but I wasn't oblivious. I knew I hadn't seen anyone on the street.

"I was upstairs." His gaze darted briefly to the ceiling of the coffee shop. "The proprietress here has graciously consented to rent me her storage room for an exorbitant daily sum. It is a small space, and uncomfortably chilly. But it affords a direct view across the street and into the windows of your office and staff room."

My jaw dropped. "You've been *spying*—"

He waved his hand impatiently. "Any one of your employees might have murdered my brother. You are the only one at that theater who surely did not kill him, as you were in Los Angeles. Specifically, you were attending a meeting with your lawyers on Wilshire Boulevard that afternoon, a fact that was well documented by the pack of paparazzi who were following you."

His accent became more pronounced when his temper flared. I stared at him, not really believing that he had apparently investigated me and probably every single person at the Palace.

"Have you—"

"Getting back to the events of this morning," Hector deflected what would have been the first of many questions. "By the time I got to the street you were already in the building. I assumed you would be going to your office, and I had observed the intruder already there from my window. I knew you to be in danger."

Well, that part was accurate. Todd hadn't actually raised his fists to me, but I'd absolutely felt in danger.

"Unfortunately," Hector went on, "you locked the lobby door behind you, and I have many skills but rapid lock picking is not among them. So I was forced to run around the block to the alley and enter the same way the thief had. By the time I got to the top of the back stairs I saw the intruder rushing down the hallway to the lobby stairs. I heard your voice from the staff room and glanced in, but you didn't appear to be harmed so I chose to pursue the intruder."

I must have been checking on Trixie by that point. My back would have been to the door. I hadn't even heard Hector.

"I take it you caught him," I said, looking pointedly at the recovered laptop. "Is he...did you..." Something about asking a person whether they had committed murder that morning was a little unnerving.

Hector rubbed his jaw ruefully, and I now noticed a darkening under his stubble. "He evaded me. My associate and I managed to relieve him of your laptop, but we were unable to pursue him."

"Why?" I asked. "And for that matter, why didn't your associate go up the back stairs after him? Why wait for you to get there?"

"Because Gabriela is in a wheelchair," Hector said. "Her job was to observe, which she can easily do. But pursuit was out of the question. The thief had a car and was gone before the police arrived. At which point I sent Gabriela away and I myself went back to my observation post to wait until you were free."

"And you asked me to come alone because you still think someone at the Palace killed your brother?"

He shrugged. "That has not been ruled out. Although this morning's activities raise other strong probabilities."

"You mean like Todd Randall being the murderer?" I said. "That had occurred to me."

Hector looked thunderstruck. "Todd Randall? You know who this man is? Where is he?" He rose, grabbing his jacket, as if ready to charge off right that instant.

"Calm down," I said. "I know who he says he is. But I'm pretty sure everything he's ever told me has been a lie, and I have no idea where he is." I blew out a breath. "Or what he's up to."

Hector sank back into his chair. He ran a hand through his hair, but it was so well-cut it just fell back into place. "I need you to tell me absolutely everything you know about this man."

I did, which didn't take long, since I didn't know much.

"So," I concluded. "Let's assume that whatever Randall was looking for is the reason he killed your brother and Kate—that's assuming he killed your brother and Kate, which I think we reasonably could."

Hector nodded. "Although he might not have been working alone," he cautioned.

"Fair enough. Now," I continued, "the only thing I know to be objectively valuable in that theater is the equipment." Particularly that new projector, which I still had questions about. "But Randall wouldn't have been looking under desk drawers for anything that big, and he wouldn't have taken the laptop if what he was looking for was equipment, right?"

Hector looked doubtful. "So it might be something small. Jewels, or even cash. But it could also be a piece of information, leading to this valuable thing. He could have been looking for something taped to the underside of the drawer. A bank code or safety deposit key or some sort of password."

I felt like I'd been looking for a password ever since I'd gotten to the Palace. "That would explain why he took the laptop," I said, placing my hand on the laptop in question. "There might be something in Kate's emails. I just need to get a hacker to get into them."

That caught Hector's interest. "You require someone who can hack into an email account?" He smiled and sat back in his chair. "Nora. In this I can be of help."

I stared at him. "You know how to hack an email account?"

"Me? No," he said modestly. "But I would be delighted to introduce you to my cousin Gabriela."

CHAPTER 23

Hector and I stepped out onto the sidewalk and I shivered after the warmth of the café.

"Where is your coat?" he asked.

"I lived in Los Angeles until last week," I reminded him.

He gave me a look, then draped his leather jacket over my shoulders. It was possibly the softest thing I'd ever felt. I was warm and cozy for the full fifteen steps across the street to the Palace.

I carried the laptop hugged to my chest. Hector had told me that his cousin Gabriela, who was the "associate" in the wheelchair who had been staking out my theater with him, had a degree in Computer Science from Cal Poly. She would undoubtedly be able to make quick work of Kate's email password. But, as much as Hector seemed like an ally, and as lovely as his jacket was, I wasn't letting anybody walk off with Kate's laptop again. Gabriela could come to the Palace.

Hector hadn't been thrilled, but he'd understood and had sent Gabriela a text. She'd gone to work, he told me, after their stakeout that morning. She was a software engineer at one of the big tech firms in Silicon Valley.

"Oh." I was disappointed. I'd had brief visions of Hector's cousin sporting a dragon tattoo and helping me wreak vengeance on Kate's killer in a cyber-spectacular way. But probably not.

"There is something I must ask you," Hector said as we entered the lobby. "This morning when I was in the hallway, following the intruder, I heard you speaking...but you were alone in the room, right?"

Uh oh. I'd probably been talking to Trixie when Hector had

glanced in to make sure I was okay. I didn't think he'd buy the "I was just working on dialog for a screenplay" story that I'd used when Marty had overheard me in similar circumstances.

"Oh, look, Callie's here," I said instead.

She was at the top of the balcony stairs. "Soooo, I hear you've had a morning."

"What are you doing here so early?" Unbelievably, it was still only nine o'clock. I willed her to come down to the lobby, if only to distract Hector from his questions about why I'd been talking to myself in the break room.

"I have a new cut of my doc," she said. "I was going to show it to Marty." She came down, gravitating toward Hector. "I'm a filmmaker," she told him, doing a flirty little thing with her fingers in her hair that you can only pull off when you're gorgeous and in your twenties. Then she said something in what sounded like flawless Spanish. I didn't understand it, but it sounded sexy.

"How nice," he replied. Then he turned to me. "You will take care, yes? I'll return with Gabriela this evening."

"I'll be fine," I assured him.

He placed his hands briefly on my upper arms. It felt strong and reassuring and somehow intimate in a way I didn't have time to figure out. "Until this evening." And he was gone, leaving me still hugging the laptop and still wearing his jacket.

"Oh. My. God." Callie said. "He is so totally hot."

"Do you think?" I said casually.

"Speaking for all women everywhere, yes," she said. "And you two are totally vibing."

"Do you think?" I said again, less casually. Then I came to my senses. "Don't be ridiculous."

She raised an eyebrow, but blessedly changed the subject. "Marty told me what happened. Are you, like, okay and everything?"

"I'm fine," I told her. "But we need to let everyone know that if they see Todd Randall they should call the cops."

"Cool," she said. "Um, do you maybe have a picture of him or something?"

Right. That would help. "Let's see if there's one on his web site," I suggested. Callie's phone was, of course, already in her hand. We moved over to the candy counter as she went to the *Real on Reel* website. We saw there was a grainy photo of Randall—or whoever he was—which was better than nothing, if barely. Callie sent the photo to the printer upstairs in the break room.

"Thanks," I said, then I remembered that I was in search of another photo.

"Callie, do you have any decent pictures of Kate? I want to post some flyers around Stowe Lake in case anyone might have seen her."

Callie's eyes widened. "Oh. Wow. Kate *hated* having her picture taken."

This much I'd figured out on my own. Every single shot of her online—and there weren't many—was blurred, with her seeming to turn her face away from the camera just as the picture was taken.

"I don't think she'd ever even taken a selfie." Callie shook her head in Millennial awe.

My heart sank.

"She had a scar." Callie gestured to the area along her left jawbone, back toward the ear. "It looked kind of like a crooked Z. She joked about it, said Tyrone Power gave it to her." She smiled, and so did I. Tyrone Power had played the dashing masked bandit in *The Mark of Zorro* (1947, Power and Linda Darnell).

"But she totally hated it," Callie said. "I think that's why she didn't like seeing herself in pictures."

"What was it from?" I asked. "Was she in an accident?"

"I think she had, like, a skin cancer or something removed. But she liked the Zorro story better."

I would have, too.

"I really miss her," Callie's expression, normally so studiously bored, softened. "I still expect to see her every time I'm here. Or to hear her, you know, yelling something down from upstairs?"

"I know," I said. I had still expected Ted to call "That you, babe?" every time I went into our house after he left. Which was an excellent reason never to go back to that house.

"She was learning Italian," Callie said. "For the last six months everything was *grazi mille*, and *come stai?* and *fa bene, fa bene, fa bene.*"

"Was she planning a trip to Italy?" I asked.

"She talked about it, but I don't think she actually, like, *planned* anything."

"Marty said her favorite movie was *Summertime.*" Set in Venice.

Callie nodded. "She said she wanted to be able to watch all of Sophia Loren's movies without subtitles." She swallowed. "I wish she'd been able to."

"I do, too."

I went upstairs to make copies of Randall's picture and to call a locksmith for the back door. I couldn't send Kate on a trip to Italy, but I could do whatever it took to protect her theater.

I could and I would.

I sent a text to Robbie, letting her know about the break-in. She called immediately, and I'd just gotten off the phone with her when Detective Jackson called. So I went over it all again, even though I got the feeling he was reading along from the statement I'd already given the police. He drilled for details in a couple places, and then seemed ready to hang up without telling me a single thing.

"Hey, wait a minute," I said. "What have you found out? Who is Todd Randall? What did he have to do with Kate or Raul Acosta?"

There was a pause for a moment and I thought I'd lost him. Then I heard the unmistakable sound of a soft drink can being popped open. The detective gulped before answering.

"Your man's a ghost," he told me.

"He's not my man," I said. Privately, I felt that calling Todd Randall a ghost was an insult to ghosts everywhere, but I didn't pursue that with the detective.

"The strongest lead we have is that website," he went on. "We've filed for court orders to get the hosting company to cough up any information they have on him."

"Like a credit card?"

"Exactly. He must have paid for that site somehow, and that information may get us to his real name."

"How long will that take?"

"I hope we'll get it today or tomorrow," he said. What he didn't say is that Todd Randall could be long gone by then.

But I didn't think he would be. He still didn't have what he'd come looking for.

And I still didn't know what that was.

Marty found me sweeping out the balcony after the first show. "2812," he announced.

"And a 1924 to you," I replied, having no idea what he was talking about.

"It's the new alarm code," he explained. "I called the security company and set it up. And I'm only telling you and Albert and Callie."

"Got it," I said. We'd agreed that only the senior staff should have the new code. None of the other employees should really need it since they shouldn't be at the theater unless one of us was. "Why 2812?"

"Because of the Lumière brothers, of course." He leaned against a column and crossed his arms, his smug expression indicating that he intended this exchange to be some sort of pop quiz on cinematic history. The Lumière brothers had been French filmmakers—the first 'real' filmmakers, by most accounts. At least the first to make any money at it.

Okay, I was up for a quiz. "So why not 1895?"

He looked surprised but recovered quickly. "You mean because they showed the first set of films in 1895?"

I shrugged, as if to say any simpleton knew that.

"They showed them on December twenty-eighth," he said. And he really enjoyed saying it.

"And they were French," I realized. "So they wouldn't say 12/28. They'd say—"

"2812," Marty finished. "You're welcome."

"And you're hilarious," I told him. Then I handed him the broom and told him not to skip the back row.

I closed the office door for the call with Robbie and Naveen. I also closed the blinds, waving goodbye to Hector, or at least to the window of the room above the café across the street. If he was there, and thwarted in his observations, he had only himself to blame. He was the one who'd told me to be careful.

And on that subject, I took extra care with the laptop. Up until that point I'd always just left it on the desk in the unlocked office, but now, in the absence of a wall safe or a better idea, I tucked it behind the couch. It wasn't exactly a genius hiding place, but at least it wasn't in plain sight.

Once Robbie and Naveen and I had chatted for a while in that meaningless Hollywood way that establishes all sorts of territorial nonsense, Naveen got down to telling us what he'd figured out about the Palace's finances. And he put it in terms even I could understand.

"Your theater is taking in way too much money."

"That's what I thought," I said. "I couldn't figure out how it all added up."

"It doesn't," he said. "To bring in the kind of revenue on these books, you'd have to be playing to packed houses on multiple screens, pretty much twenty-four hours a day."

I thought of the handful of elderly regulars who were currently settling in for the 2:15 showing of *The Mad Ghoul*. "Yeah, that's not what's happening."

"So what does that mean?" Robbie asked. "It doesn't sound

like Kate was stealing. If anything she was doing the opposite."

"Right," Naveen said. "It looks to me like she's been padding the accounts by grossly overstating the income from cash ticket sales and cash concession sales. And she'd also been selling off some assets."

"Like the espresso machine," I said. "And the printer."

"Right." Naveen said. "She'd been selling large items fairly regularly. I don't see receipts for the purchases, but when she sold them she logged the proceeds."

"What are we talking about here?" Robbie asked. "If Kate was cooking the books, she was doing it in our favor, but where was the money actually coming from?"

"And where did it all go?" I asked.

Naveen gave us the answer as if he thought it was glaringly obvious.

"Your theater has been laundering money," he said. "That's the only thing that makes sense."

"*How*?" I asked, at the same time Robbie said "*What*?"

"Look," Naveen said patiently. "It's simple. Somebody has dirty money. They run a card room or deal drugs or whatever. They can't take that income to the bank without answering a lot of questions about where it came from. So they buy another business—a legit business—one that does a lot of cash transactions, like a cupcake shop or a nail salon. That business takes in the dirty money and pads their books to show a lot more cash income than they actually make selling cupcakes or doing nails. Nice clean income."

"You're saying I'm invested in a front for the mob?" Robbie's voice went up about an octave.

"Hold on, don't panic yet," Naveen said. "Nobody said 'mob.' And the scenario I just laid out would mean that you or one of the other owners was the criminal mastermind behind the money laundering." He took a breath. "What's more likely is that Kate was pressured, or even threatened, into doing it by some third party who then—"

"You think someone was *threatening* Kate?" Robbie sounded horrified. "Some drug dealer or—"

"We don't know," Naveen cautioned her. "That's just one possibility. But trust me when I tell you that you don't want to mess around with this. We should absolutely take a look at the other owners. And we might want to go to the Feds, if only to establish your—"

"The *Feds*?" Robbie sounded like she might be hyperventilating.

"That's just a possibility," Naveen said soothingly, but Robbie was clearly beyond soothing. I was, too. Because I'd just realized, with all Naveen's talk about money laundering and drug dealers, that I'd believed everything Hector had told me without questioning it. I'd taken the word of a self-confessed criminal that he and his brother were reformed. How stupid did that make me?

"Okay, okay, what about the other owners?" Robbie asked, as if reaching for a lifeline. "Mitch is the only one I really know. He asked if I wanted in when one of the others wanted to sell, and it sounded like fun. Fun!" she now wailed.

Mitch was Mitchell Black, a sitcom director I'd met a few times. "Who are the other owners?" I asked.

"I barely know them," Robbie said. "One made a fortune selling some sort of travel app. I've met him once or twice, but just briefly. The other is the newest investor. She owns a business up there. I haven't even met her. Shit, shit, shit! I'm such an idiot!"

That made two of us.

"Now, let's just keep our heads," Naveen said. I could hear him shuffling papers. "The tech guy is Charlie Zee. He lives in Palo Alto." He paused, presumably reading something. "Oh, I love that app. The last time I was in New York—"

"Who's the other owner?" I cut him off.

"Uh...Here it is. M. Chen. It looks like she owns a florist shop. The Potent Flower. Is that anywhere near the theater, Nora?"

I couldn't speak. Everything was suddenly blindingly clear. M. Chen. M for Monica. Monica was a part owner of the Palace.

Monica, who owned the Potent Flower and was definitely not a florist. She owned a cannabis shop that probably brought in a huge amount of cash. Cash that, even though it was legally earned, couldn't be deposited in a bank until it was laundered. This I knew, because Hector had explained it to me.

"Nora?" Robbie said, probably not for the first time. "Are you still there?"

Everything suddenly made sense. Everything about the weird look that flashed across Monica's face every time I saw her. The look, I now realized, was fear. Fear that I'd take a look at the books and realize Kate had been laundering money for her? Maybe fear of something more.

"Nora?"

It even might explain what Raul Acosta had been doing at the theater. What if he hadn't actually retired from the family business? What if everything Hector had told me about their going legit was a lie? Raul could have found out what Kate was doing for Monica and tried to force her into laundering the Acosta family money as well.

"Nora!"

"I'll call you back," I said. "I need to check on something." I hung up to yells of protest from Robbie and Naveen.

I had to find Monica. I had to ask her if I was right about Raul. About all of it. Because if I was right, and Kate had refused Raul, it could have gotten violent. He might have attacked Kate. She might have killed him in self-defense.

And who had then killed Kate?

I glanced at the darkened window, feeling Hector watching me from the room across the street.

Who indeed?

CHAPTER 24

"We need to talk."

The smile that Monica had initially greeted me with vanished as she registered my tone of voice. It was replaced with a look I now recognized.

Fear.

I'd gone straight to the Potent Flower from the theater. Well, not straight there. I'd taken the back stairs and slipped out the basement door into the alley, checking to make sure cousin Gabriela wasn't parked out back.

If there even was a cousin Gabriela.

I went up a few blocks before cutting over toward Divisadero, stopping in doorways to check behind myself, no doubt looking like every guilty hoodlum in every B movie Peter Lorre ever made, trying to be sure I wasn't followed.

Now, from behind the counter of her busy shop, Monica nodded. Without a word, she led me through to the lounge where I'd had my mini breakdown the day before. There were a handful of people in the lounge, and Monica walked through the space without slowing. She used a touchscreen to unlock a door at the far end of the room. She must have understood we'd need privacy for this conversation.

We entered a short hallway with three doors, each of which had a touchscreen lock. She punched in a code at the farthest door to unlock a windowless room that was painted in warm saffron and orange tones and furnished simply with a desk and two guest chairs. Beyond the desk area, a golden Buddha head was mounted on the wall, gazing serenely at a colorful pile of floor pillows. The room seemed equal parts office and meditation nook. Under other circumstances I would have found it soothing. But under other circumstances I wouldn't have been asking Monica about money laundering and murder.

"What can I do for you, Nora?" Monica asked when the door closed behind us. She lifted her chin with something like defiance but gripped the back of a chair with white knuckles.

"You can tell me how long Kate had been laundering money for you."

I hadn't been sure of it, not completely, until I saw Monica react. She swallowed, the attempt at defiance leaving her body as she slumped in resignation, or maybe in relief. She sat, shakily, on one of the guest chairs.

"I need you to tell me everything," I said, sitting opposite. "When did it start? How exactly did it work?"

She nodded, looking blankly into space, as if gathering her thoughts. When she eventually looked at me again I got the sense that she was glad, in some part, to finally be telling someone.

"It just...happened," she said. "You know that banks won't accept money from cannabis businesses, right?"

"I know." Because Hector had explained it to me. Even though running a licensed pot shop was legal in California, selling cannabis was still illegal under federal law, so the federally-regulated banks couldn't take their deposits.

She nodded. "I was always moaning about how much trouble it was to have to deal with everything in cash. You have no idea. I knew other people were making regular trips to casinos or all kinds of crazy things, doing whatever they could to launder their profits, but that just seemed so *underhanded*, behaving like we were *criminals*." The look she gave me begged for understanding. "But I was in the same bind as everyone else. I had to do something."

Something to get her money clean. Something at the Palace. "Who's idea was it?" I asked.

Monica looked away. "I don't even remember. Kate and I talked about it. We were always wondering about what would make a good front. A business that takes in most of their earnings in cash, so you could just pad their books with extra income. Nice legal income that you could deposit. I was thinking of buying a yogurt shop, just to funnel the money through it. And there Kate was, with the theater barely scraping by..."

"But for it to work you had to own at least a piece of the Palace," I reasoned. "How did you convince one of the co-owners to sell?"

"I didn't have to," she said. "One of the partners told Kate he was thinking of selling. He thought she might want to buy in. He figured she did all the work, so she should have some equity. Which was true."

"But you bought it instead."

"It just seemed so perfect," she said. "Like it was meant to be. The whole thing just sort of...blossomed."

She made it sound so natural. Organic. But two people were dead.

"I want to make one thing clear," Monica said. "I am scrupulously honest about my bookkeeping for this shop. I have never fudged one dime about my reported sales or expenditures and I'm in total compliance with every single state regulation. You would not believe the kind of scrutiny a cannabis business gets and I've never so much as bent one single rule." She'd straightened her spine as she told me this, but having made her point, she sort of wilted. "It's just the damn banks that are the problem."

I nodded. "So you bought into the Palace and Kate started over-reporting ticket sales."

"And concessions," Monica nodded. "How she expected anyone to believe there was that much popcorn in the world..." A smile flickered briefly before fading.

"What about the equipment?" I asked.

"That came later," Monica said. "There was *so much* money. She couldn't realistically account for it all in sales, so she'd buy equipment with cash and then sell it to other theaters as second-hand, recording the income. That worked with less expensive things, but then she spent a fortune on a fancy projector, and nobody she knew could buy something that expensive."

"So it's still sitting on a shelf in the projection booth," I said. At least that was one mystery solved.

"Nora, I'm so sorry." Monica reached for my hand and held it with both of hers. "After Kate died I didn't want the theater to get in any legal trouble. I thought, if I just stopped, and left things alone, maybe nobody would ever have to know."

"And Kate handled the Palace finances on her own," I worked it out. "So when she sent the owners their quarterly checks, yours was just bigger than the rest."

"And I could finally deposit it in a bank," Monica affirmed.

"Did she keep two sets of books?" I asked. "And use some of your money to make it look like the theater was more profitable that it was?"

She nodded, biting her lip. "She kept twenty percent of the cash that went through the theater."

Albert had told me on my first day that Kate had kept the Palace solvent "by hook or by crook." He didn't know how right he was. Unless..."Did anybody else at the theater know about it?"

She shook her head. "No. Kate used her share to keep the lights on and the salaries paid, but she didn't tell anyone. She didn't want anyone else to be compromised, legally, if it ever came out."

Right. But Robbie was feeling more than a little compromised at the moment.

"Well, somebody knew." I looked at her closely. "Raul Acosta knew."

I said this as a fact, but I was really just trying to see if my guess was right—Raul Acosta had found out what Kate was doing for Monica and he wanted in on the scheme.

Monica nodded, biting her bottom lip. "And now he's dead, and Kate's dead, and it's all my fault."

No, it wasn't. At least not all of it. "Monica," I said. "I have to tell you something. Raul Acosta is part of a Columbian crime family. He must have—"

She straightened, blinking and shaking her head as she wiped her eyes. "Oh, no, I mean, yes, he used to be, but he wasn't anymore."

Now I shook my head. "He might have told you he was going legitimate, just like his brother told me, but—"

"But he was!" Monica protested. "He'd been working with a whole collective of cannabis business owners. He had a team of lawyers and lobbyists working in Sacramento."

"I'm sure he said—" I started patiently.

"No, really," she insisted. "He was trying to get the state to approve a bank for us," she said, "That wasn't just some story, it was real. I went to one of the hearings at the state legislature."

I sat back, stunned. If what she was saying was true, everything that had made sense earlier was suddenly thrown into confusion again. Had Hector been telling me the truth after all? That thought caused a warm rush of emotions that I didn't even attempt to identify, but the very appeal of it made me reject it.

"That can't be," I told Monica. "Raul was trying to intimidate Kate into laundering the Acosta family money—"

"No," she insisted. "He was trying to help her straighten out the books so nobody would ever know what she'd been doing."

"Well, then..." My mind seemed to be incapable of sifting through the changing facts one more time. "How...?" I shook my head. "Who...?" Yes, that was the question: Who?

"Then who killed Kate and Raul?" I asked Monica.

This caused her eyes to fill again. "I never should have let her keep the money," she said. "I knew it was dangerous, but she said she had it all figured out."

"What money? You mean her twenty percent?"

"No, the rest of it."

"What rest of it? There was more?"

"There was so much!" Monica wailed. "All of the cash that had piled up before we started using the Palace for the day-to-day proceeds. By the time we started that I already had months of cash that needed to be cleaned. Way too much to be accounted for by ticket sales or equipment deals. She couldn't move that until the remodel."

"*What remodel?*"

Monica put her hands up, as if physically warding off my questions.

I gave her a moment, telling myself that I *would* figure this out. When I spoke again it was with a massive attempt at composure. "Tell me about the remodel."

She nodded and gave me a relatively steady look. "Kate was going to remodel the theater."

"I know," I said. I'd seen the plans. Now I knew how she planned to pay for it. But I still didn't get how that would benefit Monica.

"She was going to hire painters and plumbers and electricians and designers and dozens and dozens of workers to do it."

"Sure." That seemed obvious.

"And most of them would do the work," Monica explained. "But some of them wouldn't. Because some of them wouldn't actually be real." She blinked, looking at me through wet lashes. "Some of them would just exist on paper, working for MC Design, which is a company that I'm in the process of incorporating."

I stared at her.

"Instead of a yogurt shop," she said.

My jaw dropped.

"So let me get this straight," I felt like it was about the hundredth time that day that I thought I understood. "Kate was going to get the work done using your pile of cash to pay both the real contractors and your nonexistent ones."

Monica nodded hesitantly. "That was the plan. We figured there would be so many bills nobody would ever look at who actually did what. We'd be able to move the rest of the money that way. MC Design would invoice, the Palace would pay, nobody would ask where the Palace got the money to pay, and all of the stored-up cash from the Potent Flower would turn into perfectly legal profits for MC Design."

I thought it through. It made sense. It was, in fact, kind of brilliant. But it had to be illegal, right?

"Hang on," I said, trying to put the rest of it together. "The remodel hadn't started yet. So where's your great big pile of cash?"

Monica wiped her nose and nodded. "Oh, Nora. Don't you see? That's what got Kate killed."

CHAPTER 25

I stared at Monica. "How much money are we talking about?"

"Well..." she said. "It's a little hard to say, but I think, probably, what was left was..." She hesitated, her voice growing smaller. "Somewhere around seven million dollars."

That number took a moment to register. Seven million dollars. There was seven million dollars hidden somewhere in the Palace. Seven million dollars that had gotten Kate and Raul killed.

"Where—" My voice squeaked, so I cleared it and tried again. "Where did she hide it?"

Monica shook her head. "I don't know, but—"

"You don't *know*?" I demanded. "It was your money. How—"

"It doesn't matter!" Monica cut me off. "Don't you see? It doesn't matter where Kate hid it, or what she bought, because somebody must have found out! Somebody must have found out and—" She stopped abruptly, shuddering. "Whoever killed Kate and Raul has it now. That's the only thing that makes sense."

I couldn't sit a minute longer. I got up and started pacing as well as I could, given the size of the room. I thought Monica was probably right, up to a point. But I didn't think the killer had gotten what he'd come for. Because after everything I'd learned that day I had two candidates for the killer: Todd Randall and Hector Acosta. And both of them were still hanging around the theater. Todd had been looking for something in Kate's office, and he wouldn't have been looking if he'd already found it. And just because Raul was going straight didn't necessarily mean Hector was. I had only Hector's word that he'd been keeping the theater under observation to find his brother's killer. Maybe he was his brother's killer. Maybe he, too, was after the money.

I stopped. Something Monica said had just caught up with me. "What did you mean when you said, 'what she bought?'"

Monica blinked. "What?"

"Just now, you said Kate hid the money or 'what she bought.' What does that mean?"

She blew out a breath. "Nora, do you have any idea how much space seven million dollars in cash would take up?"

I could honestly say I didn't.

"Think about a bank vault," she said. "What do you picture? Nice neat stacks of cash? Tidy bundles of hundred-dollar bills? That would be so easy. A ten-thousand-dollar bundle of crisp new hundreds isn't much bigger than your cell phone. But I don't take in crisp new hundreds. I mostly take in crumpled tens and twenties, small bills and lots of them. With the kind of bills I take in, seven million dollars, however neatly you bundled it, would be about the size of that desk."

I looked at the desk. It wasn't small.

"Wait. Are you saying there's a safe big enough to hold that hidden somewhere in the Palace?" I asked.

"No. I'm saying that Kate bought something. Something that was much easier to hide."

Oh. Of course. I was back to the MacGuffin.

Monica leaned forward in her chair. "We knew it wasn't safe or practical to keep that much cash around, so we had to do something with the money until I got the new company together, which was taking a lot longer than either of us thought it would. But Kate figured out something she could buy. She said it was so simple she could have kicked herself for not seeing it earlier. What she bought was easier to store than cash, and she could hide it in plain sight, no gigantic safe required. She said when the time came to sell it we might even make a profit."

Finally. I was just about ready to jump out of my skin. "What was it?"

"I..." Monica looked to the serene Buddha head on the wall behind where I stood. "I don't know."

"What?" I yelled. "How is that *possible*?"

She shrugged, a bit of her earlier defiance returning. "She said it was safer that way. If I knew what it was, or where it was, I'd look at it differently. I'd draw attention to it every time I walked past, whether I meant to or not. So I just...left it to her."

I stared at her. "Seriously?"

Monica lifted her chin again. "She was my best friend."

And now she was dead.

What could you buy for seven million dollars in cash, hide in plain sight, and be able to easily sell when the time came? That was the question I asked myself as I walked around the city after leaving Monica.

I had to think, and I've always been better at thinking while moving. When I was a TV writer I'd always paced the writers' room. Robbie had once told me that just watching me work had been exhausting. And when I wrote now it was usually in furious bursts after coming in from a long walk, where I'd already figured out what I wanted to say. So now, with a thousand questions sloshing around in my mind, I walked. And I thought. And I sent the occasional text.

To Hector:

Change of plans. Don't bring Gabriela over. I've figured out something else. I'll talk to you tomorrow.

What I'd figured out was that he might have killed Kate and his brother. He replied immediately but I didn't look at it. I'd gotten good at ignoring texts lately, what with all the practice I'd had with my husband and the lawyers. I kept walking.

The October days were short, and it was getting dark and

chilly. I had a brief moment of missing Hector's warm leather jacket, which I'd left in the office, then I stepped into the next open clothing shop I saw and bought the thickest warmest sweater they had. I didn't need Hector.

Hector. Suppose he was still the head of a crime family. What if he'd tolerated his brother trying to go straight, but when Raul had mentioned the lengths his future customers went to in order to process their earnings, Hector had gotten an idea. What if he'd wanted in on the money laundering scheme at the Palace? Could he have gone to the theater that night? Maybe lied to Raul, telling him that he'd decided to go straight too? That he wanted to meet Kate? And then what? Had there been a fight? Maybe Raul had resisted, maybe Kate had tried to run? Maybe, maybe, maybe.

I sent a text to Detective Jackson:

Have you verified Hector Acosta's whereabouts on the day of the murders?

I doubted the detective would tell me, but it was worth a shot. And I'd never used the word "whereabouts" before in my life, but I used it deliberately here. I hoped it would sound official and police-like. Maybe Jackson got so many texts that he'd answer without realizing it was me that asked. Maybe.

If Hector was still in Columbia when Raul and Kate were murdered I could eliminate him as a suspect. Although crime lords were well-known for having henchmen, weren't they? Think of Sydney Greenstreet in *The Maltese Falcon*. Think of Sydney Greenstreet in just about anything.

But back to the point: Hector had found out that I was at my lawyer's office on the day of the murders. I could try to find out where he was, too.

Oh. Wait a minute. Hector had found out where I was. That meant he was investigating the murders. Why would he be investigating the murders if he'd committed them?

This thought made my head hurt. I stopped on the sidewalk,

not having any idea where I was. In the past week I'd only gone a few blocks in either direction from the Palace. Now I was on a bustling street of shops and restaurants, patronized by a hipster-looking clientele. A check of a street sign told me I was on Fillmore, but that meant nothing to me. I turned uphill and kept walking.

Okay, putting Hector aside for a moment, what about Todd Randall? He'd been lying about who he was and why he'd been in contact with Kate. And he'd broken into the office in search of something.

But all that still left me with the question of how he fit in. Why had he really been in contact with Kate? Because it certainly wasn't for a film festival. How could he have found out what was going on between the Potent Flower and the Palace? How could he have known about the money? If Monica, Kate, and Raul were the only people who knew, where did Todd Randall come in?

This would all be a lot easier if I knew who he actually was. I thought about texting Detective Jackson again, but decided that might be pushing my luck. Instead I tried Monica.

Did Kate ever mention Todd Randall to you? Do you have any idea how she knew him?

There was so little I knew about Kate herself. When I'd originally looked her up online I'd been surprised by how little information about her I'd found. Even Albert, who'd known her the longest, didn't know anything about her life before the Palace. At one point I'd wondered if she might have been fleeing from some sort of criminal past or might even be in the witness protection program. Now all those thoughts combined to present another possibility. What if Todd was someone from Kate's past? Could he have tracked her down somehow? Had he been blackmailing her over some secret?

I shook my head, worried that I was just being a screenwriter and spinning out increasingly fantastic scenarios. What I needed were facts.

I also needed a hot meal and a warm, safe space to keep thinking. I thought about summoning a ride share car to take me back to Robbie's guest house, but with as much as Hector seemed to know about me, I was pretty sure he'd have found out that I was staying in an isolated house made largely of glass. Until I heard back from Detective Jackson I had no desire to see Hector again. Particularly alone, where nobody could hear me scream.

Okay, now I was just freaking myself out. Nevertheless, I refused to be Barbara Stanwyck in *Sorry, Wrong Number* (1948, Stanwyck and Burt Lancaster) trapped and waiting for my killer to come find me. Instead I pulled out my phone and saw that I was five blocks away from a hotel with decent ratings. It was five blocks back in the direction of the Palace, so I turned left at the next street and set off toward comfort. And safety.

I spent those five blocks thinking about the MacGuffin. Something valuable that could be hidden in plain sight. And Monica had said Kate didn't want her looking at it differently every time she went past it. So it was in plain sight in a commonly used area.

What small thing would I buy with seven million dollars? First I thought about jewels, and then I thought about gold. In its heyday, the interior of the Palace had been dripping with gold leaf. Not much remained, but there were still glints and glimmers in the carved woodwork, holdovers from past restorations, if not from the original grandeur. What if Kate had bought something like gold coins and just stuck them around here and there, high in the crown moldings or along the proscenium arch? Would they have blended right in? Would anyone have noticed?

That hit all the criteria. Small, check. Valuable, check. Hidden in plain sight, check. And they might even be worth more by the time Kate sold them. Of course, they might also be worth less, but still.

I started walking faster as I became more and more convinced I was on the right track. I'd grown to appreciate the way Kate's mind had worked, the way she'd put movies together and the quirky tableaus she'd created in the theater to celebrate them. Did that mean I'd come to understand the way she'd thought? Had I tuned into her personality enough to figure out how she'd hidden the money? I asked myself whether decorating the theater with genuine gold would have appealed to her sensibilities, and the answer was a strong yes. I ran up the steps to the hotel when I got there.

I couldn't wait to talk to Robbie.

CHAPTER 26

"Where the hell have you been?!"

"Robbie, I have so much to tell you!"

I'd gotten a room at what turned out to be a very nice hotel and asked the guy who checked me in to have room service send up a pot of coffee and the biggest cheeseburger they were capable of producing. I hadn't had anything except a cup of Marty's tea all day and feeling like I'd finally figured something out had made me ravenous.

"Where are you?" Robbie demanded. "I've been texting you for hours!"

"I'm sorry," I said. "I'm in a hotel not far from the theater. And I'm fine. I'm wearing a fluffy white robe and hotel slippers and everything."

"How could you just run off like that? We're in the middle of talking about organized crime and murders and you just say 'gotta go' and bail? What were you thinking?"

"I'm sorry," I said again, and I meant it. Robbie sounded truly upset and I hadn't meant for her to worry. "I just suddenly realized something, and I had to check it out before I told you and Naveen about it. I had to be sure I was right."

"I'm texting Naveen right now," she said. "We've been debating calling the cops all afternoon." I heard her start tapping.

"Sorry," I said again. "But tell Naveen he doesn't need to start any investigation of the other owners. I know who Kate was laundering the money for."

The tapping stopped. "What? How? Who?"

So I told her everything, and finished just as the cheeseburger arrived.

"So my first instinct was to run back to the theater immediately and start shimmying up ladders to look at anything gold," I told Robbie between bites. "But we're smack in the middle of the 6:50 show, so I figure I'll wait here until after everyone goes home. If I go back after midnight I should have the place to myself."

"You will do no such thing!" Robbie said. "Have you forgotten what happened the last time you went into the theater alone? When Todd Randall—"

"Well, sure, I know," I said. "But we changed the alarm and fixed the lock, so—"

"Nora Paige!" she yelled. "I forbid you to go back to the theater tonight!"

I stared at the phone. "You *forbid* me?"

"Yes. I just realized you work for me. So I forbid you to take any more stupid risks. Go check out the gold tomorrow, in full daylight, with the whole staff of the theater and the entire San Francisco police department with you. But do not even *think* of skulking around with a flashlight by yourself in the middle of the night!"

"Okay, okay, calm down." She made a good point. Not about being my boss, but about the flashlight. I'd see much more if I could turn the house lights all the way up, and if I did that tonight it would alert the presumably watchful Hector that I was up to something. And alone in a big empty theater. "You're right," I told her. "Tomorrow will be better. Just because I figured it out doesn't mean Hector has. Or Randall."

"Just because you *think* you figured it out," she said. "You may not even be right. Because, one, the killer may already have the MacGuffin, and two, if it's still in the Palace it might not be in the form of gold coins glued to the rafters."

Well, when she put it like that…"What do you think it is?"

"I don't know. Maybe gold coins glued to the rafters, but maybe literally anything else. Listen," she went on, "I want you to promise me you'll wait until tomorrow. Seriously, Nora."

Ugh. As much as it killed me to admit it, the smart thing to do was to wait. "Maybe I shouldn't have gotten a whole pot of coffee from room service," I said.

"Girl, you pour that down the drain right now," she advised. "And see if there's wine in the minibar. Then get a good night's sleep and don't go in tomorrow until other people are there. Promise."

I promised. I didn't like it, but I promised.

I checked out of the hotel in the morning and was waiting outside the True Value hardware store on Divisadero when it opened at ten. I'd located the store on my phone, and the guy who unlocked the door seemed unfazed when I asked him for flashlights, binoculars, and acetone nail polish remover. Maybe it wouldn't be his weirdest request of the day.

It was Friday, which meant the movie lineup would change and the first show would be at 11:30. I figured everyone working the early shift would be in about an hour before that. I breezed past the ticket booth and up the poster-lined entryway at exactly 10:35, pleased to see two things: the lobby door was locked and Brandon was behind the candy counter.

"Hey Nora," he said as I used my keys—Kate's keys—at the door. "Everybody's been looking for you. Are you okay?"

"Everybody who?" I asked, more sharply than I'd intended if his startled reaction was anything to go by. I just hoped "everybody" didn't include either of my prime suspects.

"Um, Callie and Marty and Albert?" he said, turning his signature shade of splotchy crimson. "They're all upstairs."

"Oh, good. Yes, I'm fine, but I need your help with something before the first show. Can you go find the tall ladder?"

"Sure," he said, not sounding sure at all. "Um, should I tell everyone you're here?"

"Yes," I put the hardware store bag on the counter. "I got enough flashlights for all of us."

Searching for the hidden gold took a little longer than I'd planned, mainly because I had to spend some time convincing everyone that I was A: just fine despite having vanished without a word the day before, and B: not clinically insane for thinking there was gold in the rafters.

I didn't think anyone had to know that Kate had been laundering Monica's cash. They only needed to know that someone had killed her for something valuable.

"Look," I explained to everyone as they assembled and sat (Albert) stood (Callie and Brandon) or glared (Marty) in the balcony. "We know Todd Randall came here looking for something. He said it was something she bought with his money."

Albert harrumphed.

"I don't believe that either," I told him. "But I've found out that Kate *had* bought something valuable recently, and it was something small that she hid in plain sight in the theater."

I was assaulted with questions from all sides and I held my hands up in protest. "Later—I promise I'll explain everything later, but right now we have just about half an hour to start looking for anything that glimmers with these." I passed out the flashlights and binoculars. The house lights were all the way up, but we could use all the help we could get.

"If you think you see something, we'll go up on the ladder for a closer look," I told them. "And if it really is something, and it's glued to the woodwork, we can use nail polish remover to dissolve the glue without hurting the gold." I'd spent quite a while thinking through the details of the operation before I'd finally fallen asleep at the hotel.

Everyone was staring at me as if they weren't quite sure whether I'd lost my mind. I couldn't really afford to care about that now.

"Go!" I yelled at them. "Look!"

So they did.

And we found nothing.

"So when you said there were gold coins glued to the woodwork, what you meant was there was something somewhere in the theater," Marty said. "Which we already established yesterday."

"It could be anything," Callie said.

"Anywhere," Brandon concluded.

"That is, unless the killer already has it," Albert reminded us.

We were in the break room gathered despondently around the table. The 11:30 showing of *Dial M for Murder* was underway, and I'd called Claire and Mike to come in and help out so the rest of us could talk. My staff was less than thrilled with me. I was less than thrilled with myself.

"Okay. Well. I apologize," I said. "I may have gone a little bit down a rabbit hole with the gold idea." And with thinking I could read Kate's mind.

"It was a good idea," Albert said comfortingly.

"Sure," Marty said. "A great idea. Based on absolutely nothing."

I couldn't actually dispute that, so I didn't. The truth was I'd gotten completely carried away with one possibility when there were a thousand others.

"Okay, so, can someone explain why Kate had something so valuable that somebody, like, killed her over it?" Callie asked.

I'd decided what to tell them when I'd thought everything through at the hotel the night before. Kate had wanted to shield them and the theater from any hint of criminal conspiracy. So did I.

"She'd been saving money," I now said. "With the goal of remodeling the Palace. That's why she hadn't been keeping up with the routine repairs. But then she invested the money in something. Something small that she hid in plain sight. Something that she thought would be worth more when she sold it than it was when she bought it."

Marty, who had been lounging dejectedly, now stirred with interest. "How much money are we talking about?"

There was no way in the world they'd believe Kate had saved anything like seven million dollars. So I glossed over that, too.

"Enough to start a remodel of the building, so probably quite a bit."

"As much as that monstrosity of a projector that's taking up room in my booth?" Marty asked pointedly.

"I thought about that, and it is in plain sight, but really only your plain sight. No, the projector is valuable, but I don't think it's the MacGuffin." Nor was it worth seven million, I didn't add.

Albert smiled at my use of the term. "I always did fancy myself as Sam Spade." He rubbed his hands together with relish. "Let's figure this out, shall we? Something small and valuable, hidden in plain sight."

"You all knew Kate," I said. "You know how she thought." Which apparently I didn't. "What do you think she would have done?"

"What's been done in the movies?" Brandon asked. "Kate knew everything about movies."

"And she loved a good caper film," Albert agreed.

"What was that one where they melt down stolen gold into, like, souvenirs of the Eiffel Tower?" Callie asked.

"*The Lavender Hill Mob*," Marty and I said in unison (1951, Alec Guinness and Stanley Holloway). I gave Marty a glance that recognized a kindred spirit. He just looked startled that I'd known the film.

"I love the idea of looking to the movies for clues," I said. "What are some other capers Kate liked? Anything you showed recently?"

"I don't know about recently, but there's always *Topkapi*," Albert said (1964, Peter Ustinov and Melina Mercouri). "But that's all about stealing the dagger, isn't it? Not hiding it somewhere."

"*How to Steal A Million?*" Brandon contributed (1966, Audrey Hepburn and Peter O'Toole).

"Again, that's about stealing the statue, not hiding it," Marty said dismissively.

"But it's a good thought," Albert patted Brandon's arm.

We considered and rejected *The Asphalt Jungle* (1950, Sterling Hayden and a glimpse of Marilyn Monroe), *To Catch a Thief* (1955, Cary Grant and Grace Kelly), and *The Ladykillers* (1955, Alec Guinness and Peter Sellers) before Callie jumped to her feet.

"Oh. My. God," she said, her eyes wide. "Omygod, omygod, omygod!" She turned to me. "*Family Plot!*"

It took just a moment until I was with her. *Family Plot* (1979, Karen Black and Bruce Dern) was Alfred Hitchcock's last film. It involves a sham psychic and kidnappers, and in the last scene of the film the camera pans to a chandelier where we see an enormous diamond hidden among the crystals. The MacGuffin. Hidden in plain sight.

"The chandelier!" We tumbled all over each other rushing out of the room to the top of the balcony stairs. From that vantage point, we could see directly across the lobby to the hundred sparkling facets of the glittering chandelier.

How To Steal A Million
1966

Oh, how I love a caper movie! And this has to be the prettiest one ever made, with Audrey Hepburn as Nicole Bonnet, Peter O'Toole as Simon Dermott, a wardrobe by Givenchy, jewels by Cartier (yes, the jewels get a screen credit—it's that kind of movie) multiple tiny convertibles, and Paris, Paris, Paris! It's fun, gorgeous, and sophisticated, three words that also describe Audrey Hepburn.

Audrey is everything you want from her here. OMG, the white bubble hat, the white sunglasses, the little white dress and the tiny red convertible that she's tooling around Paris in the first time we see her—you will die. And don't even get me started on the black lace outfit she wears to meet Peter O'Toole clandestinely in the Ritz bar. A black lace dress with black lace tights and, I swear to you, a black lace mask barely obscuring amazing silver glitter eye makeup. I may pass out from fashion overload. Did I mention the clusters of diamonds at her ears? Cartier clusters, people.

So, okay, there's also a plot. Nicole (Audrey) comes from a long line of happy-go-lucky art forgers and lives in a Parisian mansion with her father and the family collection, the center of which is the "Cellini Venus," a small statue forged by her grandfather. All is well until her father loans the Venus to a museum, which means it will have to be authenticated. Which means Audrey somehow has to get it back before the expert arrives from Zurich. Which is where Peter O'Toole comes in. And he comes in as a very fashionable burglar.

The two meet cute when she finds him attempting to rob her house in the dead of night. He's in a tuxedo and she's in a pink nightie. Only Audrey Hepburn could totally rock a pink nighty and black rubber galoshes. And he's no slouch himself. The word "debonair" comes to mind. The first shot of him is those Peter O'Toole blue eyes peering over the top of a forged painting. Burgle me, Peter, burgle me.

The Venus is installed at the museum under (of course) elaborate security, but Audrey is (of course) able to convince O'Toole to rob the place. The plan he devises involves a boomerang, a magnet, and the two of them spending a great deal of time together in a very small broom closet. Which is fine. They're both so slim.

Will they retrieve the statue and live gorgeously ever after? You'll have to watch and see. And by that I mean *you have to.*

Parisian Thoughts:
The statue is watched over by very French guards. You know they're so French because of their mustaches.

The look on Audrey's face after being kissed by O'Toole is the look we all imagine we'd have after such an encounter. Pure dazed bliss.

No two people have ever made smoking look sexier. Is that how they stayed so thin? This is not a productive line of thought.

Is this movie the reason I started calling my father

"Papa?" Audrey is beyond adorable every time she says it.

So Many Good Lines:
This movie is so pretty you could watch it with the sound off. But then you'd miss lines like these:

"I'm a society burglar. I don't expect people to run about shooting me."

"It's national crime prevention week. Take a burglar to dinner."

"You know, for someone who started lying just recently, you're showing a real flair."

And delightful exchanges like these:

A: "Well, you don't think I'd steal something that didn't belong to me, do you?"
P: "Excuse me, I spoke without thinking."

P: "Ah, yes. That does it." (on seeing her in her burglary disguise)
A: "Does what?"
P: "For one thing, it gives Givenchy a night off."

Movies My Friends Should Watch
Sally Lee

CHAPTER 27

The lobby chandelier hung on a clever cable system that allowed it to be lowered down slowly for cleaning. I didn't know this at the time, but Marty did, and he tore down the stairs, heading straight to the little metal box in the wall by the doors. The box held the alarm system keypad, the master light switches, and another control that I'd never really noticed.

"Keys!" Marty turned to me. "Where are Kate's keys?"

They were in my backpack, which I'd left on the break room floor. Brandon ran back up for it, and then I had to dig around in all its pockets while everyone fidgeted nervously, craning their necks toward the light fixture.

I found the keys and handed them over to Marty, who tried two before fitting the right one into a small keyhole. He turned it and we heard a low rumble as the cable system engaged.

We had about forty-five minutes before the film would end and people would start filing out into the lobby. I've never seen anything move more slowly than that chandelier. It was agonizing. We automatically formed a circle around where it would arrive, looking up and straining to see any extra hidden sparkles. I realized Claire was standing next to me, looking up with the rest of us. I'd forgotten all about her, but she'd been covering for Brandon at the concession stand.

"Why don't you go take care of the ticket booth?" I said. "People could start showing up any time."

Nobody would show up an hour before a show, not to the Palace, but the teenager ambled off obligingly, asking no questions about the sudden urgent need to clean the chandelier.

The rest of us were just about ready to jump out of our skins. I had a moment of worrying about Albert's heart. Then the chandelier finally arrived at eye level and the five of us leapt on it like lions on a wildebeest. I held my breath as we examined each and every crystal.

And found nothing.

Again.

I went up to the office to text Robbie with news of my defeat. Sick of rooting around in my backpack, I just dumped its entire contents onto the desktop and picked the phone out of the pile.

No gold in the woodwork. No diamonds in the chandelier. No MacGuffin.

Robbie sent one word back.

Yet.

Which is why I loved her.

Everybody else had gone back to work after the chandelier fiasco. I sat in the office alone, trying to clear my head.

The phone pinged with a text, and I glanced at the cracked screen. It was Detective Jackson, finally getting back to me about Hector's whereabouts. Or not.

You will be kept informed of developments in the case as the need arises.

Well. So much for tricking him into telling me anything useful.

Hector himself had sent about a dozen texts and left three voicemails, all variations on a theme of "where are you?" If he wasn't a crime lord and coldblooded killer I would owe him an apology for making him worry. I sent him a quick text saying I was fine and that I'd be in touch. Hopefully that would keep him at bay, crime lord and coldblooded killer or not.

I scrolled through my texts, selectively ignoring the ones I didn't want to deal with and realized that Monica had never answered the one I'd sent her about Todd. Which meant I was in exactly the same spot I'd been yesterday afternoon, except exhausted from the misspent adrenalin of two consecutive wild goose chases.

I might never find the MacGuffin. If this were a movie, it might end with a scene set a hundred years in the future, with the Palace being demolished to make room for a robot factory or something. The camera would pan in on something small and valuable in the rubble, and the audience would cry "No!" as a bulldozer covered it forever. What would that something be?

"Hey, Nora. Watcha thinking about?"

I jumped about a foot when I heard Trixie's voice.

"Oh!" she said. "I didn't mean to startle you!" She was perched on the arm of the sofa.

"It's fine." I put a hand over my racing heart. "How are you?" I hadn't seen her since she'd run through Todd the morning before, trying to defend me.

"Fine. What happened with that fella? Did the police come?" She craned her neck to see behind the closed blinds out the window. "The pictures are different. How long have I been gone?"

"Just since yesterday." Marty must have changed the marquee earlier that morning to show the "ladykillers" weekend lineup: *Dial M for Murder*, which had ended as we'd raised the woefully diamond-less chandelier back up, and *Gaslight,* which was currently underway.

"What happened?" Trixie scooched forward, her eyes wide with curiosity.

I filled her in, editing the details to avoid the things that might take too long to explain to a 1930s usherette, like legal pot shops that couldn't use banks.

"So we need to find what Kate hid in the theater," I concluded. "Do you have any ideas? Did you ever see her doing anything that looked odd, or see her tuck something away anywhere?"

Trixie made a face while thinking. "I don't know. All I can think about since you said 'diamonds' is diamonds."

"Diamonds are like that," I acknowledged.

Trixie thought some more. She was the most fidgety thinker I'd ever seen. Eyebrows were raised and lowered, lips were arranged in a twist or a pout. Ears were tugged. Finally, she looked at me and shrugged. "*Allora*," she said. "That's what Kate would say when she was stumped, and brother, am I stumped." She sighed. "'*Allora, allora, allora.*"

"Is that Italian?"

Trixie nodded, chewing daintily on a fingernail. "Kate was learning it. She listened to lessons on her contraption, so I was learning it, too." She recited: "*Roma è così bella! Dov'è l'hotel? C'è l'hotel. Fa bene!*"

"Trixie, that's amazing! You learned all that from listening to her lessons on the laptop?" Which reminded me, where was the laptop? I got up and pulled it out from behind the couch where I'd stashed it the night before.

She waved a hand modestly. "Oh, it's nothing. I took French in high school, and Italian isn't that different. I figure I could find my way to my hotel in Paris or Rome any old time." She blinked, her smile fading. "Not that I ever will."

"Oh, sweetie." My heart went out to her. After eighty plus years of loneliness she was still bright and inquisitive, and, although it was weird to say this about a ghost, lively. I couldn't imagine how hard it must be for her to know she was trapped within these walls for all eternity.

I had a sudden vision of a bulldozer knocking down the Palace at the end of its story. What would happen to Trixie then?

"It's not so bad," she said. "I can see Paris or Rome anytime in the movies."

Okay, now she was ripping my heart out.

"Maybe I'll go watch the picture," she said. "That might help me think." Then she sat up straight. "*Gaslight!* We're showing *Gaslight!*"

I didn't see what the excitement was about. "Right. You missed the beginning, but—"

"Nora! *Gaslight!* The jewels! The jewels are in the dress!"

I caught up with her. In the movie Charles Boyer is trying to make Ingrid Bergman think she's losing her mind. She hears something in the attic every night and he tells her there's nothing there. What she hears is Boyer, the fink, in the attic looking for the fortune Ingrid's aunt left her. But none of that matters. What matters is that in the end we find out the fortune is in the form of jewels, sewn into an elaborate costume the aunt had worn as an opera singer.

Jewels. Hidden in plain sight.

And we had a rack of old costumes downstairs.

I'd already leapt to my feet before some modicum of sense kicked in. I held up both hands.

"Wait!" I yelled, more to myself than to Trixie. "I *cannot* go running all over this theater like a crazy person again."

"Okay," Trixie nodded, eyes shining. "We'll walk."

All we found hidden in the costumes of the Palace was dust. And some well-fed moths.

We'd gone down to the prop room where I'd looked through the posters a few days ago with Albert. I didn't get my hopes up (okay, that's a lie) and didn't tell anyone what I was doing.

Once downstairs, Trixie and I methodically went through every article of clothing, every accessory, every belt and boot and umbrella. I spotted a pair of earrings—cheap costume things—and wondered if this is what Monica had been doing the day I met her, when she said she'd come to the theater to recover the earrings she'd loaned Kate.

It bothered me that I hadn't heard back from her.

There were a few cloudy old mirrors and dusty paintings hung haphazardly on the walls around the room. After exhausting the possibilities of the costumes and props, I took a good close look at every single gilded frame, but couldn't convince myself that anything was real gold. Nor were any of the paintings lost masterpieces. At least as far as I could tell.

Trixie had helped, as much as she could without being able to physically move anything. This was her first wild goose chase of the day, so she was more optimistic than I was, but eventually even she had to admit that we were wrong.

"*Allora,*" I said. "What now?"

"I'll keep thinking," Trixie said. Then I got a text and when I looked up from my phone she was gone.

The text was from Hector.

Clearly something has caused you to mistrust me. When you realize you are wrong in this, I will be here.

Which really made me hope he wasn't a coldblooded killer. Because if he was just a nice guy, he was quite a nice guy.

I went back up to the office. The contents of my backpack were still spilled all over the desk. I noticed the page torn from Kate's notepad among the rest of it.

Something had bothered me about this list when I'd looked it over at Stowe Lake. There were too many movies for it to be a regular lineup.

"Win," "M," "Lace," "Sorry," and "Gas."

The words hadn't registered when I'd looked at the list before. But now, given the films we were playing, two of them jumped out at me. "M" could be *Dial M for Murder*, and "Gas" could be *Gaslight*. Both were movies where husbands plotted to kill their wives, which is why this weekend's lineup was dubbed "ladykillers."

What if the rest of the titles on Kate's note had the same theme? "Sorry." That could be *Sorry, Wrong Number*, which I'd just been thinking about the night before. Another husband plotting his wife's murder.

This made sense. With the unifying theme, "Lace" suddenly clicked in my mind as *Midnight Lace* (1960, Doris Day and Rex Harrison), where the suave English husband is trying to drive his rich American wife to suicide. And "Win" had to be *Rear Window* (1954, Grace Kelly and Jimmy Stewart), where the two leads think they witness Raymond Burr disposing of his wife's body and set out to prove a murder.

I sat back, stunned. Now that I saw it, how had I not seen it before? And what did it mean? Marty had torn this page off the notepad on Kate's desk. That meant it was probably the last note she had written. Possibly on the day she died.

We were showing *Gaslight* and *Dial M* now. She wouldn't have wanted to show them again any time soon. So the list probably wasn't for a lineup. It meant something else.

If Kate had been married I would have leapt to the conclusion that this was her dying clue and that her husband was her killer. But Kate hadn't been married.

Had she?

CHAPTER 28

Monica, text me back. I need to know if Kate was married. If she was ever married.

The answer came two minutes later.

Are you all right? They just gave me my phone back.

They? They who? I was replying when her next text came in.

I'm in the hospital. I was attacked last night.

While I'd been hanging out at the hotel the night before, Monica had been bashed on the head from behind as she'd entered her house. She didn't regain consciousness until she was at the hospital. Which was after someone had ransacked her home and attempted to break into her shop.

"Thank God for the guards," she said, propped up in her bed. The hospital was only a few blocks away from her shop. I'd slipped out the back door of the Palace and called for a ride share the minute I'd gotten her text. When I got to her room she'd been surrounded by visitors. She sent them all away as soon as she saw me in the doorway.

"They took my keys," she told me. Her head was bandaged and she had an IV in her arm. "They must have thought they could just disarm the alarm at the shop, but I have guards on duty around the clock."

I could see why. Cannabis shops must be tempting targets for break-ins, what with all the drugs and cash and everything. The thief had run off at the first shout from the guards but they still called the police, which led to a patrol car being sent to Monica's house where she was found unconscious.

"Thank God," I agreed. She'd taken a blow to her head, which had knocked her out. If she hadn't gotten to the hospital she might have died. Just like Raul.

Monica gripped my hand. "I was so worried about you. If they came for me..."

I squeezed her fingers gently. "I was too paranoid to go home," I told her. I didn't want to think about what might have happened if I had.

She gave me a weak smile. "Paranoid is good." She took a deep breath and shifted her position in the bed. "I guess this means you were right. Kate's killer doesn't have the money."

"No." Whoever had attacked Monica was obviously still looking for the MacGuffin. "What did the police say?"

She snorted. "Something amounting to the opinion that I was asking for it by running a drug den."

"That's insane," I protested. "You run a legal business!"

She grimaced. "Welcome to my world."

"Did they even tell Detective Jackson?" I asked. "Did they even make the connection to—"

"Well they wouldn't, would they?" she asked. "Not without knowing about the money laundering."

Oh. Right. The money laundering. The illegal money laundering. Right.

I rubbed my eyes. "I think we have to tell them."

Monica gave me an agonized look. "I can't do that to Kate," she said. "I'm responsible for her death. I can't be responsible for destroying her memory."

I opened my mouth to tell her that she wasn't responsible for Kate's death, and that nothing could destroy the memories of the people who loved her. But then I thought about everything I'd learned that day, and I said something different.

"You've kept all of Kate's secrets."

I gave her a steady look. She held it for a moment before turning away.

"I think it's time you tell me," I said. "Tell me about Kate's past. About Kate's husband."

It was a guess, but Monica swallowed, squeezed her eyes shut, and nodded.

I held my breath until she spoke.

"Kate Winslow wasn't her real name," Monica said. "She chose it when she was staying in a shelter in Winslow, Arizona."

I held myself back from asking questions. She would tell me in her own way.

"It was the last in a network of shelters she'd stayed in, moving across the country, relying on good people who risked their lives to help women like her escape."

I made a small sound. Monica glanced at me and nodded.

"She was running," she said. "Running for her life. I don't know where she was running from, but it didn't matter. She was running from the man who would have killed her if she'd stayed." She looked straight ahead. "From her husband."

I swallowed.

"She'd been in shelters and safe houses for two years by the time she got to Arizona, and the people who ran the network believed she was finally safe. They gave her new paperwork, a new identity, and told her to build a new life. She built it here."

Monica looked me in the eye. "You cannot understand what it's like to live with that fear. He becomes superhuman in your mind. He's every monster in every movie you've ever seen, and he'll never stop looking for you. When he finds you, he will hurt you beyond imagining. Over and over again. Until he kills you."

This is why Kate dodged having her picture taken. This is why she'd passed on high-profile opportunities to promote the theater. She couldn't let herself be seen. She couldn't let herself be found.

"He beat her," Monica said. "He burned her. He tried to carve his name into her flesh."

I felt sick. The Z scar Callie had told me about. It hadn't been from removing a skin cancer.

"He would have killed her if she stayed," Monica told me. "It was just a matter of time. I know it." Her eyes burned into me. "Do you hear what I'm saying? *I know it.*"

I gripped her hand, feeling her whole body tremble. I understood what she was saying. She knew what Kate had been through. Knew it firsthand.

"I didn't come here through a network," she said. "I wasn't that lucky. But when Kate and I first met we saw it in each other." She smiled grimly. "Like knows like."

She turned to me, her words fierce. "What we did, we did to help," she said. "There was *so much* money, and it could do *so much* good."

My eyes widened. "You've been giving back."

She nodded. "We have. Supporting the safe houses and shelters that are helping other women escape. We didn't even have to launder that money. I had cash and Kate knew how to funnel it to the network. Together we've saved lives. The lives of women and children. The lives of women like us."

When I got out of the hospital I pulled my phone from my backpack with shaking hands. I sent a text to my husband.

Ted. We should talk.

He had cheated on me and publicly humiliated me. But there were worse things a husband could do. I shuddered, thinking of everything Monica had told me.

My marriage was over, but compared to Kate and Monica and millions of others, I was a very lucky woman.

CHAPTER 29

Back in the office, I thought long and hard about calling Detective Jackson. Did he already know that Kate had been living under a false identity? Did he know her real name, or her husband's? Because Monica didn't. Kate had never told her, and Monica had believed the past should stay in the past.

But what if it hadn't? What if the past had gotten Kate killed? Because if I was right about the cryptic list of movie titles she'd left, husbands killing their wives had been on her mind. Had Kate's husband finally found her?

"*Allora*," I muttered, pulling out my phone to call the detective. "*Allora, allora, allora.*" I was stumped. And admitting it felt better in Italian.

"Now you sound just like Kate."

Once again Trixie's sudden appearance just about made me jump out of my skin. She was as bad as Marty's early-morning overture. I didn't know if I'd ever get used to either of them.

Trixie was standing near the door. "She used to do just that," she said. "Sit in front of the contraption and talk to herself. On a good day it was "*Fa bene, fa bene, fa bene.*"

I'd seen enough Italian movies to know that *fa bene* meant something along the lines of "it's all good" or "everything will be fine." I hoped Kate had had a lot of those days.

"But on other days it was *allora*." Trixie came over and alighted in one of the chairs facing the desk.

"Say that again," I said, something clicking in my mind.

"*Allora?*" Trixie asked. "You had it right. Your accent is a little—what are you doing?"

I was opening the laptop. Because I had a crazy idea. Kate had muttered to herself in Italian while working on her laptop. Kate had muttered to herself *in Italian*.

I clicked on the email icon and was presented with the login prompt. I typed Kate's email address as the user name, and then held my breath as I typed "allora" in the password box.

Nope.

"Allora." Capital "A."

Nothing.

This was stupid. Even I knew that most passwords required a number or some sort of special character somewhere. But, since I'd come this far, I tried "fabene."

The email opened. I was in.

An hour later, rethinking everything, I went looking for Marty. I found him in the projection booth, scrolling through his phone while onscreen, in *Dial M*, Grace Kelly struggled for her life with the man her husband had blackmailed into attacking her. The struggle, I knew, would not end well for him.

"Hey." I stood in the doorway, hugging Kate's laptop to my chest.

Marty jumped at the sound of my voice. "Don't do that!" He put the phone down in disgust. "And you know that blog I told you about? Don't bother. He hasn't updated it in weeks."

What? I hadn't thought anything could distract me from my news, but this did.

"He?" I said. "I thought you told me the blogger's name was Sally."

"Did I? Well, not that it matters now, since he's obviously given it up, but that had to be a fake name—Sally Lee?" The look he gave me was a now-familiar challenge to my classic film knowledge.

I shook my head.

"That was Eleanor Powell's character in *Broadway Melody of 1938*," he said smugly. "Eleanor Powell, who Fred Astaire said danced like a man?'" He raised his eyebrows, his case made.

"Cool," I said, not pointing out that Astaire had meant that as high praise. I had other things to discuss. "So, do you want to know what I found in Kate's emails?"

He goggled. Which I have to say I enjoyed.

"How did you...?"

I put the laptop on one of his tall tables and opened it. "I'll give you the highlights," I told him. "I didn't find any Swiss bank accounts or stashes of Bitcoin. We're still no closer to figuring out what Kate bought. But I did find out something else."

I paused, mainly to irritate him. Which it did.

"What?" he finally demanded.

"Todd Randall was telling the truth."

Hi Kate,

My name is Todd Randall and I'm writing because I've heard that you're the go-to person in San Francisco if I want to put on a classic film festival. I'm tentatively targeting early next year, and since this is my first attempt at something like this, I'd love to get the thoughts of an expert. Would you mind letting me pick your brain sometime?

Best,
Todd

Marty stared at me after reading this first of many emails that Todd and Kate had exchanged. "That isn't possible," he said.

I showed him the whole thread. "He first wrote about six months ago. It started out all about the festival, but he was charming and flirty, and it was clear that she liked him. Over time the emails get more personal."

Marty had started shaking his head almost as soon as I spoke.

"No," he insisted. "She would have told me if she was planning a film festival."

"Not if he asked her not to." I found an email from near the beginning of their exchange.

Dear Kate,

I'm sure your staff is amazing, and I'm looking forward to meeting them (though not as much as I'm looking forward to meeting you). But for now, do you mind keeping this under your hat?

I hope you don't think I'm being too presumptuous, but I can't help feeling that I've found a kindred spirit in you. And maybe something more...? This festival feels like our baby right now. Do you mind if we keep it just ours for a while longer?

With affection,
Todd

"She'd suggested introducing you to him," I explained when Marty had finished reading. "And this is how he convinced her to keep it a secret."

"Kate was no fool," Marty said. "She would have looked up that bogus website. She would have found him out in five minutes."

"She was no fool," I agreed. "But he had answers for everything." I opened another email. "Here. He asks her to forgive the state of his website. His web designer's kid had just been diagnosed with cancer, and Todd was giving him all the time he needed, because as much as he cared about his business, he cared about people more."

"Ugh," Marty snorted. "So he isn't a liar and a fraud. He's a humanitarian."

"And here," I clicked again. "When he said something about

Edward Everett Horton in *Topper*—"

"Ah ha! That was Roland Young!" Marty exclaimed, breaking his cardinal rule about no raised voices in the projection booth.

"I know. And when Kate called him on it he said..." I scanned the email. "'Of course! How silly of me. I'll never be able to match your encyclopedic knowledge. This is why I need you so much. Why I'm so glad you've come into my life.'"

"Pardon me while I throw up." Marty shoved the laptop away, a pained look crossing his face. "How can Kate have fallen for this schmuck?"

"He's got a good line," I said. "If I hadn't caught him in the office, I might have fallen for it myself."

Todd had set off my warning bells when he'd flirted with me in the lobby the other day, but I'd chalked that up to my newly-maybe-available jitters. But with time, if he hadn't broken into the office? If he hadn't confronted me in the break room? Who knew?

With Kate he'd taken the time he'd needed. He'd let her keep her distance, which would have been crucial for earning the trust of someone with her abusive past. He'd made her feel safe and appreciated. And then he'd reeled her in.

"He's clearly a con man," Marty had gone back to the emails. "And, by the way, I don't see any mention here of him giving Kate a deposit for anything, so that was a lie. But what was he after? It's not like Kate had—"

He broke off from the screen to stare at me.

"The MacGuffin?" I said.

"How could he have known?"

I shook my head. "No idea. But a con man doesn't string someone along like this without a goal in mind."

He sank onto a stool, squeezing his eyes closed and rubbing his forehead. "How did I not know? How could I not have noticed? Was this guy wandering around the theater for the past six months without me even—?"

"No," I said. "It all happened over email. He said he lived in Chicago."

Marty looked confused. "Are you saying they never met?"

"He planned a trip out here," I said. "They made a date."

Marty looked at me sharply, hearing something in my voice.

"It was for the day after she died."

CHAPTER 30

Talking to Marty hadn't shed any more light on anything, mainly because he didn't have all of the pieces of the puzzle that I did. He didn't know Kate had fled from an abusive husband. He didn't know about the money laundering. He didn't know how Raul fit in, or if Hector was still a criminal mastermind.

To be fair, I didn't know those last two things either.

Marty had leapt to the conclusion that Todd had targeted Kate because he was after the money she'd "saved." He didn't know about her past, but did her past matter? The only thing that tied in the idea of her husband coming for her was the cryptic list of movies I'd found. And I might be wrong in my interpretation of it. I'd been wrong before. At least three times just that day.

One thing was for sure: I couldn't hang around in the office stewing all night. I tucked the laptop back behind the couch again, swept everything off the desk into my backpack, and headed down the lobby stairs, where I found Albert and told him I was leaving. I didn't want everyone worrying about me again. Although it was kind of nice that they worried.

Then I got lucky. I'd planned to slink out the alley door again, but it turned out I didn't have to. Because the 4:15 of *Dial M* had drawn the biggest crowd I'd ever seen at the Palace, a good sixty people, and they were all mingling with those arriving for the 7:30 *Gaslight* as I said goodbye to Albert. I just attached myself to a group of middle-aged women who were swooning over Grace Kelly's dresses and left with the crowd, counting on Hector being more focused on the windows upstairs than the moviegoers spilling out into the dusk.

I blended in with the women until I got to the corner, then broke off and turned uphill. I had three goals for the evening: Buy a change of clothes, as I had no intention of going back to Robbie's guest house alone until the murderer was behind bars. Walk until I was sure I wasn't being followed and then find another hotel for the night. Figure out who had killed Kate.

Two out of three should be easy.

I walked back toward the busy shopping area around Fillmore, where I'd been the night before. I went into a boutique, bought what I needed, and then asked them if they had a back door I could use to leave. I hadn't watched every Humphrey Bogart movie ever made without learning a thing or two about not being followed.

Then I kept walking, generally heading east while gaining an increased respect for San Francisco's hills. Eventually I arrived at a giant cathedral on top of a steep hill. The church was beautiful, but more interestingly, it was across the street from Kim Novak's apartment building from *Vertigo* (1958, Novak and Jimmy Stewart). I may not have known my new city, but I knew my Hitchcock movies. I took it as a sign and got a room at the huge Fairmont hotel next door.

I'd left Kate's computer back at the Palace, and my computer at Robbie's house, so I used the hotel's writing paper to gather my thoughts. There was a lot to gather. I had about a million theories zinging around in my head, so I picked my top three and started trying to make sense of it all. Sometimes just seeing things in an outline form can help.

Scenario A: Todd is a con man
- He knew about the money laundering and was after the money
    - But how did he find out about it?

- He used a fake name because duh, that's what con men do.
- He avoided meeting Kate in person for months.
    - o Because it's classic catfish behavior.
    - o Because it let her imagination do a lot of his work.
- He killed her because she wouldn't give him the money.
    - o Or maybe she threatened to turn him into the police? Or to the Acosta brothers?
    - o Or maybe he didn't intend to kill her, but she fell when he chased her up Strawberry Hill? But why was she there in the first place???
- He killed Raul because...???
    - o Raul tried to defend Kate? This is pure speculation.
    - o Raul saw him kill Kate and had to be eliminated? More speculation.
- He attacked Monica because...???
    - o He found out about the money? Again, how?
- He acted all interested in me because...???
    - o He found out about the money and thinks I have it? How? How? How?

Starting to get freaked out by all the unanswered questions, I abandoned that theory and moved on to the next one.

Scenario B: Todd is Kate's husband
- He's about her age, so that fits.
- He somehow found her after more than twenty years.
- He used a fake name when he contacted her, obviously.
    - o His real name starts with "Z," based on the scar on her neck.
- He avoided meeting Kate in person for months.
    - o Because he enjoyed toying with her.
    - o Because as soon as she saw him the game would be over.
- He killed her out of hatred, not over money.

  o But if he didn't know about the money, why was he still in town looking for the MacGuffin?

  o And if he did know about the money, how did he find out?

- He killed Raul because...???

  o Same speculation as with Scenario A.

- He attacked Monica because...???

  o He's still looking for the money.

- He acted all interested in me because...???

  o He's still looking for the money.

Okay, once again I had way more questions than answers. And there was still another strong possibility.

Scenario C: Hector is the killer

- Hc kncw about the money because Raul told him.

  o Raul might have told him if he really believed Hector was going straight.

- He wanted in on the money laundering.

  o Because he wasn't going straight—he's still a drug kingpin.

- He killed Kate because...???

  o She wouldn't go along with his plan?

  o He wanted the money.

- He killed his brother because...???

  o Raul really was going straight. Maybe he threatened to turn Hector in?

  o An argument that go out of hand?

- He attacked Monica because...???

  o He's still looking for the money.

- He's been so nice to me because...???

- He's still looking for the money.

  o It's easier for him if I'm a trusting idiot.

Sometimes seeing things in outline form can help. And sometimes it can't. I stared at the three scenarios until my eyes stung. They all seemed equally plausible. They all seemed equally farfetched. I even saw that A and C could both be true. Todd could have been trying to con Kate out of the seven million while Hector was trying to get in on the money laundering.

It also occurred to me, probably because of *Dial M for Murder*, that either Todd or Hector could have been hired by Kate's husband to kill her. That sort of thing did happen. At least in the movies.

And I had to admit the possibility that I had Kate and Raul's roles reversed. I kept thinking of Kate as the main victim, and Raul somehow caught up in it all—in the wrong place at the wrong time. But it was equally possible that someone from Raul's past (like his brother, perhaps) followed him from Columbia to kill him for some reason and Kate had just gotten caught up in that. Maybe *she* was just in the wrong place at the wrong time, in which case her past had nothing to do with anything.

My frustration knew no bounds. And I was frustrated mainly with myself for not being able to see what I was sure was right in front of me.

Eventually I did the only reasonable thing I could. I opened a bottle of wine from the minibar and called Robbie.

"It all comes down to the money."

We'd been talking for a while before Robbie came to this conclusion. Long enough for me to have outlined my three major scenarios and finished more than half the bottle.

"I think it does," I agreed. "But will finding the money point us to the murderer? Who knew about the MacGuffin? And how? And when?"

"And where is it now?" she finished.

"Well, it's not glued to the woodwork in the form of gold," I said. "Or diamonds in the chandelier, or jewels sewn into costumes."

"Okay, so that's three things down. That just leaves anything else."

"Thanks," I said. "That's helpful."

"Do you know what I thought of this afternoon? Diamonds in the ice machine. I had this amazing visual of the soft drink machine just spewing out diamonds all over the concession stand."

"Cool." I'd had nuttier thoughts.

"And then I wondered if they could be hiding in plain sight in the ice that Raul was found on."

"You have no idea how good it makes me feel that you're as crazy as I am," I told her. "But the police drained the ice machine."

"And didn't find seven million in diamonds?"

"If they did, they didn't mention it."

She sighed.

"Oh, and I haven't even started in on Strawberry Hill. How did Kate wind up in the park?" I asked. "I mean, could she have buried something up there?"

"Anything is possible." Her tone said anything really wasn't. "But that wouldn't be something in plain sight that Monica would have seen all the time, which is the one clue we have from Kate."

"Right," I admitted. Just as well I hadn't stopped for a shovel in my wanderings.

I heard Tia's voice in the background.

"My daughter has just pointed out the time," Robbie said.

I glanced at the alarm clock on the nightstand. "It's three in the morning. Shouldn't she be in bed?"

"Shouldn't we all?"

"Goodnight, Nora!" I heard Tia yell.

"Goodnight, ladies."

There was no scenario in which I would sleep that night. I kept feeling like I was just on the edge of seeing something that had been staring me in the face all this time. Something in plain sight.

I wandered around the hotel room, watched the lights of the city from my window for a while, and finally turned on the TV, looking for Turner Classic Movies. I found it, and recognized *The Innocents* (1961, Deborah Kerr and Peter Wyngarde). TCM, like the Palace, was making the most of the lead-up to Halloween.

I stayed with it for a while, but trying to figure out if Deborah was seeing a ghost or losing her mind hit a little too close to home. I looked around the room again, craving a distraction.

I'd thrown the bag from the boutique on a chair when I'd gotten in, but now I put away the clothes I'd bought: undies, a pair of jeans, a couple tee shirts, and a hoody. That took all of three minutes.

I'd also bought a new purse. The backpack with all its compartments had driven me crazy long enough. Now I took a simple one-pocket messenger bag out of its tissue, tossed it on the bed, and dumped the contents of the backpack out next to it.

When I'd left the office I'd swept everything from the desk into the backpack, and it looked like I'd taken more than I'd intended. Included in what I now spilled onto the bed was Kate's notepad, several extra pens, and the small ledger of movie posters that I'd brought up from the basement days ago and never looked at since.

I thumbed through the book now, half paying attention to Deborah's mounting dread on the TV, but getting increasingly absorbed in the collection of poster art Kate had put together. I'd seen the *Gilda* in the first drawer I'd opened, and the *Frankenstein* still hung in the tiled entryway of the Palace, along with *Dr. Jekyll, Gaslight,* and *Dial M.* Every lineup we'd shown since I'd gotten to the Palace was represented in the locked glass cases lining the way from the ticket booth to the lobby doors.

The slate would change again on Tuesday, to the theme of "monster mash." I flipped through the pages of the book, looking to see if there was a poster for *Dracula* (1931, Bela Lugosi), *The Wolf Man* (1941, Lon Chaney Jr.) or *The Creature from the Black Lagoon* (1954, some poor actor in a rubber costume).

We had all three, and many more, each entry annotated with

where and when they'd been purchased. I wondered where we could display more of them. Maybe hang them on the way up the lobby stairs? This really was a great collection. If they were real they'd be worth a fortune.

On the TV, Deborah Kerr screamed.

If they were real.

If they were real, would they be worth seven million dollars?

I dove for my phone and did a search. The first hit I found was from an auction house, and it was enough to make me gasp out loud. A *Frankenstein* had sold recently for over $350,000, and that wasn't even a lobby-sized poster. A *Dracula* was up for sale, with a reserve bid of over half a million dollars. How many posters did Kate have? Hanging in plain sight, where Monica might have stared at them every time she passed, if she'd known what they were worth.

"Calm down," I told myself out loud. I'd been absolutely sure of three things that hadn't panned out. I refused to get all excited again. But I couldn't stop my heart from practically thumping out of my chest.

I looked at the clock. It was after four in the morning. There was nobody to call. If I was right, a poster worth a fortune could be hanging outside the theater with nothing but a sheet of glass and a single lock to protect it. But if I was right, it might have been hanging there for weeks. I needed to calm down. Think rationally.

Kate had usually handled the posters herself and had insisted on treating them as carefully as if they'd been originals. I remembered Albert telling me that, as he'd gingerly lifted them out of their drawers and placed them on clean archival paper. And he'd told me that they didn't use pins to hang them up. They used magnets, to avoid damage. Again, because Kate had insisted.

An authentic vintage poster would have damage. It would have been hung in some lobby back when the movie was new. It could have creases, stains, or age spots. I'd noticed the *Gilda* didn't have any of those signs of legitimate wear. But I hadn't looked at the others.

I grabbed the ledger again. *Gilda* had been bought several years ago, before Kate would have started laundering money for Monica. But *Frankenstein* had only been purchased a few months ago. And now that I was looking, I noticed that *Frankenstein* had a tiny dot next to the name, in blue pencil. *Gilda* didn't.

But *Dracula* did. A check of the rest of the pages told me that twenty-eight posters had blue dots. And they were all bought within the last year. All but three were from the same seller, noted only as Sasha.

Was I absolutely sure I was right this time? I couldn't say. But was I sure enough that I absolutely had to go take a look at the posters that very instant?

Damn right I was.

CHAPTER 31

I may have been out of my mind with excitement, but I hadn't forgotten that Hector was probably still keeping watch on the Palace. Even in the wee small hours of the morning. Especially then. With that in mind I had the taxi let me out two blocks away.

I really wanted to go take a close look at the *Frankenstein* poster hanging in the theater's entryway. But if Hector were the murderer, going out front would amount to hanging out a flashing neon sign reading "Please Come Kill Me." Instead I ducked down the side street and peeked into the rear alley. There were no parked cars containing Hector's watchful associates. At least as far as I could tell.

I used my new key to open the back door and heard the urgent beeping of the alarm, giving me ninety seconds to enter the code. I felt my way along the wall to the keypad, where I punched in the number 2812, grateful that Marty had made such a production about telling me the new number. I might not have remembered it if he hadn't. Once I entered the code the beeping stopped. The silence, and the dark, was absolute.

I continued feeling along the brick wall until I got to the stairs. I knew the prop room was windowless, so I'd be able to turn on lights once I got there. But the thought of inching my way along the maze of basement corridors in the dark was more unnerving than I'd expected. What I needed was a flashlight, and I'd stashed a bag of them behind the candy counter after the fiasco with the search for gold. I decided fumbling up the dark stairs to the lobby was preferable to fumbling around in pitch-black hallways, so I gripped the cold metal railing and made my way up.

The empty expanse of the lobby was eerily lit by four green Exit signs. They provided the only illumination aside from the dim outline of the lobby doors, the light from the streetlamps barely making it up the entryway. I found the cache of flashlights under the candy counter and grabbed one. When I turned around I caught my breath. There was a dim glowing light at the top of the balcony stairs.

"Nora!" The light waved, calling my name in a whisper.

"Trixie!" My response was hushed, but still carried like a gunshot.

I'd never seen her in the dark before. She came down the stairs, the details of her outline indistinct, surrounded by a faint glow. If I hadn't known her to be my bubbly usherette friend, she would have scared the living daylights out of me.

"What's going on?" she whispered excitedly. "What are you doing here this early?"

I supposed it had gone from being very late to being very early.

"I had another idea," I told her. "And this time I'm pretty sure I'm right."

She clapped and glowed a little brighter. "Oh, I knew you would! Gee, you're clever. What did you think of?"

"Come with me." I headed for the basement stairs. "Let's go see together."

I didn't turn the flashlight on until we were in the stairway, the door closed behind us. Only then did I feel safe. Not that I felt safe at all. But I did feel better with Trixie by my side.

We went back down the stairs and navigated the warren of hallways to the prop room while I told her what I'd figured out. What I thought I'd figured out.

"Golly Moses!" She stopped in front of the prop room door, staring at me. I'd just told her how much an original *Dracula* poster was worth. "For a *poster*? Why, we used to throw them out after the picture closed! We'd maybe give them to one of the kids sometimes, but we were supposed to throw them out."

"I think everybody was supposed to throw them out," I told her. "That's why originals are so scarce now, and why the ones that are still around are worth a fortune."

"Well, I never." She shook her head, her curls shimmering in the darkness.

"I know," I said, opening the door. "Now, shall we go see if I'm right?"

"Gee, Nora, I sure hope you are."

So did I.

The prop room was creepy with the lights out, and almost creepier with them on. I jumped when I saw my own reflection in a mirror hung crookedly on the brick wall. The racks and piles I'd ransacked the day before, looking for hidden jewels, now seemed sinister somehow. Probably because it was near dawn and I was operating on pure adrenaline.

Trixie and I had gone through everything in the room the day before. Everything except the posters. Had we been in the presence of a fortune in art as we'd sighed in disappointment at not finding a fortune in jewels?

There were a few random lamps and vases on the table near the poster cabinet. I moved them to the floor and got several sheets of archival paper from the top drawer, laying them out on the tabletop to create a clean surface.

Then I turned back to the cabinet, almost afraid of what would come next.

"Go on!" Trixie hopped from one foot to the other in excitement.

I could have started alphabetically. The first poster marked with a blue dot in Kate's book was *The Adventures of Robin Hood* (1938, Errol Flynn and Olivia de Havilland). But as enticing as that was, I was after a bigger prize.

I opened the drawer marked "D-G" and again saw *Gilda* on

top. She was gorgeous, but there was no blue dot next to her name in the ledger. I moved through the stack, sliding each poster a few inches aside, not bending any corners, being incredibly careful. The posters were flat in the shallow drawer, each sandwiched between sheets of archival paper. Finally, I saw the corner of the poster I was looking for. *Dracula.*

I rubbed my hands on my jeans, wishing I had a pair of the cotton gloves that they use in museums, then lifted the poster out of the drawer.

I laid it face up on the table.

Yes.

Bela Lugosi's mesmerizing eyes dominated the image, but I wasn't looking at him. There were several uneven pinholes in each corner, signs that the poster had at some point been hung. More importantly, there were creases. They were faint, but they were there—one down the center and three across. I hadn't had time to do any real research on how to authenticate posters, but I had done a quick search on my phone while in the taxi. These creases were a very good sign. Before the 1970s, I'd read, posters were almost always shipped from the distributor folded.

"Gee, he gives me the creeps." Trixie was on the other side of the table, peering intently at the poster. "Is it real? An original?"

"I don't know," I said. "I think it could be." I turned it over. Carefully. It was heavier than a normal poster and had some sort of reinforced backing. The top of my head started to tingle. A backing was another good sign. Somebody had thought the poster was worth preserving.

"Oh, no," Trixie said. "It's ruined." She was looking at a mark in the lower left corner. "Somebody stamped it."

"Right," I said, my mouth suddenly very dry. "A gallery stamped it. I think that means it's been authenticated. Trixie," I whispered, hardly daring to say it. "I think it's real."

Her eyes grew enormous. "Oh, Nora. You did it."

I turned the poster back over and looked back down at Bela, not sure I could believe it. If the other posters Kate had marked in the ledger also looked this good...I'd finally found the MacGuffin.

Which might have been my last thought on this earth if Trixie hadn't screamed.

CHAPTER 32

"Nora! Duck!"

I reacted without thinking, dropping and dodging as something went whooshing past my ear and slammed into the table with a deafening crack. I turned and saw Todd Randall wielding an iron bar like a club and looking at me like a killer.

"Nora!" Trixie shouted again.

"Todd!" I backed away from him, realizing that he stood between me and the door. I was trapped.

He smiled. At least, he probably thought it was a smile. "Nora. I guess I should thank you." He nodded toward the poster on the table. "I was getting damn sick of this place."

"How did you get in?" Which maybe wasn't the most urgent question, but it's the one that came tumbling out of my mouth as I looked frantically around the room for an escape. Or a weapon.

"I bought a ticket," he said. "I've been here since the second show yesterday."

So much for relying on grainy pictures of him to warn the staff.

"I guess I owe you," he said, his eyes flicking past me. He was probably also looking for anything I could use as a weapon. "I had no clue how Ellie hid all that money." His eyes returned to mine. "But I figured a clever bitch like you would figure it out. I just had to wait."

"Nora," Trixie shimmered into view behind Todd. "I can't hurt him. I wish I could but I can't." She swiped a fist through his torso.

"I know," I said.

"You know what?" Todd looked at me narrowly.

"I know you're Kate's husband."

I hadn't known that, not until he'd just called her Ellie. But now, watching the stunned look on his face, I absolutely knew him to be the violent predator Kate had run from. Run for her life.

"How did you find her?" I asked. I'd surprised him. Maybe I could use that to keep him off guard.

He made a guttural sound, low in his throat. "Something you should know about hunting," he said. "The trick is knowing how to wait."

While he spoke I took a step to my right. He did the same, unconsciously mirroring me, and I felt a surge of hope. If I could move slowly around the room, keeping him across from me, eventually I'd have my back to the door. And then I'd just have to run.

"That's what separates the good from the great," Todd said. "Waiting. Keeping a sharp eye out. Holding for your moment."

Trixie appeared at my side, facing him with me. "I'm going to get help," she said. "I don't know how, but I promise I'm going to. Please just keep him talking. Just don't let him near you until I get you help."

I nodded and she vanished. Where she would get help at dawn in an empty theater was something I didn't want to think about. I just hoped she could do something.

"So you found Kate," I said. "And then what? Why the whole lie about 'Todd Randall' and a film festival? Why not just come for her? And what's your real name, anyway?" Another step to my right.

He moved forward. Damn. "You ever see a cat with a mouse?" His eyes glinted. "That cat never has more fun than when the mouse realizes how stupid she is." He weighed the iron bar in his hand. "That space between when she knows she's going to die and when the final swipe of the claw comes..." He sliced the bar through the air. "That's the magic time."

I swallowed. "What about the money?" I asked. "How did you find out about it? And what about Raul?"

"Oh, is this the part where I confess everything?" His lips

twisted.

"I'll tell you what I think." I stepped to the right again. This time he followed. "I think you made a date to finally meet Kate in person. I've seen the emails. You were going to meet at the café across the street." Another step. "But you didn't stick to that. You came a day early. Why?"

"You just keep going, honey. You're doing fine." He took another step.

I now had the door on my right, but I'd have to navigate around the poster cabinet and table to get to it. Todd would have a clear path. I had to keep him moving.

"It doesn't matter," I said. "The fact is you showed up at the theater a day early. Kate wasn't expecting you. Was Raul already there?"

A flash of annoyance crossed his face. Or was it jealousy?

"Is that why you didn't stick to the plan? Did you come a day early to watch Kate without her knowing it? Did you see her meet Raul in the lobby and go up to the office? Did you think there was something between them?"

Definitely jealousy. And now matched with rage.

He struck out with the iron bar, shattering one of the glass lamps I'd moved.

"That bitch!" he seethed. "Throwing herself at me over email and all the while she was spreading her legs for that—" Whatever derogatory term he used to describe Raul was lost in another smash of the bar.

"So you followed them up to the office," I said. "While *Random Harvest* was playing and everyone else was busy." I took another step. "Then what did you do? Hit Raul from behind? That seems to be your—"

The bar shot out, smashing a mirror.

"She had no right!" he shouted. "She was *my* wife!"

"So you knocked Raul unconscious," I said.

This seemed to take him by surprise.

"Didn't you know? You didn't kill him. When you put him in

the ice machine he was still alive."

Todd recovered quickly. "He's dead now, isn't he?"

"What happened?" I asked. "How did Kate wind up with a broken neck?"

"It was her own damn fault," he said. "I wasn't going to kill her. Not before I made her pay for everything she put me through."

"Oh," I said without thinking. "What *she* put *you* through."

The bar came crashing down again, this time on the table. On the *Dracula* poster.

"That slut thought she could buy me off," he snarled. "Once she saw I meant business she couldn't wait to tell me about all the money she had. She'd give it to me, she said, if I'd just go away." His voice took on an ugly, mocking tone. "She wouldn't tell anybody what I'd done. She'd give me the money if I'd just leave her alone. Yeah, right." He wiped his mouth with the back of his hand. "But I played along. I let her think she could win."

There was nothing I could lay my hands on that would stand up to that heavy iron bar. I had to run. It was probably about fifteen steps to the door, then through the dark hallways to the back door and escape. If I didn't take a wrong turn.

"She told me I could use the back stairs and hide the body in the ice machine down here." Todd said "She wouldn't tell anyone. It could be months before it was found, and I'd be long gone by then, with all that money in my pocket."

I could imagine this conversation, Kate pleading for her life, trying desperately to figure a way out, to find her chance to run.

"I made her drag him from her office to the stairs," Todd went on. "But then she got stupid and made a run for it." He held his head up, pointing the bar at me. "I did not kill her. The bitch tripped. Fell down all those stairs and broke her damn neck."

My stomach turned. Kate had died on the hard concrete stairs. Running from him, as I was about to.

"So you hid Raul's body, like you'd planned," I said, fighting to keep my voice even. "And then what? The ice machine wasn't big enough for both of their bodies?"

"I went looking for some other place to put her," he said. "And instead I found a wheelchair."

I made a small, strangled sound of understanding. Albert had told me the wheelchair had gone missing from the prop room.

"Why the park?" I asked. "Why did you take her to—"

He laughed, an ugly, rasping sound. "She'd broken her neck," he said. "I thought I could make it look like an accident. If she wasn't found here, nobody would look around for clues here, and nobody would find the other guy until I was long gone. And San Francisco is supposed to be full of hills, isn't it? So I checked the map on my phone for the nearest one."

"That's so..." *stupid*, I thought. Then I got a vivid mental image of him pushing her up to the top of the hill and throwing her over the side. It wasn't stupid. It was cold-bloodedly horrific.

My mouth had gone dry. "And you've been looking for the money ever since."

He twisted his lips into a smile. "And now there's nothing left to do, is there, sweetheart? Except for one last little thing." A light glinted in his eye.

I ran. It was pure instinct. I didn't even think.

I was halfway across the room before he grabbed me from behind.

CHAPTER 33

He caught me by my hair, whipping me around until I crashed into the brick wall. A nearby mirror rattled with the impact.

Dazed, I staggered back. He caught me, dragging me over to the mirror where I saw a bloody gash on my cheekbone. He stood behind me, holding me by the neck, grinning into the mirror.

"Aren't you pretty," he said. "I like a girl with a little color in her cheeks."

He wiped the edge of the iron bar across the cut on my face, then held the bloody tip to my neck.

"You asked me before what my name is." His mouth was at my ear. His voice was low and husky. "It's Nate. Nate Campbell." He moved the bar, drawing a capital "N" on my neck in blood.

An "N." Kate's scar hadn't been a "Z" after all. It had been an "N." It only looked like a "Z" because when he'd carved it into her skin he must have been holding her head at an angle. The angle he was now holding mine.

"I'm just sorry we don't have more time, sweetheart. There are things I'd like to do—"

Suddenly the entire room was filled with the deafening sound of the 20th Century Fox overture, louder than I'd ever heard it. Todd jumped and loosened his grip on me, swearing. In that split second I took my chance. I ran.

"Marty!" I shrieked. Out the door and down the hallway, with a murderer crashing along behind me. The halls were still pitch black, but I got the turns right and the darkness seemed to slow him down. I'd planned on escaping out the back door, but now, knowing someone else was in the theater, I sprinted up the stairs instead, shouting for help.

I felt Todd behind me as I raced to the top of the stairs, to the lobby-level landing. I could hear his heavy breathing and with just a few steps to go I felt the bar swiping at the back of my jeans. It didn't connect, but the next strike would.

I kept my eyes on the top of the stairs, and suddenly a blinding light blazed on the landing above. It was Trixie, incandescent with fury, her form blurred and burning, opening her mouth in a scream as she rushed forward, passing through me, howling an unearthly "*NO!*"

I heard Todd scream behind me as she appeared to him, terrifying in her glorious blinding rage. I felt as much as heard him crashing backwards down the stairs. Almost at the top, I turned to look and stumbled. I could feel myself about to fall down the stairs after him when I was grabbed by the wrist from behind.

"What the hell?" Marty shouted.

I hugged him like I'd never hugged anyone before in my life.

CHAPTER 34

Marty and I stared down at the body of Todd Randall, lying at the bottom of the stairs. His head was twisted in a way that said he wasn't going to be a threat to anyone ever again.

Trixie was nowhere to be seen.

"What the hell?" Marty said again. "Is he dead? What the hell?"

I loosened my grip on his flannel shirt and looked up at him, intending to try to explain, but it freaked him out more when he saw my bloody face. "Holy shit, Nora! What happened?"

Which is when we heard the sound of shattering glass from the lobby.

"Nora!" A voice called. Hector's voice.

Marty and I stumbled out of the stairway in time to see one of the lobby doors shattered and Hector sprinting up the grand lobby stairs.

"Hector!" I yelled. At least I tried to. It came out as more of a squeak.

But it was enough. He turned, took one look at the two of us, and said "I'll kill you."

It took me a moment to realize he was talking to Marty.

"No!" I yelped as he slammed back down the stairs. "It wasn't him! I'm fine! Marty saved me!"

"I did what?" Marty looked even more confused.

"What happened?" Hector crossed the lobby, pulling me away from Marty and touching the area around my cut cheek surprisingly tenderly. "I saw the lights flash and knew you were trying to signal me."

"What lights? How did you even know I was here?" His gentle touch was really, really nice.

"I saw you from the cameras I put in the back alley," he murmured. "I've known each time you have entered or left the building."

"You *what?*"

"*WHAT THE HELL IS GOING ON?*" Marty yelled.

I withdrew from Hector's attentions, taking a step back to look at them both.

"You." I pointed to Hector. "Have a lot of explaining to do. And you." I pointed at Marty. "Deserve all the doughnuts in the world and a full explanation. But do you mind if I call the police first? Because there's a dead killer in the basement, and I think they'll want to know."

I was very collected when I said this. Then the lobby started to sort of swirl a bit and my legs seemed to lose the ability to keep me standing. They each grabbed an arm as I slumped against the candy counter.

I didn't faint. I feel I need to make that perfectly clear. I just got a little woozy. And if Hector or Marty thought it was strange that I murmured the name "Trixie" as I drifted in my wooziness, they didn't say anything about it. At least not then.

Many hours later, after a trip to the ER for stitches and X-rays—which thankfully revealed an unbroken cheekbone—I went back to Kate's office hoping Trixie would appear, but there was no sign of her. I had no idea how much it might have taken out of her to show herself the way she had. I just hoped she was okay. And yes, I did realize how weird it was to hope that a ghost was okay.

I opened the blinds for the first time in days and raised my hand to the window across the street where Hector was presumably still keeping watch. He'd left before the police arrived, preferring not to get involved if it wasn't absolutely necessary. The police made the assumption that Todd/Nate had broken the glass lobby door, and Marty and I didn't correct them.

"Are you okay?"

I jumped when I heard Marty's voice, and turned away from the window.

"I'm fine," I said. "Thank you again."

He shrugged, then closed the door behind him and took a seat in the chair opposite the desk. "Is it true?" He crossed his arms and waited.

The police had questioned us separately, Marty at the theater and me at the hospital. But I assumed by now he'd heard at least part of what I'd told Detective Jackson.

I sat on the couch facing him. "Todd Randall was Kate's husband," I confirmed. "She ran from him over twenty years ago. His real name was Nate Campbell, and her real name was Ellie." My voice faltered as I said this. It filled me with an unexpected surge of emotion to speak her true name out loud.

Marty blinked rapidly, nodding. Then he looked at me, raw. "Why didn't she tell me?" For the first time since I'd known him his defensive shield was torn. "She was—" He swallowed, hard. "She was my best friend."

"She was," I said. "But her past was her past, and she'd gone through a lot to keep it that way."

He swiped at his eye, his pain turning to anger. "And that bastard hunted her down and killed her."

Technically, the way Todd had explained it, Kate's death had been an accident. But in my mind that technicality didn't matter. "Yes," I said. "He killed her. And Raul."

"And he would have killed you if he hadn't tripped."

Or if he hadn't been frightened half out of his mind by a vengeful ghost.

"He would have killed me if he hadn't jumped when you blasted your morning music," I said. "That damn overture probably saved my life."

Marty raised his head, his defiance returning. "That damn overture *is* my life."

"And I will never say one word against it again," I promised. "I'm just glad you came in so early."

He shrugged. "I'm always early."

"Right," I said slowly. "But not dawn early. Why *were* you here that early?" Had Trixie succeeded in sending out some sort of psychic cry for help?

Marty shifted in his chair. "I had an idea, all right? I wanted to check it out."

"An idea?"

"About the MacGuffin. I got to thinking in the middle of the night."

"Oh! Marty—"

"I got the idea from *Gaslight*," he went on. "What if the MacGuffin is jewels sewn into some of those old costumes down in the prop room?" He leaned forward, willing me to slap my forehead and call him a genius.

"Yeah. I thought so, too," I told him. "I checked them out yesterday."

This took a moment to register, then he sat back, deflated. "Oh. Well. Sure. It was just an idea."

"Marty," I tilted my head. "Why don't you ask me why I was here so early?"

"I—" He was about to continue blustering, then he stopped, and looked at me closely. "Why *were* you here so early?"

"The police are all gone, right? Because we're going to have to cross the crime scene tape. I need to show you some posters."

About two minutes later he let out a whoop that could probably be heard across the entire city of San Francisco.

By the time the 4:15 of *Dial M* started the broken glass in the lobby had been swept up and the door covered with a sheet of plywood. Callie and Albert had been told everything—well, mostly everything—and all of the original posters were safely stored in in a large safety deposit box at the nearby First Republic Bank.

Albert and Marty had looked up online estimates of what the collection was worth while Callie had hovered over them saying a lot of things like "Wait, *What?*" They were dumbfounded at the roughly seven-million-dollar result. I didn't think I'd be able to stick to my story of Kate having saved that amount out of the Palace's petty cash but luckily they hadn't asked about it. Yet.

With everything under control, I grabbed Hector's leather jacket and went across the street to Café Madeline, where I found the crime-lord-turned-rescuer at a table by the window.

I dropped the jacket on the chair next to him and sat opposite. "What the hell do you mean you installed cameras at the theater?"

He smiled, which was really irritating, mainly because it was such a good smile. "May I get you a coffee?"

"You may answer my question." I folded my arms and waited, then realized I was acting like Marty and unfolded them.

Hector sipped from his own coffee cup. "I know you suspected me, and I didn't blame you. I would have suspected me too."

"If you expect an apology—"

He held up a hand. "I expect no such thing. You would have been a fool to trust me. I, however, had the advantage of knowing that I was not a killer. Nor were you. Therefore, someone else was. That someone was still a threat, and I had no intention of letting you or anyone else at your theater be his next victim."

I opened my mouth, then closed it, having no clear response.

"Your security is laughable. After the morning of the break-in, I realized you needed more surveillance than my cousin Gabriela and I could provide."

"There really is a cousin Gabriela?"

"She looks forward to meeting you," he nodded. "I installed two small cameras in the alley behind the theater, with live video feeds going to my phone. Also," he took the jacket from the chair. "There is a small voice-activated listening device in this pocket." He took something that looked like a thumb drive from the jacket and held it up briefly. "Which has been in your office since I loaned it to you."

My jaw dropped.

"As I said," he sipped again. "Your security is laughable. As are your attempts to avoid being followed as you wander about the city. I would say I hope you enjoyed your stay at the Fairmont hotel last night, but I don't believe you got any sleep."

"How—"

"One can purchase many services in this, the 'gig' economy," he shrugged. "One simply needs to know where to look."

I surprised myself by being more curious than outraged at his unrepentant violations of my privacy. "Is that how you knew I was in trouble this morning?"

For the first time, Hector lost his I-know-everything attitude. "No. I knew that you had entered the building, but I did not know that Randall was already there. When I saw you go in, I expected to see a light in the office soon thereafter. When I did not, I became concerned. But it wasn't until you flashed the lights that I knew I had to take action. I had no patience to pick the lock, so I threw a brick through the glass of the door."

"What do you mean, I flashed the lights?"

He looked bemused. "All the lights in the building flared on then off all at once. I assumed you'd thrown some master switch, just for a moment, to signal me."

I nodded. I hadn't done any such thing. I'd been down in the basement with a killer.

"Had Marty gotten in by that time?"

Hector shook his head. "He must have arrived after the lights flashed, as I was going down the stairs here. That's why, when I saw him with you, and the blood on your lovely face, I assumed the worst."

I was momentarily distracted by the phrase "your lovely face," then I focused on what he'd just told me. There was only one other person who could have flashed the lights. Someone who had promised me she would find a way to call for help. And she had.

"And now I must ask your forgiveness," Hector said.

"Damn right," I told him. "I can't believe you had me followed."

He waved a hand. "Not for that. But for not taking the same precautions over Kate's friend Monica. I deeply regret what happened to her. And also for thinking one of your friends might have killed my brother." He reached for my hand, which I didn't give him. He left his palm-down on the table. "Please forgive me, Nora."

I looked at him long and hard. He had no remorse about spying on me, following me, bugging my office. But he'd also thrown himself into danger to save me when I was threatened, and everything he'd done he'd done to find his brother's killer. I'd done some questionable stuff myself for the same reason.

I still didn't fully trust him. But I didn't fully not trust him, either.

He was waiting for an answer.

"Louie," I sat back in my chair. "I think this is the beginning of a beautiful friendship."

He looked confused, not recognizing the last line Bogie says to Claude Rains at the end of *Casablanca* (1942, Humphrey Bogart and Ingrid Bergman). But that was okay. I was kind of looking forward to showing him some old movies.

CHAPTER 35

"Hi Nora. Do you want me to staple some posters to the plywood? I mean, you know, new posters. I mean, you know, old posters but not *real* old posters. You know?"

Brandon was stationed in the ticket booth, and he glanced up the entryway—where an original *Frankenstein* poster was no longer hanging—to the hastily-repaired lobby door.

The thought of shooting staples through one of Kate's posters, even one of the reproductions, made me a little queasy. "Please don't," I told him. "We'll get the door fixed on Monday."

He nodded. "I'm glad you're okay." A blush swept over his face like an incoming tide.

"Thanks, Brandon. I'm glad we're all okay."

The movie was in progress, so the lobby was empty of customers. Claire was behind the candy counter but didn't look up from her phone as I came in and headed for the balcony stairs. No wonder Todd had been able to just breeze in with the crowd the day before. I shuddered at the memory of him grabbing me and sprinted up the stairs to dispel it.

I found Marty in the projection booth.

"I brought you something." I held a white paper bag up to show him. I'd picked up several of the yummiest looking pastries at the café where I'd left Hector.

"You promised me doughnuts." He took the bag and looked inside. "A hazelnut croissant is not a doughnut." Nevertheless he took it out and devoured half of it in one bite.

"I'll bring you doughnuts every day from now on," I told him. "I'll also hire you a real assistant—one that you get to pick. And I'll still never be able to thank you enough."

He looked at me with profound irritation, which was somewhat compromised by the flakes of pastry at the corner of his mouth. "I didn't even know you were here. I would have played my music whether—"

"It wasn't just the music," I said. "I was about to fall down those stairs. If you hadn't grabbed my wrist I would have gone right after Todd. Admit it, you saved me."

He shrugged, a full-body twitch, looking even more irritated. "It was just instinct."

I beamed at him. "That's what you say. But do you know what I say?" I moved closer and sang softly. "You saved me, you sa-ved me..." to the tune of "Good Morning," from *Singin' in the Rain* (1952, Gene Kelly and Debbie Reynolds).

This nearly caused Marty's head to explode in irritation. Which was what I'd been going for. "Are you going to be cheerful now? Because I was just starting to not one hundred percent hate you. But if you're going to be cheerful, all bets are off."

I laughed and left him alone in the booth. Because that's the way he liked it.

There was still no sign of Trixie. I told myself that it had taken her a while to recover from the effort of breaking a coffee mug the first time I'd met Todd Randall. It would probably take her longer to recover from the morning's superhuman efforts. But I still felt a little lost without her keeping me company in the office.

"Albert," I popped my head into the break room, where the ninety-year-old ticket taker was jabbing purposefully at the screen of an iPad. "I'm going to go out for a—"

"Oh, Kate. I'm glad you're here. I've just spoken to Sasha."

My look must have said "Who's Sasha?" pretty clearly.

"Sasha Roth. He owns a gallery in Sonoma," Albert explained. "It's on the main square, opposite the Sebastiani Theater. Have you ever been?"

I came into the room, realizing this wasn't going to be a quick conversation. "No," I told him. "I've never been to wine country up here."

"Oh, you must go," he said. "It's lovely. This time of year it's a little bare, after the grapes are harvested, but—"

"Albert," I said gently. "Who's Sasha?" The name rang a bell, but I couldn't place it.

"He's the dealer who sold Kate most of the posters," Albert said.

Of course. I'd seen his name in the ledger. I sat at the table. "Tell me everything."

He grinned. "Well, around the holidays last year his gallery was in a bit of a financial pickle. He'd done well carrying vintage advertising posters for wine and liqueurs, so he'd gone all-in on a very impressive collection of classic film posters, thinking that people who came to see the Sebastiani—it's a lovely old theater— would be a good clientele for movie memorabilia."

"But not so much," I guessed.

"They only wanted reproductions," Albert said. "He couldn't move the originals. He paid attention to the online markets, and when he noticed Kate had bought four originals in the space of a few weeks, he got in contact with her. He sold her three lots over three months, all for cash."

I sat back in the chair. "And they've all been authenticated?"

He nodded. "Nora," he said carefully, "that's a lot of cash."

I looked at him. "Yes it is."

"I've been asking myself whether I want to know where Kate laid her hands on that much cash." He glanced at me, then at something over my shoulder.

"Well, I want to know." I turned to see Marty standing in the doorway, arms crossed and chin lifted defiantly.

Callie stood beside him. "I mean," she said. "I kind of think we probably should know." They both moved into the room and sat at the table. "Because we're talking about Kate, right? So, no matter what it is, we're going to, like, understand. Right?" She looked at the others.

"Are you sure?"

They were. So I got up and closed the door. Then I told them Kate's story.

Later, after hugs (from Albert), tears (Callie), and a long stoic stare (Marty), I knew what I had to do.

"Monica?" I called her from my office. "I need to talk to you about the money."

I'd told them where it had come from. And I'd told them why Kate had done what she'd done. That she'd been using her twenty percent not just to keep the Palace going, but also to support a network of safe houses that helped abused women escape. And why that cause had been so important to her.

"Kate's share of the money," I now told Monica. "It should be just under a million and a half dollars, right?"

"Twenty percent of whatever we get for the posters," Monica said. "So somewhere in that neighborhood. Which won't be enough for a full remodel, but you can start, right?"

"Right, except we don't want to use it for that."

"What do you mean? And who's 'we?'"

"I told the gang. Albert and Callie and Marty. I told them all of it." I ignored Monica's sharp intake of breath. "And they made a decision. They don't want to keep Kate's share. They want to give it to the shelters." My voice broke. It had taken all my strength not to dissolve into a weepy mess when they'd come to their incredibly generous decision. "They think it's what Kate would have wanted. They want to donate it in her memory."

"Oh, Nora." At which point we both dissolved into weepy messes.

It took a while for me to pull myself together after getting off the phone with Monica. I hadn't told her what else I'd talked about with Albert and Callie and Marty.

"Are you sure you don't want to use the money for the Palace?" I'd asked.

Marty squared his shoulders. "We'll be fine. I don't need an assistant."

"We'll, like, figure something out," Callie agreed.

"By hook or by crook," Albert nodded.

"Probably not by crook," I cautioned. However nice it would have been to continue getting supplemented by Monica's money laundering, it didn't seem safe to keep it up. Not with all the police attention the Palace had been getting lately. "But you're right. We can figure it out. We will figure it out."

Although I had no idea how.

My phone pinged with a text, startling me out of my thoughts. The text was from my lawyers, and it was just one line.

Read your email.

I swallowed. If I'd been able to deal with a crazed killer in the basement I should be able to deal with a simple email from a lawyer, right? But I still tapped the envelope icon with a thudding heart.

I found the right email quickly. It contained a draft of a preliminary financial settlement, agreed to by Ted's lawyers. Both "draft" and "preliminary" told me that there was a long way to go, but they also told me that this was happening. My marriage was really over.

My eyes blurred with tears, which I blamed on last night's lack of sleep. I blinked them away and looked at the settlement. It was a lot of money.

With this amount of money came freedom. Not just from my philandering husband, but from everything. I could start my life over anywhere.

I blinked and looked around the cluttered office. This was where Kate had started her life over. Could I do the same? I'd made friends here. Albert was possibly the sweetest man on earth, Callie was wry and observant when she put her phone down, and Marty was a supreme curmudgeon, but I couldn't think of anyone I'd rather talk old movies with.

And then there was Trixie. Maybe I could leave the Palace, but could I leave her? And what if the Palace didn't make it? What would happen to her?

"Trixie?" I said out loud.

But my best friend at the Palace was silent.

CHAPTER 36

I went out walking as evening settled over the city. Walking and thinking, not paying attention to where I headed, not really having a direction in mind. But eventually I looked up and found myself on the sidewalk in front of Robbie's house.

I went around to the guesthouse to pick up my laptop and a few other things, but I was too unsettled to stay in. I headed back to the theater and arrived as the 9:40 *Gaslight* began.

Callie was behind the candy counter. "I thought you left."

"I'm back," I said. "I'll be in the office if you need me." Because I had things to do.

I stopped in the break room for coffee, then took my laptop to the office and opened it up at the desk. The first thing I did was answer the lawyers. Then I went to my blog, because Marty was right. It had been far too long since Sally Lee's last post. And walking all over the city had given me a lot to write about.

Marty and Callie both dropped by to say goodnight when the last show was over, but I barely glanced up. I was on a roll. Alone in the office in the empty theater I might have been afraid. I might have been creeped out by everything that had happened, hearing every little creak and rattle as a murderous maniac on approach. But I felt just the opposite. As midnight came and went I found myself relaxing into my writing. Alone at the Palace, I felt at home.

I was just wrapping up a new posting when a voice startled me. An incredibly welcome voice.

"Nora, you're all right! I'm so glad! How long have I been

gone?"

"Trixie!" I jumped to my feet and ran to hug her, remembering just in time that I couldn't do that. I stopped awkwardly in front of her. "Are you okay? How did you do that? You saved my life!"

"Did I?" Her eyes grew huge, sparkling. "I don't remember anything but watching him chasing you up those stairs and being so furious I could have killed him. Then I must have gone *poof*. What happened?"

"You really don't remember?"

She shook her head. "Did the police come? Did they arrest him?"

I hesitated for an instant, making a quick decision. "No. He fell down the stairs. He died."

She gasped, putting her hands to her mouth. "When he was chasing you? Oh, Nora." Then her shock turned to indignation. "Well, it serves him right."

It did serve him right. And if she didn't realize she was responsible for it, I wasn't going to burden her with that knowledge. I thought she might have blocked out her part in saving me because her mind couldn't cope with it. She'd been glorious and terrifying. Maybe too terrifying for her to deal with.

"You were amazing," I said. "Your trick with the lights got me the help I needed."

"Did it?" Her face glowed with happiness. "Oh, Nora, I just couldn't bear to think of him hurting you. And I couldn't bear not being able to help."

"You helped, sweetie. You helped so much."

More than she would ever know.

"And the posters? Are they real?"

"They are," I told her. "We found the MacGuffin and solved the murders."

"Well! That's not too bad for the new girl and a ghost." She stood up tall, the gold braid on her cap glinting in the light from the desk lamp.

"Not bad at all," I agreed.

Maybe it was for the best that Trixie couldn't remember what had happened. It would probably figure in my nightmares for years. Maybe her inability to remember also accounted for something else I hadn't been able to understand. She had no memory of Kate's death. Was that something else that she'd actually seen and blanked out? Had it just been too painful? I'd probably never know.

A light rain had started earlier, and the wind must have been picking up, because we both heard a banging coming from downstairs.

Trixie flitted to the window and looked down at the dark wet street. "I don't see anything." She looked at me. "Are you sure he's dead?"

I'd seen them take the body out. "I'm sure," I said. "But the glass on the front door got broken. I bet the plywood came loose in the wind." I looked around the room for anything I'd be able to use to secure it.

"Are you sure?" Trixie said. "I think it sounds like someone knocking."

Now that she mentioned it, the banging did have a certain rhythm.

"Who—" Trixie asked.

"Hector," I guessed. He'd probably been watching me walk around the office having a conversation with no one from his room across the street. "Wait here," I said. "He's probably just checking up on me." And thinking I'd lost my mind.

"He's that dishy Latin Lover type, isn't he?" Trixie dimpled. "You take all the time you want, honey. When you come back I'll tell you about a dream I once had about Gilbert Roland."

I grinned at her, glad beyond words that she'd come back.

As I loped down the balcony stairs I admitted to myself how tired I was. I had a hotel room at the Fairmont and a bed in Robbie's guesthouse. I should pick one of them and get some sleep. And in the morning, maybe I should start looking for my own place. Because it looked like I was going to stay.

Callie had left the lights on over the candy counter, knowing I was still upstairs. That was enough light for me to make my way across the lobby to the doors, where I saw the plywood was still in place on one and the outline of a man backlit by the streetlights was visible through the glass of the other. He waved when he saw me.

I waved back, then entered the alarm code and opened the door. "Hector—"

But it wasn't Hector.

"Babe."

Ted Bishop, movie star, husband, and paramour of Priya Sharma, stepped into the lobby and swept me into a cinematic embrace. He inhaled deeply, muttering in my ear in a way that sent well-remembered shivers skating down my spine. "Babe, I've missed you so much. I've been so, so stupid."

Ted. Here.

What the hell was I going to do now?

San Francisco
1936

San Francisco is set in the months leading up to the earthquake of 1906. The opening title card describes the old city as "splendid and sensuous, vulgar and magnificent." Damn right. It still is.

The movie is about high culture versus low, faith versus cynicism, good versus evil. There's something approaching a "B" plot that I promise you won't care about. There's a rivalry between the Palace saloon and the highfalutin Opera theater, and prize money is at stake at something called the Chicken's Ball. But it's really only about Blackie Norton (Clark Gable), the "most godless, scoffing, and unbelieving soul in all of San Francisco" falling for the sweet opera singer Mary Blake (Jeanette MacDonald) as she learns how to put over a number in his saloon (hint: it involves a lot of feathers and outsized arm gestures).

But I'm getting ahead of myself. We begin on New Year's Eve. Showgirls! Confetti! Streamers! Gable's Blackie is king of the Barbary Coast. He owns a joint called Norton's Palace where the swells go to have fun—not the kind of place where a preacher's daughter should be singing. But the little lady is new in town and looking for a job. Blackie asks to see her legs before he asks to hear her sing. And when she sings, boy, she sounds just like Jeanette MacDonald. Which may or may not be a good thing, depending on your feelings about operetta. Blackie's into it.

Oh! I haven't even mentioned Spencer Tracy! He's Blackie's childhood friend—and a priest! Father Tim Mullin, who can beat Blackie at fisticuffs. He lives for the day when Blackie will stop thinking that God is for suckers. Will the preacher's daughter be able to get through to him? Or will Blackie succeed in corrupting her? It sure looks like it, much to Tracy's dismay. When Gable talks MacDonald into leaving the Opera to come sing "San Francisco" at his joint (wearing a darling little military number with a capelet and spangled hot pants), Tracy is appalled, telling Gable "You can't take a woman in marriage and then sell her immortal soul." I mean, come on. They're just spangled hot pants.

It's going to take a major act of the sucker's God to get everybody together again. Which brings us to The Earthquake. Considering this film was made in 1936, the special effects are pretty amazing. There are a lot of quick editing cuts, which weren't too common at that time. Brick walls collapse, an entire theater is turned to rubble, people are crushed while running for their lives, and Jeannette (unhelpfully) faints. The aftershock is even more impressive, as is the widespread fire that overtakes the city.

With the city on fire, will Blackie finally find some faith? Okay, that's not a fair question. But I have to say, when he's reunited with Father Tim and Mary, even these jaded old eyes got a little misty. Mainly because of the look Tracy gives Gable. Spencer Tracy. Yes. Every time, yes.

"We'll build a new San Francisco!" someone shouts in the crowd. And in the final shot, as "Glory, Glory, Hallelujah" morphs into the fifth version of "San Francisco" of the film, we see the smoldering wreckage of the old sinful city turning into the modern (and blessedly still sinful) city of 1936. It really is amazing what 30 years can do. I'd love to see the view from that site now.

Don't blink or you'll miss it:
Gable shirtless in high-waisted short shorts as he spars with Spencer Tracy in the boxing ring. (Tracy wears sensible leggings and a turtleneck, no fashion victim, he.)

Where you'll cringe:
Oh dear. The Chicken's Ball. The opening number looks like a minstrel show. Mercifully, we only get a glimpse of it. Another thing we glimpse is the obligatory Asian "houseboy" who exists to make chop suey for Gable upstairs at the Palace.

Best line about my new home:
"They call us the wickedest city in the world. And it's a bitter shame it is, for deep down underneath all our evil and sin we've got right here in San Francisco the finest set of human beings that was ever rounded up on one spot. Sure, they had to have wild adventure in their hearts, and dynamite in their blood, to set out for here in the first place. That's why they're so full of untamed deviltry now."

Movies My Friends Should Watch
Sally Lee

Want More Sally?

If you enjoyed Sally Lee's movie blogs, check out the Movies My Friends Should Watch website for more.

Visit www.moviesmyfriendsshouldwatch.com.
And watch good movies!

MARGARET DUMAS

Margaret Dumas lives in the San Francisco Bay Area, where she reads and writes books when she isn't watching old movies.

**The Movie Palace Mystery Series
by Margaret Dumas**

MURDER AT THE PALACE (#1)

Henery Press Mystery Books

And finally, before you go...
Here are a few other mysteries
you might enjoy:

LIVING THE VIDA LOLA

Melissa Bourbon

A Lola Cruz Mystery (#1)

Meet Lola Cruz, a fiery full-fledged PI at Camacho and Associates. Her first big case? A missing mother who may not want to be found. And to make her already busy life even more complicated, Lola's helping plan her cousin's quinceañera and battling her family and their old-fashioned views on women and careers. She's also reunited with the gorgeous Jack Callaghan, her high school crush whom she shamelessly tailed years ago and photographed doing the horizontal salsa with some other lucky girl.

Lola takes it all in stride, but when the subject of her search ends up dead, she has a lot more to worry about. Soon she finds herself wrapped up in the possibly shady practices of a tattoo parlor, local politics, and someone with serious—maybe deadly—road rage. But Lola is well-equipped to handle these challenges. She's a black-belt in kung fu, and her body isn't her only weapon. She's got smarts, sass, and more tenacity than her Mexican mafioso-wannabe grandfather. A few of her famous margaritas don't hurt, either.

Available at booksellers nationwide and online

Visit www.henerypress.com for details

FIXIN' TO DIE

Tonya Kappes

A Kenni Lowry Mystery (#1)

Kenni Lowry likes to think the zero crime rate in Cottonwood, Kentucky is due to her being sheriff, but she quickly discovers the ghost of her grandfather, the town's previous sheriff, has been scaring off any would-be criminals since she was elected. When the town's most beloved doctor is found murdered on the very same day as a jewelry store robbery, and a mysterious symbol ties the crime scenes together, Kenni must satisfy her hankerin' for justice by nabbing the culprits.

With the help of her Poppa, a lone deputy, and an annoyingly cute, too-big-for-his-britches State Reserve officer, Kenni must solve both cases and prove to the whole town, and herself, that she's worth her salt before time runs out.

Available at booksellers nationwide and online

Visit www.henerypress.com for details

I SCREAM, YOU SCREAM

Wendy Lyn Watson

A Mystery A-la-mode (#1)

Tallulah Jones's whole world is melting. Her ice cream parlor, Remember the A-la-mode, is struggling, and she's stooped to catering a party for her sleezeball ex-husband Wayne and his arm candy girlfriend Brittany. Worst of all? Her dreamy high school sweetheart shows up on her front porch, swirling up feelings Tally doesn't have time to deal with.

Things go from ugly to plain old awful when Brittany turns up dead and all eyes turn to Tally as the murderer. With the help of her hell-raising cousin Bree, her precocious niece Alice, and her long-lost-super-confusing love Finn, Tally has to dip into the heart of Dalliance, Texas's most scandalous secrets to catch a murderer before someone puts Tally and her dreams on ice for good.

Available at booksellers nationwide and online

Visit www.henerypress.com for details

MURDER IN G MAJOR

Alexia Gordon

A Gethsemane Brown Mystery (#1)

With few other options, African-American classical musician Gethsemane Brown accepts a less-than-ideal position turning a group of rowdy schoolboys into an award-winning orchestra. Stranded without luggage or money in the Irish countryside, she figures any job is better than none. The perk? Housesitting a lovely cliffside cottage. The catch? The ghost of the cottage's murdered owner haunts the place. Falsely accused of killing his wife (and himself), he begs Gethsemane to clear his name so he can rest in peace.

Gethsemane's reluctant investigation provokes a dormant killer and she soon finds herself in grave danger. As Gethsemane races to prevent a deadly encore, will she uncover the truth or star in her own farewell performance?

Available at booksellers nationwide and online

Visit www.henerypress.com for details

CPSIA information can be obtained
at www.ICGtesting.com
Printed in the USA
BVHW042027030219
539376BV00006B/36/P